SINGLE GLANCE

A SINGLE DAD, BASEBALL ROMANCE

ERIE CITY HAWKS
BOOK 1

K.C. BROOKS

For my dad.
Never thought our afternoons at Shea Stadium would lead to this, but here we are. Thank you for making some amazing memories with me.

And for the ones who feel a little lost.
Sometimes you're right where you're meant to be.

PLAYLIST

Listen Now on Spotify!

1. Medusa- Cameron Whitcomb
2. Settling Down- Miranda Lambert
3. Why Should We- Chase Wright
4. Night Falls- Sam Riggs
5. Worst Way- Riley Green
6. Eyes on You- Chase Rice
7. The Archer- Taylor Swift
8. It's Not Your Fault- Max McNown
9. When You're Down- Sam Riggs
10. I Want Us- The Road Below

AUTHOR'S NOTE

While this book might be a baseball romance, it is a romance book above all else. While it is the author's intention to honor the sport, some rules or guidelines may have been tweaked to allow for the characters' relationship to thrive.

This book also contains on page, sexually explicit situations. It also contains elements of strained family relationships, childhood trauma and abuse, manipulation, and unplanned pregnancy.

While it is the author's intention to broach these topics with sensitivity, it could still be triggering for some readers. If that is the case, please skip this book.

Protect your peace, lovelies.

ONE

Hadley

Seven Years Ago

"What do you mean, it's on the sixth floor?"

The heathen behind the desk just smirked as she passed over my room key. "Number 612," she repeated, as if that was the part I had trouble comprehending. She pointed around the corner, where a massive group congregated. "And *that* is the line for the elevator."

I groaned and dropped my head back, regretting not stopping for one last cup of coffee. After three days in my car, I couldn't resist driving that final stretch, excited to check out my dorm room and meet my roommate in person.

Whatever. At least I was finally in Austin, a world away from my home in Massachusetts, and that was what mattered most.

I never planned on moving to Texas for college. I never planned on any of this. If you had asked me a couple of months ago, I would have laid out every part of my five-year plan: graduate from Yale with my law degree, get engaged to Josh, the love of my life, and leave my past behind.

Too bad none of that was in the cards for me now. First,

I'd forgone Yale in favor of attending Stanford with Josh because that was *his* dream, and he didn't want to spend the next four years without me. *Should have been the first red flag, but you know what they say about hindsight being* 20/20. Maybe that *would* have been the start of our story— *if* I had gotten into Stanford. Despite my grades and my personal statement detailing how I'd worked my butt off at the diner the past four years to save every penny in the hopes of attending, none of that mattered to the admissions office. I cringed just thinking about that rejection letter, the lasting bitter sting of each of the words.

We regret to inform you...

The door slammed closed on that dream. After a lifetime of disappointment, I should've been used to it, but reading through that letter crushed me.

Growing up, whenever I needed to get out of my house, I'd walk the two miles to the local library. I'd lose myself in the pages of different fairy tales, loving how the characters only needed a little magic to change their fate. While magic wasn't an option in real life, I'd substituted it with hard work and dedication, thinking that would be enough to shift my story from the girl from the wrong side of the tracks into the princess in the gilded castle.

Too bad happily ever afters only exist on the pages of those stories. In my story, the heroine was too stubborn to listen to her advisor's suggestion of applying to more than one college.

Foolishly, I'd bet *everything* on Stanford, not even bothering to apply to any other schools before I turned in my early decision application, thinking it was just a formality. I'd checked every box, did everything I was *supposed* to do.

And my rejection wasn't the worst part. No, that was the look on Josh's face when I told him I wouldn't be part of the freshman class with him. He'd gone cold, talking about his future in terms of "me", instead of "we". There were so many signs I missed. Naïve little Hadley still believed after all that, I'd end up with Josh, that we'd have our picture-perfect wedding, and everything would be right in our world. We'd leave behind our divided town and shape our new lives. Together.

At least, until I walked in on him balls-deep in Deidre Panamater at our graduation party.

The picture didn't have the same appeal after that.

On the one hand, it was good I found out the so-called "love of my life" was a philandering asshole who planned to spend his college years as a perpetual fuckboy extraordinaire. But the words he slung at me as he pulled up his jeans still stung, as if he'd inked them for everyone to see.

"Dating you was fine for high school, but I have to think about my future, Hads. My parents like you, but they'd never be okay with me settling down with some townie chick from Maple Ridge."

Fine—not like I hadn't heard it before. When you grew up in my section of town, people made assumptions. The crumbling apartment buildings and boarded-up windows didn't exactly inspire warm, cozy vibes. But if you never looked beyond the surface, you failed to see all the good in that community. So many of our neighbors helped raise me —it was a family. Still, kids were cruel, and adults were even worse. I'd heard comments about where I lived since kindergarten; given my mom's reputation, I was used to the sneers.

But hearing that pour out of the boy I loved? That brought every negative thought to the surface, breaking down my tough façade.

Luckily, that was months ago, and I refused to let the

memories of Josh sour my new experience. Austin hadn't been my original plan—hell, it wasn't even my back-up plan. However, after Stanford rejected me, I couldn't bring myself to even think about a different Ivy. I'd gambled and lost; I was in no hurry to repeat that mistake.

Thank goodness for rolling admissions and glowing recommendations from my teachers. I didn't even remember how I learned of Walker University. It must have been one of the safety schools my advisor insisted I apply to, even though we both thought I would get into Stanford. But during the lowest moment of my life, there the brochure was, sitting on my desk like the answer to all my problems.

It turned out to be the best thing that could have happened to me.

Maybe in the future, I'd regret my decision, but today, I was ecstatic. This was it—day one of my new life. Despite my new RA's shitty attitude and saccharine smirk, I was determined to get through it with a smile on my face.

"Stairs?" I asked, trying to hide my grin when her eyes widened. She pointed off to the far hallway, and I grabbed my cart, shoving my belongings away from the crowd. When I found the stairwell, I poked my head up, debating if the wait for the elevator would be worth it.

I leaned back into the hallway and sucked in a sharp breath. Somehow, the line seemed to have tripled in the last five minutes. A couple of fathers battled carts, trying to fit more than was physically possible into the elevator car. When one of them gave up, the elevator closed its doors with a weary groan, as if exhausted by the day.

No way in hell. The idea of being trapped inside an elevator was bad enough, but squeezing in with ten other college students determined to bring their stuff in as few trips as possible? That sounded like my absolute nightmare.

At least the dorm's entrance was on the second floor, leaving only four flights of stairs to my room.

"You got this, Hadley." I turned to face my belongings. God, why did I bring *all* my clothing? Not that there was any other option. When I lived at home, my room was small, and the lock on my door had seen better days. I'd invested in a deadbolt early on to make sure my mom didn't "borrow" any of my stuff. If I left anything behind, it wouldn't be there when—*if*—I ever went back.

As I stared at the flights of steps in front of me, I second-guessed that decision. Maybe the risk would have been worth it. At least then, I wouldn't be stuck trying to drag everything up the stairs. I turned, placing my hands on my hips as I decided what to tackle first. Fine. I had this. It was only six suitcases. Six suitcases up four flights of stairs. Which meant—

"If you're thinking about the math, don't," a deep voice chuckled from behind me.

"Oh my God!" I jumped at the voice, my hand flying to my frantically pulsing heart. "You scared me half to death—"

When I turned, the rest of my words cut off as the most gorgeous man I'd ever seen stood only a few feet away. The guy was tall, barely able to get through the doorway without ducking. He'd tucked his short brown hair under a baseball cap, but pieces of his curls peeked out from the front. With his tanned skin and bright eyes, it was impossible to stop staring. My eyes darted down, unable to stop myself as I scanned the rest of him. Tight, lean muscles covered his entire frame, and my thighs clenched a little at the idea of being thrown around like a rag doll. When my eyes darted back to his face, his smile knocked me off my axis.

All my life, I'd known plenty of people who'd perfected

their fake smiles. Too many teeth, dead eyes. With the town laughing stock for a mom, you learned quickly who you could trust and who would talk shit as soon as you turned around.

But this stranger? Goodness radiated out of him, an easy, charismatic charm that put you at ease. As I tried to remember how to form sentences, his eyes roamed down my body.

Oh, fuck.

Look, after over seventy-two hours on the road, I was not the best version of myself. Sure, I had showered before leaving the motel that morning, but I piled my long, wavy blonde hair on top of my head, and more than one stain marred my vintage t-shirt.

"You okay?"

"Me?" I squawked. "Yeah, yeah. Of course. Just tired after a long drive. Sorry about that." I cleared my throat, moving my attention back to the man in front of me. "Are you moving in too?"

He smiled and leaned in closer. "Nah, just helping out. Didn't want to take the elevator?"

"Nope." I popped my hip to lean on the stair railing. "Have this thing about small spaces, especially when other people try to squeeze in too."

"Can't blame you on that one." He held out his hand. "I'm Cam."

"Hadley." As our palms collided, I tried to ignore the jolt of electricity that trickled through my veins. It was disjointing, unexpected, and my cheeks flushed as I averted my gaze. I hiked my thumb over my shoulder. "I should get these up to my room."

"Let me help." He motioned toward my largest suitcase. "Save you a trip or two."

"You would be my hero." I passed it to him, and he didn't flinch, even motioning for another.

"Shit, Hadley. What do you have in these things?"

"I have an unhealthy obsession with clothing and shoes," I joked, knowing he'd most likely write me off for that comment alone. I'd heard it all—plenty of people labeled me as vapid or shallow because I liked fashion, but those people didn't have to choose their clothes based on the church's donations. After a lifetime of having few choices, I wanted to try every style and figure out what I liked most on my terms. "I like options," I shrugged. "Plus, I'm from Massachusetts, so I didn't know what to expect when I got to Texas."

"Damn, you're a long way from home," Cam chuckled. "And my mom freaked out about me moving an *hour* away."

"My mom wasn't happy about it either." Understatement of the century. She hid my car keys the morning I left, and it took me almost three hours to track them down. "But I think she understands why I wanted to come out here."

"Which is?"

"Escaping the cold winter," I winked as I started up the first flight of stairs. Cam laughed below me, and for a moment, I regretted the lie. The truth about my reasons for moving to Texas sat on the tip of my tongue, but I shoved them back down. That was not first conversation material. *Keep it light and breezy, Hadley. Talk about the weather, his taste in music—not the complicated interpersonal dynamics of your family.*

Besides, when Cam stepped up to my side, I had more pleasant things to fill my mind. In fact, if Cam kept smiling at me, I'd forget I had a mother at all. We fell into step as we climbed the stairs, talking about his hometown and some local attractions. By the time we reached the sixth floor, I had a new restaurant, park, and bookstore to check out.

As we turned down my hall, I smiled back up at him. "Thank you again for your help, Cam."

"Don't mention it," he said. "My dad would have killed me if I left a beautiful girl struggling with her suitcases."

My cheeks darkened at his words. It wasn't the first time someone had called me beautiful, but it was the first time the words rang true. I spent so much of my time picking apart my appearance, hating all the ways my body changed as I grew. Over the course of two summers, I'd gone from a skinny little thing to a body with curves I didn't know how to dress or handle. That was hard enough, but then the comments started. My mother never prepared me for how to handle people leering at you, or grown men giving you skin-curling "compliments". In fact, she only fed into my insecurities, hurling hateful words, as if I'd changed just to spite her. I tried to ignore them, but there were only so many insults you could take before they were carved deep into your psyche.

I exhaled, shoving those thoughts out of my mind. When I looked up, Cam continued to watch me. His appraisal felt different from the others. When most people stared at me back home, it made me feel raw, like they were looking for some flaw or weakness to prove their internal judgments. But with Cam's gaze on me? I felt beautiful, like someone saw *me* after years of hiding behind a practiced smile.

Emboldened by his words, I took a step closer. "Well, maybe I could buy you a cup of coffee to say thanks?"

Before Cam answered, a door down the hall burst open, and a brunette sauntered into the hallway with a laundry basket. When she got closer, her face broke into a wide smile. "Wait, are you Hadley?"

Cam's eyes widened as he looked behind me and took a step back. The move was so unexpected, my stomach twisted, and it took everything in me to keep the smile on my face. As I turned to face the new addition to our group, I relaxed a little, recognizing her from social media. "Victoria?"

She nodded, placing her laundry basket at her feet. "Yes! But you can call me Tori. I'm so excited to finally meet you." She raced over and pulled me into a hug. At first, I didn't know how to respond. I wasn't used to hugs. My arms reached out, and I patted her back, hoping she wouldn't think I was weird right off the bat. We were stuck together for the year, and after our conversations online, I had high hopes we'd get along.

After we pulled apart, she moved to my side. Victoria smiled up at Cameron as she nuzzled against him. "Did you help with her suitcases?"

My eyes tracked their closeness, trying not to rush to conclusions. Still, my stomach already swirled into a sour knot, unable to look away, no matter how hard I tried. Maybe she was his sister? A close friend from home? I mentally searched through Victoria's social media pages, but I hadn't spent a lot of time on them, knowing they usually only showed what a person wanted to project into the world.

"Yeah." He cleared his throat, no longer meeting my eyes. "The elevator line is still ridiculous. I didn't know she was your roommate."

I waited for his eyes to meet mine, to relay on some unspoken message that this was a misunderstanding, that I hadn't read him completely wrong.

Instead, he leaned down and kissed the top of Victoria's head as she placed her hand on his chest and looked to me. "Hadley, this is Cam, my boyfriend."

Angry lashes of guilt and disgust flowed through my veins. How had I been so wrong about this guy? Was my internal barometer so off, I couldn't see through another fuckboy? My hands clenched at my sides, and all I wanted to do was scream at Victoria to get away from him.

Then again—what had Cam really done? He'd helped me out when I needed it, and sure, maybe our conversation had veered into flirtation territory, but he never made a move on me. If anything, *I* made a move on *him*. That wild anger simmered down to quiet guilt, hating that I'd already messed up with my new roommate.

As Cam turned and finally faced me again, I lowered my head, refusing to meet his eyes. Hot shame colored my cheeks. It brought me right back to seeing Josh cheating on me, giving new life to the words my mother loved to spew at me. Of course, Cam wasn't interested in me. He was the good kid, probably from a stable home, with a planned out future and the right girl at his side. That moment we shared was all it would ever be—a passing moment, a single glance, nothing more.

When Victoria picked up her laundry basket and headed down the hall with Cam, I made myself a promise. This mistake was a sharp reminder of why I wasn't cut out for a relationship, at least not right now. I needed to keep my head down and focus on school.

Nothing could get in the way of that.

Especially not my roommate's boyfriend.

Present Day

Some memories etch themselves into your brain, the rare moments you instinctively know are life-changing. The ones you're going to reflect on for the rest of your days. When I'm old and grey, looking back on my life, I already know what's going to come back to me.

Back in elementary school, when my dad handed me a baseball.

Six years ago, when the doctor placed my daughter, Emilia, in my arms.

The last moments of our college championship, when I stepped up to bat and hit the ball over the fence, earning our team the win and the trophy.

And now, this one.

I stared out over the brand new green field of Erie City stadium. From the box perched behind home plate, you could see almost everything. The place was pristine, which made sense. Construction finished three months ago—a minor miracle, considering the city only gave them two years to turn the old minor league stadium into one fit for a major league team. But somehow, they did it, and all it needed now was fans filling the seats, ready to cheer on their brand new team.

Disbelief filled my veins. After years of waiting, praying for the chance, I got the call to come up to the majors. The season had barely begun, but I'd already resigned myself to another year in the Triple-As. Not that it was a bad gig—at least I was on the Hawks' farm team. It was more than what most guys got to say. But the dream was always the majors—to feel that rush of playing at the top of the class. So, when my coach sat me down two days ago and told me my card had been pulled, I almost had to pinch myself.

My disbelief amplified when the door opened, and a voice I knew all too well filled the space between us. Grayson Anders smiled as he walked over to me, holding out his hand. "Good to see you again, Cam. Sorry if I kept you waiting." He motioned to the bar-height table in the center of the room. "Please, have a seat."

I nodded, still trying to keep my cool. As I settled into the chair, I glanced up, looking at my idol on the other side of the desk. God, I was going to puke. Even though I'd met Grayson Anders a handful of times, during those instances, he was just Gray, working at his family bar—a far cry from the major league world he'd left behind. It was easy to separate the man from the legend, to forget he was one of the best ballplayers of the last decade.

But seeing him here now?

Gray's dark eyes crinkled as he watched my jaw fall open. "Something to say, Cam?"

"I, uh..." I ran my hand through the back of my dark hair, wondering if I should have cut it. My father was always strict about our attire and how we presented ourselves to society. He'd probably kill me if he saw me showing up here without shaving, or at least trimming, my face. "I'm kind of in shock. Vic didn't mention you'd be the one greeting me."

"Called in a favor with Benny so I could be the one to welcome you aboard." Gray smirked back at me. "As for Tori, I asked her to keep it between us."

That didn't surprise me in the least. My ex, Victoria, knew Gray was my hero. When she moved to Gray's hometown, the woman didn't even try to warn me; she let me walk into his bar like it was a normal occurrence. She still laughed about how red my face turned when I saw him for the first time.

I probably had the same dumb-founded look on my face now.

Gray leaned back in his chair, his tattoos poking out from his rolled-up sleeves. His dark metal wedding ring grabbed my attention, but he spoke before I could ask about his wife. "I've seen your tapes from the minors. You're fast as hell, kid."

"Thank you, sir," I said, clearing my throat.

Gray shook his head. "Cut that sir shit out. It's Gray— Anders, or Coach if we're on the field. And this isn't me blowing smoke up your ass, Cam. Our manager, Bennett Weber, is a hard guy to impress, and he liked what he saw. We're excited to see what you'll do up here."

"Th—" My words cut off when Gray gave me a look.

"Like I said, this isn't me telling you anything new. You're talented; you wouldn't be here if you weren't. But getting to the game—that's just the first part of this battle. It's a long season, and we've already had our share of ups and downs." He nodded to the window behind him. "You sure you're ready for this?"

"Hell yes." I didn't hesitate for a second. Nothing would keep me from that field.

Especially because this deal meant getting to be closer to my daughter. Almost three years ago, the league had announced it would add four new teams: two in the National League and two in the American League. I didn't pay it much mind at first, mostly because I thought I'd still be in Texas. But after my ex moved up here, and they announced they'd be creating a team in upstate New York, it clicked. This was my shot at the dream—getting to play professional baseball and be close to Emilia. I fought like hell to get moved to Erie City's farm team, and my agent had come through right after Boston made me an offer.

Not that playing for Boston's farm team wouldn't be great, but the city was never home. I'd visited long enough to get a sense of the place, but in my heart, I was a country boy. I couldn't relax with that much noise around me. Also, the fans with the legacy teams were vicious. They'd eat you alive if you messed up a play.

But none of those issues mattered most. No, that was the distance from my daughter. I hated being five hours away from Emilia. She was in kindergarten now, and it affected how much time I got to spend with her.

Playing for the Hawks meant I could see her as much as possible—the stadium was only forty-five minutes from Saint Stephen's Lake, where my ex and daughter lived with her new boyfriend. I was already looking at apartments halfway between the two, hopeful I'd get to spend most of my free time with Emilia.

"I'm ready for this, Gray."

Gray nodded and tapped his hand on the top of the table. "I'll be honest with you, Cam—this is a young team. A lot of these guys are coming up from the minors, just like you. Everyone is looking to make a name for themselves, but we don't need a group of superstars. We need a team, one that can come together when we need it. Counting on you, kid, to be a leader, both on and off the field."

My throat tightened, the pressure mounting on my shoulders. "I'm ready for it."

He stood, holding out his hand. "Then welcome to the Hawks, Cam. Let's make this a great fucking year."

THREE

Cameron

Twenty minutes later, the team's social media manager led me around the stadium, checking out the place that would hopefully become my second home over the next few years. We'd already gone out to the field and up to the stands, and now she guided me toward the locker rooms.

As she pushed open the door, I inhaled sharply, hoping this would be a great season. I might have done well in the minors, but I was a long way from that now. Nerves hit me like a freight train as we walked down the painted hallway, where the rest of the guys would file in shortly.

It was one thing to start the year as a rookie. It was something else entirely to come in once the season already started. The rest of the team had time to build chemistry during spring training, to learn each other's strengths and weaknesses. While baseball teams were often like revolving doors, most had a core group of guys who would lead us to victory. Were they pissed I'd been called up?

Teamwork was everything, especially when you were already starting at a disadvantage. Many of the teams we'd face were franchise teams and had been playing together for years. They communicated silently on the field—would we even speak the same language?

As I walked inside, I sucked in a sharp breath, not quite believing the sight in front of me. In the minors, we'd had nice locker rooms, but nothing like this. Dark green flooring covered the space, with the Hawks' logo etched in white in the middle of the room. The center of the room had four dark leather couches, and rich mahogany wood lockers lined the walls. Each one had a little spotlight over the top of it, proudly illuminating player's names. Some taken lockers only said Erie City Hawks, a reminder that everyone had to earn their name on the wall. Staring at one of the blank placards, resolve settled in my gut. My name would go up there.

This was real. This moment, the one I had fought for years to achieve, was finally in my grasp. All the hard work, all the days away from home, all the milestones I'd missed—they had all been for this.

I was a major league baseball player.

Fuck, that felt good.

As I walked further into the room, I found my locker instantly. If the balloons and signs weren't enough of a hint, my daughter stood in front of it, holding her mother's hand.

"Daddy!" Emilia exclaimed as she burst across the room and leaped into my arms. I happily caught her, taking a whiff of the strawberry shampoo she loved so much. Even though it had only been two weeks since I last saw her, I missed her terribly. No amount of FaceTime calls would match the feeling of having my little girl in my arms. She pulled back and put her palms on my cheeks, squeezing them together. "Do you like our surprise? Mommy helped me make the poster."

"I love it, baby girl," I said as I kissed her nose. After I put Emilia down, I hugged Victoria. "You guys didn't have to drive out here for this."

"Are you kidding?" Victoria said. "We've been here every time you started with a new team. It's practically a family tradition at this point. No way we'd miss this one, especially with you being so close now." She beamed at me, tears forming in the corners of her eyes. "You did it, Cam."

I squeezed her a little tighter before I let her go. I cleared my throat, trying to hide my emotion at her words. Victoria had been my high school girlfriend and my first love. She'd been there from the very start—from my first junior varsity game to the call I got about joining the Hawks. She was the most stable person in my life, despite the shift in our relationship.

When we were younger, our paths seemed so clear. We'd attend the same college, then get married right after we graduated. But life had other plans, and we ended up getting pregnant with Emilia during our freshman year.

Although we tried to make things work, as we got older, it became clear Victoria and I were better off as friends. It hurt like hell at first, but over time, we made it work. Now, I couldn't imagine my life without her.

"Where's Adam?" I asked, looking down at her still-bare ring finger. "Is he avoiding me? He knows I'm going to kick his ass if he doesn't make an honest woman out of you soon." Victoria's boyfriend, Adam, was one of the biggest movie stars in the world. He'd taken a break last year and moved to the same small town as his best friend, Victoria's brother. Their paths crossed, and the rest was history.

When we first broke up, I dreaded the idea of Victoria with another guy. I thought it would be this painful moment, like it might shatter our friendship into something entirely different. But none of that happened when she fell for Adam. In fact, it was like he'd always been a part of our family, completing Victoria in a way I'd never seen before. He made her happier than ever, and he loved Emilia just as fiercely.

"Oh, hush." She rolled her eyes. "No, we're not engaged. Not yet, at least. He'd get married tomorrow if he thought I'd say yes. But you know the plan—MBA first, and then we can focus on wedding planning."

"Are you sure it's okay if I stay in your guest room?" I grinned at Emilia, who was climbing down my legs to explore the room. "Cause I can make other arrangements—"

"Don't you dare," Victoria said. "We meant it. Stupid to waste money on rent when you want to buy a house. And we have plenty of room. Plus, Adam is looking forward to having another guy around. He's been outnumbered for a while."

"What do you mean?"

Emilia tugged on my sweater, and I forgot the question. She pointed to the hot pink poster hanging from the top of my locker. She'd written the words "Good Luck, Daddy" in an obnoxious amount of glitter. "Auntie Hadley helped me make it. She told me you loved glitter and that we should use it all."

"Of course she did," I grumbled, shooting an annoyed glare at Victoria. She just shrugged. While I loved Victoria, her best friend was another story. Hadley had been trouble from the day we met, chaos wrapped up in a beautiful package. Part of me hoped their friendship would fade when Victoria moved up here, but if anything, it was stronger than ever. It was becoming painfully clear I was going to be stuck with Hadley McKay for a long time. I pointed to the sign, and a burst of glitter fell over all of my stuff. Victoria rolled her lips together, trying to suppress her chuckle. I narrowed my eyes. "One of these days, I'm going to kill her."

Emilia pouted. "That's not very nice, Daddy. Auntie Hadley just wanted to make your first day special."

Oh bullshit. I needed to have another conversation with Hadley about the lies she told my daughter. She might look angelic and soft, but I knew the truth. The woman was a menace, sent from hell itself to test my willpower. She thrived on torturing me, spreading her particular brand of mayhem wherever she went. Last year, Victoria had gone away for a week to attend her brother's wedding, and because she'd never been away from Emilia for that long, she wanted to make sure I had reinforcements, mainly because we were at the end of baseball season, and I had scheduled games. So, she asked Hadley to help me with Emilia.

Big fucking mistake.

It was a week of goddamn torture. Even though our paths barely crossed, Hadley left evidence of her presence all over Victoria's house. Paint and glitter covered every surface, and the whole place smelled like that sickeningly sweet gum she loved to pop. It took almost three weeks to get the cabin back together.

Before I could launch into another diatribe about Hadley, a bunch of guys walked into the locker room, smiling at the recent addition on the wall. One guy stopped at the locker next to mine, tossing his bag inside. He chuckled, "Now that's a welcome sign." He nodded to Emilia. "Did you make it?"

"Yup." She beamed. "My mommy and Auntie Hadley helped."

"You're a talented little girl. You think you could make some more for the locker room?"

"Really?" she squealed as she looked over at her mother. When Victoria nodded, Emilia turned back to the man. "I'd love to."

He nodded as he turned toward me. "Hey, man. Damien Ramos."

"Cam Seda," I said back, trying to keep my cool. Not that long ago, I had Damien's poster on my bedroom wall. The guy was a monster on the field, and in real life, he was almost as intimidating. Most people considered me tall at six foot three, but Damien had a couple inches on me. Tattoos covered his dark skin, pictures of angels and other elements I couldn't quite make out, but I'd read enough interviews to know he'd gotten most of them in honor of his family.

After pulling on a hoodie, Damien motioned behind me, where Emilia stood staring at all the men shuffling inside. "Your kid?"

"Yeah," I smiled. "She's my girl."

Damien nodded and started dropping his stuff in his locker. Holy hell, I was playing with *the* Damien Ramos. He was a legend on the New York Rebels, notorious for his home runs and aggressive attitude on the field. I never thought he would have left that team, but when Gray asked him to join this fledgling one, he couldn't resist playing with his former teammate and friend. The guy was getting close to retirement, but he was still lethal on the field, and the Hawks would take any advantage they could get.

"You have any kids?" I spit out, trying to keep my cool.

"Nah." He grinned as he dug through his bag. "Not sure it's in the cards for me. But my sister and her wife have five girls, so I've got a lot of experience babysitting if you ever need a hand." He walked over to Victoria and introduced himself. "Wife?" Damien asked.

"Nope," she said. "We're not together, but we're Cam's family. We wanted to come to cheer him on." She turned back toward me. "But this one's getting a little tired, so I think we're going to head out. Family dinner tonight? Say yes."

"Wouldn't dream of missing it." I leaned in to kiss her cheek. "I'll text you when I'm heading back to the house."

As my family walked out of the locker room, the rest of the guys started talking, and I tried to take it all in. Coming in as the new guy was always nerve-wracking, but there was a nice camaraderie with the crew. I'd heard nightmares about hazing from some guys sent back down to the minors, but none of that seemed to happen in this clubhouse.

I sighed as I turned back toward my locker, my uniform ready and waiting for me. I ran my hand over the white jersey, tracing the green pinstripes like it was all an illusion. But when I turned it around and saw my number written in the dark green font, I couldn't help but smile.

Perhaps with some beginner's luck, we'd take this team and make it something great. Maybe I'd prove myself and get to stay here as long as possible.

As I looked at Emilia walking out of the locker room, she turned and gave me a wide smile. For me, there was no other option. I needed this team to work out, needed to bring everything to the field every day.

My daughter and the game were the only things that mattered.

FOUR

Hadley

"How long you planning to stay up there?" My mother coughed through the phone. "You promised you'd come back here after you graduated. What's everyone going to say when they find out my kid's abandoned me?"

That I have no interest in being around you? I sighed as I slapped my palm to my head. This was my penance for answering the phone during the school day. My once-peaceful forty-five-minute lunch had turned into a barrage of questions, all accompanied by my mother's sneer. From the moment she lit up the screen, disapproval painted her face. My mother hated my choices, even down to the sand-wich I'd made for lunch.

"Mom, I already told you. I can't take off work right now. Go to the church. Call up some of your old friends. You'll be fine without me." Not that anyone would answer her calls after the shit she's put them through. Colleen McKay used to be beautiful, the world at her fingertips, but time had made her selfish and entitled—believing the world owed her for how her life had turned out. When she wasn't able to cloak her disappointment, she'd started drinking, and now, I was pretty sure her only steady relationship was with Johnny Walker.

My mother's voice lowered. "I know you don't like it here, Hadley—"

"Then you know better than to ask," I bit out, finally losing my patience. After talking in circles for way too long, I was tired and so fucking hungry. I swear, I loved my mother; I really did. In her heart, I had to believe she wanted what was best for me. But her version of love usually came with endless strings.

My mother's face hardened. "Fine. I get it. You don't have to worry about me. I just miss my daughter and thought she might miss me too. Stupid thought."

Familiar guilt tucked in the back of my eyes, pressing tears out from the corners. I discreetly tried to rush them away, grateful my mother was on a small screen instead of standing in front of me.

"I'll try to come home soon," I promised, unsure if I actually meant it. It had been months since I'd returned to my childhood home. After I graduated from college, the plan was to open a daycare with my best friend, Victoria. We'd done all the work, from scouting locations to drafting up a business plan. But after she fell in love, our plans seemed to go on the back-burner, and I'd had to look long and hard at my life and what I wanted to achieve.

The answer? I had absolutely no idea. There was no back-up, no alternative route. I was free-falling with no one there to catch me. So instead of making a choice, I did the opposite. Decided to embrace a more nomadic lifestyle before I put my big girl pants on and settled down. Now, the goal was to let my heart guide me and soak up any new opportunities that came my way. I'd lived in Denver for almost six months right after I got my diploma, but when

Victoria called about a substitute teaching job near her home, I couldn't say no.

As my mother hung up without another word, the door swung open, and my class poured in, already finished with recess for the day. I'd inherited this group of kiddos when their regular teacher went on maternity leave in December, and they were mine for the rest of the year. They all laughed and smiled as they found their desks, grateful to have gotten outside after a long and dreary winter.

The door closed, and my co-teacher walked over to my table. Even though Brianna and I had only been working together for three months, we'd gotten along from the moment we'd met. Despite our ten-year age gap and being in different phases in life, we'd become fast friends, at least at work. I'd asked her to come hang out with Tori and me a handful of times, but she'd always say no, twisting her wedding ring like something was holding her back.

Oh well, at least we worked well as a team. Our classroom operated like a well-oiled machine, Brianna being the more data-driven, practical teacher, while I was more about the sparkle and enthusiasm.

As our students settled at their desks, grabbing crayons and colored pencils for their post-recess calm-down time, Brianna glanced at my unfinished lunch and frowned. "Get interrupted by something?"

"More like someone," I groaned, standing to brush any errant crumbs off my dress. Now that it was finally spring, I'd take any excuse to wear my dresses. Winters in New York were no joke, and after living in Austin for the past five years, my blood wasn't used to the bitter cold. I shrugged as Brianna gave me another look. "My mother. Don't ask."

"I won't. But if you ever need any commiseration in the mother department, I'm here," she said as she moved around the tables, helping our second graders get ready for phonics.

As I gathered my materials for class, I gave Brianna a tight smile. My family history was a well-guarded secret. I was all too aware of how quick people's judgments could change when they found out about your roots. I'd grown up with the stigma my mother created, and I'd worked really damn hard to keep it in the past. Only a few people in my life knew the truth about my childhood, and I liked that I finally had a clean slate.

For years, I'd held onto the dream of freedom—of finally being free to live life how I saw fit. With no one else depending on me, there wasn't a reason to create roots just yet. As long as my bank account had enough funds, I was free to do what I wanted, spending my days soaking up everything the world had to give. My life might not have been exactly how I imagined it, but it was mine.

The thought pulled away the last icy remnants of my conversation with my mother, and I settled on the carpet with a wide, genuine smile on my face. This might not be permanent, but right now, it was exactly where I wanted to be.

FIVE

Hadley

Later that night, I relaxed on my couch and scrolled through an app to find something to watch. I was already dozing off, and judging by the rest of the week, I'd be asleep on the couch in minutes. What a glamorous life I led. No wonder I was hopelessly single. No one interested me, and the few who did weren't interested in dating someone with my schedule. *Hey baby, want to pass out before nine pm and wake up at four-thirty?* Not many people signing up for that routine.

Besides, the solitary life worked for me. I'd dated Josh for my entire high school career, and that left me unimpressed, to say the least. I'd gone on a couple of dates and had some hook-ups in college, but nothing lasted more than a few weeks. After being burned so thoroughly by Josh, I had high standards for the people I let into my life. No one had come close to matching them since, so I figured it was time to call dating a loss. Maybe to some people, it was weird to let a few awful dates sour the whole experience, but right now, it wasn't worth it to me. Maybe I was old-fashioned, but I wanted to be swept off my feet and not because of anxiety to settle down or because I felt bored or lonely. I'd rather be by myself forever than be with someone just for the sake of it.

Not that I was really alone.

As the thought crossed my mind, a soft meow came from the side of the couch as Laila brushed my toes with the top of her head. I reached down and brought my black cat into my lap. When I graduated, I hadn't intended on getting a pet, but fate had other plans. I was walking through a local farmer's market when something snagged on my sweater—a sweet little kitten with large, green eyes stared back at me, her nail tugging a hole into my cardigan. The woman from the adoption agency joked the kitten was a spitfire, and I knew it was meant to be. She came home with me that very day.

Laila quickly curled up on top of my legs, batting my hand to give her scratches on the top of her head. Okay, so maybe I was one step closer to becoming a cat lady, but would that be the worst thing? Laila and I had a good thing going, and as long as I fed her regularly, I got all the affection I needed.

Just as Laila drifted off to sleep, a knock came from the front door, the noise abrasive and obnoxious in the quiet apartment. My cat jumped up with a hiss, sticking her claws into my thighs. "Shit," I snapped as I sat up, inspecting my skin for any blood. None, thank goodness.

As I tucked my phone into my hoodie pocket, I pulled back the curtains by the door, smiling when I saw Victoria waiting on the other side. I cracked open the door, smirking at her. "Shouldn't you be off getting loved up by your real-life superhero?"

Victoria just laughed and pushed past me to come inside. One of the best perks of taking the teaching job? When I needed a place to stay, Tori immediately offered the carriage house on the edge of her property. I loved this place. It still had all the charm from the turn of the century, but they'd spared no expense bringing all the plumbing and fixtures into the modern edge. The plan was for it to be a guest house until Tori's daughter, Emilia, grew up. Then, when she was an adult, she could have a private place to stay when she came to visit.

But considering Emilia was only six, it was empty for the foreseeable future, and Tori said it was mine for as long as I wanted it.

"You know it's only five, right? Not getting loved up when Emilia's still conscious," Tori said as she plopped onto my couch. "But later...that's another story."

I settled onto the couch next to her. "Where's Emilia right now?"

"Adam took her out to get some ice cream."

"*Before* dinner?"

Tori rolled her eyes and tossed my couch pillow at my head. "Normally, he wouldn't, but Adam's leaving to meet with some studio executives for a week, so he wanted to get some time in with her."

"Good man," I said. "How's he treating you? Still a romance hero brought to life?"

I loved to tease Victoria about her love life, but inside, I felt a little jealous. No one deserved a great love like my best friend. She was all heart and deserved someone who treated her like a queen. Luckily, Adam fit the bill. When they first connected, I supported it, thinking Victoria needed a fling to move on from her ex. Instead, they fell in love, and while I was so happy for their little family, it put a pin in a lot of our plans.

For years, Victoria and I talked about opening our own daycare. With my teaching license and her business mind, I was sure we'd be successful. I'd imagined the centers we'd create, finding a balance between affordability and quality care. Growing up, there weren't a lot of options for child-care. Most of my neighbors relied on each other to watch their kids when they had to work. It was a system that worked, but it wasn't the best for the kids. They were missing out on opportunities to socialize, to learn new skills, all things their more affluent peers took for granted. I wanted to help bridge that gap, and I thought Victoria felt the same way.

At least, until she moved up here with Adam.

"He is," Victoria said, her cheeks filling with color. "But that's not what I'm here to talk to you about. I need you to come up to the main house. We're celebrating Cam's first day on his new team, and we want you there."

I rolled my eyes. No, thank you. Celebrating the golden boy was not how I wanted to spend my evening. "I think I'll pass. Plus, he's been on the team for weeks. Isn't that why he was down in Florida for spring training?"

"Technically, yes, but that was the farm team. Now, he's on the major league team. It's a really big deal..." She stood and tugged me up from the couch. "C'mon. It'll be more fun with you there. Besides, what other plans do you have? Watching *the Real Housewives of Beverly Hills* and pondering why so many guys use fish as props on their dating profiles?"

"First, rude. And second, you're wrong. I'll be watching *the Real Housewives of Salt Lake City*." She definitely had me on the fish thing, though. What was that about?

"Aren't they the same thing?"

I gasped, pulling my hand to my chest. "The fact that you even asked that makes me question our friendship."

"Get over it," Tori chuckled as she pulled me toward the door. "You're stuck with me for good."

Just the way I wanted it.

SIX

Cameron

I was drained by the time I pulled into Victoria's driveway. If I thought playing in the minors was taxing, I was a damn fool. The majors paid better, but the pressure increased tenfold, especially on our home turf. The raised stakes affected every player on the field, especially me. I only played one inning because it was a tight game. The team from Atlanta came to defend their standing, and the veteran guys defended their positions. But at the end of the fifth inning, they needed a break, so Benny called in. Outfield was new to me—I'd been a shortstop my entire career, but those spots were filled. So instead, I stood out in the right field, catching any fly balls careening my way.

I might have only gotten to play in one inning, but I made it count. I caught a fly ball and assisted in a double play that ended their run. That, tied with the couple of lead-ins I'd batted, my first game in the majors had gone pretty well.

The outfield and batting coach seemed happy with my performance. Gray might have been the pitching coach, but he'd come over to congratulate me on a good game. The one wild card? Our manager. Benny Weber's quiet, stern demeanor was notorious throughout the league. He played his cards close to his vest, at least until he got pissed. Stories still floated around from when he played for the Boston team, getting tossed out of a couple of games for arguing with the umpires.

Shit, this was going to be a long season. We still had over 100 games to play, and I was already exhausted. Muscles I didn't even know I had ached, and all I wanted was a long shower and to sleep for the next twenty-four hours.

As I drove down the long driveway, I stared at the old farmhouse, barely recognizing it with the exterior almost finished. When Victoria and Adam purchased the house last year, I was one of the first ones to come tour the property. I said nothing to them, but inside, I had doubts. They had a lot of work ahead of them, and while Adam had deep pockets, they could've been buying a money pit.

But somehow, they'd turned that dilapidated old farmhouse into their dream home, a place that would suit their family for many years to come.

I loved all the work they'd put into it, but my favorite part was the wrap-around porch. It went all the way to the back of the house, showcasing the valley and lake below. It was something out of a postcard. The whole place was calming, making you leave your worries at the door. My stress was already fading.

I pulled my truck next to Adam's SUV and noticed a third car parked there. The beat-up teal sedan was familiar, especially when I saw the cluttered back seat. No one else would drive a car with that obnoxious color and have that much crap left inside.

"Hadley," I muttered under my breath.

Hadley was the last person I wanted to see after a long day. What the hell was she even doing here?

Last I'd heard, she wanted to travel across the country, planning on visiting all fifty states before she settled down. It tracked for her. Hadley was always a bit of a wildcard. Even though we'd stopped spending time together after Victoria dropped out of school, it was impossible to ignore her. Hadley drew everyone into her orbit, making you want to get closer, even if all of your instincts screamed to stay away.

Over our four years at school together, I'd watched plenty of people fall at her feet, desperate for an ounce of her attention. It might have been her smile, the kind that made you light up inside even on your worst days. Or it was because the girl was objectively stunning. When I first met Hadley, her full lips and her freckled, tanned skin called to me. Made me want to reach out and brush her honey blond curls over her shoulder, just to see how they felt. Everything about Hadley was the perfect lure, drawing me in until my defenses went down.

And that's when she would strike with her razor-sharp tongue, trying to find all of my weak points and go in for the kill.

No matter how high I tried to put up walls between us, it didn't matter. Hadley was a hurricane, a god-damned force of nature. Even though being around her was aggravating and frustrating, keeping a distance between us was a challenge. And with her close friendship with Victoria, she'd always be around. Even more, now that Emilia was obsessed with her.

That was the one good thing I could say about Hadley. She always had Victoria's back, and, by extension, Emilia's. If my daughter needed Hadley, she would move mountains to get to her. For all of her flaws, Hadley was loyal to a fault. She'd never let anyone hurt my family.

But she didn't extend that level of loyalty to me. She'd made it clear years ago that she only tolerated me because of Emilia. Making me annoyed and uncomfortable was Hadley's favorite pass-time, and it was a battle I always lost.

With a muttered curse and a long sigh, I forced myself out of my truck, grabbing my duffel bag before entering the house. At this point, I just entered, not bothering with knocking. I called out when I stepped into the foyer, and Adam came out first, shaking my hand.

"Hey man, welcome back."

"Good to be back," I said as I slid my bag to my feet. "Thank you again for letting me stay here. If it becomes too much—"

"Nah, never too much," Adam said. "You're family. You want to settle in before dinner?"

"Yeah, that'd be great," I said. Even though I showered at the stadium, it was quick, just enough to rinse the sweat off of my skin before driving back to the house. The idea of getting under the hot spray and soaking my muscles almost made me groan.

"Take your time. The girls are in the kitchen, working on dinner. I'll let them know you'll be down soon." He clapped his hand on my shoulder, then turned back down the hall.

I grabbed my bag and headed up the stairs. Luckily, after being here so many times, I knew which room was mine for the next few weeks. Different sections divided the house, likely remnants from its days as a large, multi-generational home. Victoria and Adam's bedroom and the one I was borrowing were on opposite ends of the second floor, with Emilia right in the middle. There were other rooms also dividing our spaces, from a small, loft-style play-space to Adam's home office. Don't get me wrong—I appreciated the hell out of both Adam and Victoria for letting me stay with them instead of spending the next month in a hotel. But I was also grateful for the distance between our living areas. My ex and I might be cool, but our relationship would never be that good.

As I pushed open the door, I smiled, loving the little details Victoria must have added since she last face-timed me. When we last spoke, the room was almost completely bare. But now, there was a king-sized bed in the middle, with end tables anchoring each side. On the table closest to the door, there was my favorite picture of Emilia and me, taken during her first visit to my old stadium back home. Although, considering it was park benches and a pile of mud, it felt odd referring to that place as a stadium after spending the day in a state-of-the-art one. But it was where my career started, where I learned the meaning of the game. It would have killed me to end my career there, but I'd always be grateful for that team.

I dropped my duffel by the door. It wasn't much. I'd only brought the essentials, leaving everything else in my storage unit back in Boston. I'd barely had time to get it into storage before moving out here, and I was in no rush to pull it out now. Now that my career would hopefully be stable for a couple of years, I wanted to settle down. Put down roots. Even if I got traded, I still wanted a place here, close to where my daughter would grow up. This was her home, and for that fact alone, I'd make it mine as well.

Just as I got settled, a soft knock came on the door. Victoria popped her head inside the room. "Dinner's almost ready. You good to eat in like 15?"

"Yup," I nodded. As I stood, I pointed to the ensuite

bathroom. "Just gonna grab a quick shower, and then I'll head down."

Victoria toyed with her fingers, averting her eyes around the room. "Listen, there is one thing I might have forgotten to mention when I offered the room to you."

I arched my brow. "Do I even want to know, Vic?"

"It's about Hadley."

My jaw tensed, especially when Victoria looked at me with a sheepish smile. "Did she take off and join the circus? Because that would make my fucking day."

"Not exactly," Victoria said. "Remember how we've been renovating that old carriage house on the edge of the property? Well, it got done right as I convinced Hadley to take a substitute teaching job nearby. So...."

"So?"

"She's also staying here," Victoria pushed out. As my jaw hung open, she gave me a guilty smile. "And I might have also invited her over for dinner, so play nice, Cam."

"Me?" I said, finding my voice after that shock. "Tell her to play nice. She's the one who goes for the jugular every chance she gets."

"I already did," Victoria said. "And who knows? This could be an opportunity for you two to clear the air."

"Doubt it."

"Cam..." She rubbed her fingers over her tense brow. "Please, for Emilia, can you try to get along with her? She's picking up on the tension between you two, and she feels bad. Like she has to choose who she wants to spend time with."

That broke my heart. My issues with Hadley were ours to deal with, and I hated that my six-year-old was picking up on them. I would do anything for Emilia. Even deal with chaos incarnate, with a smile on my face.

"I'll try," I sighed.

"That's all I ask."

With that, Victoria left my room, closing the door behind her. As her footsteps faded down the hallway, I cursed, muttering to myself. Knowing that I would be spending the foreseeable future with Hadley was enough to make me repack my bag and high-tail it out of here. In fact, the only thing stopping me was that I knew that she'd see that as a win.

Maybe we could clear the air? Sorry, Victoria, that would never happen.

SEVEN

Hadley

The smell of chili reached my nose before I entered the kitchen. After weeks of surviving on microwaved meals and frozen pizza, I drooled. Tori was making a huge effort to make Cam's welcome party special. Personally, I would have fed him something a little more toxic, but I guess it's considered a faux pas to poison the guest of honor.

When I walked inside, I spotted Victoria stirring the pot on the stove, Adam leaning against the counter, watching her work. He just smiled as she spoke of her grandmother, the one who originated the recipe. I smiled to myself as I watched them, loving how in sync they were. In my life, I'd learned love like that was rare, and when you found it, you held on with both hands. My mom never had luck in the romance department. I didn't meet most of her dates—if you could even call them that—but the few who lasted longer usually left a lot to be desired.

I walked over to Emilia and kissed the top of her head, loving when she smiled up at me. Maybe she'd grow up with a good example of love and be able to open up better when it came along. With Victoria and Adam, as well as

Cam and whoever he settled down with, giving her a good example, she'd grow up to be less jaded than me.

"What are you working on?" I asked as I took my usual seat next to her.

Emilia kept drawing, but the side of her smile ticked up. "A picture for daddy to put up in his locker." She wrinkled her nose. "Everything in there is boring."

"Well, your dad needs something to brighten it up then." A smirk formed on my face as I peeked over at the craft cabinet. "You know what would make it even better—"

"Don't even think about it, menace."

My words died out as Cam entered the room. We hadn't been in the same space for over a year, and I'd forgotten what it was like when he was close. The air was sucked out of the room, making it hard for my chest to expand—especially when he came around looking like *that*.

His dark hair was damp, and his skin was a little flushed, like he just stepped out of the shower. I couldn't help but trail my eyes down his form. God, why did you have to be so unfair? Did you have to make the guy who hated me also ridiculously attractive?

It was bad enough Cam dated my best friend, which automatically put him in the no-way-in-hell column, but he also couldn't stand me. I tried to shove that into the back of my mind, writing him off for the millionth time. I didn't need him to like me. I'd dealt with plenty of people who didn't enjoy my personality. But with Cam, it grated against me, and the more he pushed me away, the more I tried to get under his skin. If I had to think about him all the time, I wanted to do the same to him, to be the gnat humming in his ear.

Cam sat on the other side of Emilia, draping his arm over the back of her chair. His body wash filled the space between us, and I hated how much I liked it. It was clean, one of those scents that threw the word *mountain* in the title, but it wasn't anything artificial or overpowering. It was just, well...Cam. Masculine but comforting. Strong but subtle.

Fuck, what the hell was happening to me?

Before I could think any more about Cam, I shifted to the other side of the kitchen, grabbing a wine glass from the cabinet. Adam turned, grabbing a bottle of red from the counter and passing it over to me. As I poured a hefty amount, he arched his brow, silently asking if I was okay. While Tori was my soul-sister, Adam had become an older brother. He was always checking in with me, and I had to admit—I liked it. They treated me like a part of the family, even though I was an intruder. I gave him a subtle nod, and his brow furrowed, like he didn't quite believe me but wouldn't push.

"So..." Tori asked as she grabbed the bowls from the cabinet. "How did your first day go?"

"Not bad," Cam said. "Still pretty surreal, but it was good to be on the field, get a feel of the stadium."

"How was it?" Adam asked.

"Pretty damn cool. It's got all the bells and whistles. Just wait until you come to a game. It's going to blow your mind."

"I'd like that," Adam chuckled. "Might have to wait a bit. I'm waiting to hear about a project I'm interested in. If it works out..." He gave Tori a look. "I might be out of town for a couple of months."

"Oooh," I said. "Please, please tell me it's another super-hero movie. You've deprived us since you all hung up your tights. I need more. The world needs more."

Cam rolled his eyes while everyone else laughed. Adam

shook his head, "Not this time, Hads. I hate to break it to you—I'm pretty sure I'm done with those types of roles. Doesn't interest me anymore. Plus—" He walked over to Victoria and wrapped his arms around her shoulders. He leaned down and pressed a kiss to her temple. "Those shoots are too long. I can't stand to be away from home that much."

"Fine," I mock-groaned. "I guess I can forgive, considering it's for true love and all."

We gathered everything up in the kitchen and then joined Cam and Emilia at the table. With the two of them already settled, I moved over to the other side, away from my usual seat. It felt weird to cram three of us together while the other side was empty. As soon as I sat down, I realized I made a mistake. Because from this spot, Cam and I were directly across from each other.

When he looked up, a smile remained on his face, left over from whatever he was talking to Emilia about. For a moment, I pretended he meant the smile for me, instead of his usual stern look. Cam's smile made my stomach churn in an unexpected way. How could I have forgotten about that dimple on the side of his face? It was one of the first features I noticed about him when we met, loving how it made him seem more boyish, like he didn't have the weight of the world sitting on top of his shoulders.

When he caught me staring, he arched a brow, almost waiting for me to make a comment. I swallowed any of the barbs sitting on the tip of my tongue, hoping this tentative peace between us could last a little longer.

EIGHT

Cameron

The truce between Hadley and me lasted twenty minutes. It started off slowly, side looks and scoffs under our breaths. By the time we were down to the last bites of our dinner, we were staring daggers at each other, our promises of peace and attempts at civility out the window.

"Are you seriously trying to argue that Professor Miller graded fairly?" Hadley scowled across the table. "The man's a fascist who only wanted his own ideologies repeated back to him!"

I leaned back in my chair and crossed my arms. I'd never admit it, but Hadley was right. Our shared philosophy professor—the one class we had in common in college—was an absolute nightmare. He'd talk down to the women in the class while praising the men when they brought up the same points. I hated the guy and had filed various complaints about him after I took his course.

But I wasn't about to let her know that.

After Victoria dropped out of school to take care of Emilia, Hadley's path never crossed with mine. At least, not until we walked into opposite ends of the philosophy class' lecture hall, our eyes meeting for the first time in a year. The moment I saw her, all those long-buried thoughts came rushing to the surface. My eyes roamed over her face, as if committing any changes to memory.

But Hadley's eyes only narrowed, her face contorting into a bitter stare. That was enough to bring our last conversation back to the surface, the one where Hadley blamed me for Victoria dropping out.

In reality, she wanted to leave school to be there for our daughter. I knew it killed her to walk away, especially when she'd just found her footing outside our hometown, but after living in the shadow of her father's career, Victoria wanted to do things differently when she became a parent. I'd tried to convince her to stay in school, even offering to drop out with her when we got the positive test result. Victoria refused to let me, and once she made up her mind, there was no changing it. I'd be forever grateful she pushed me to complete my degree. I owed it to Victoria—and Emilia—to finish what we'd started together.

"We should move on," Victoria said from the other side of the table. "College was a long time ago, guys."

That would have been smart, but I couldn't let it go, not yet. Hadley always got the last word, but she'd struck a nerve with her comments.

"And you're any better?" I scoffed back at Hadley. "You said I only got a better grade on that final paper because I was on the baseball team."

Yes, it was a stupid thing to hold on to, but the sting was still there. It was one of the few times Hadley and I had called a truce, forced to work together on a group project that took up weeks of our time. Every day, I looked forward to seeing her, thinking we were amending our friendship. Hadley warmed up to me, no longer looking at me like the devil who impregnated her best friend and forced her to drop out of school. At least, until the final grades came out.

Hadley shook her head. "Only one person got above a C. One out of sixty students. Are you telling me you deserved an A?"

Yeah, I fucking did. I worked my ass off on that paper, almost to the detriment of my team. I'd stayed up so late, I almost missed practice. Our college coach was strict—miss practice? You were out the next game. But I never wanted to be that guy, the one who got by only because he had some athletic ability. I wanted to do well in school, wanted to have something to fall back on in case baseball didn't work out.

But I didn't say any of that to Hadley.

I shrugged and leaned back in my chair. "Does it matter?"

Hadley's dark blue eyes flared, and it took everything in me not to smirk. She always had the upper hand, leaving me staring at her with that same annoyed expression. Let her judge. Let her think the worst.

But I should have known better. Hadley never did what I expected her to do.

"You're right," Hadley sighed. "I...uh. I read your paper." Shock must have colored my face, because her cheeks filled with a vibrant blush. "You left it after the last class, and I couldn't help myself. It was good. Really good."

"Wow," Victoria whispered to Adam. "I think hell just froze over."

Hadley gave her a saccharine smile before turning back to me. "You deserved that A, but I did too. I tried to argue that with Miller, and he made a sexist comment."

"He did what?" I bit out, not knowing where this protective urge appeared from.

Hadley shook her head. "It doesn't matter. Like you said —it was a long time ago. It's just stuck with me all this time because I hate when my intelligence comes with a caveat." A ghost of a smile crossed her lips. "I tried to report him, but they called it retaliation for my crappy grade. No one took me seriously, and I took it out on you. Sorry, Cam."

I kept staring at Hadley, not sure about the mixed-up emotions swirling inside me. On one hand, it felt good to hear those words after all the comments over the years. Maybe it was because she was so close to Victoria, but I hated how Hadley assumed I'd only gotten by because of baseball. After a long beat, I cleared my throat and nodded. "Thanks, Hadley."

"Okay..." Victoria said as she stood. "I'm going to clear the table while we're at a good stopping point. I don't want to shake this peace we have right now."

NINE

Hadley

Later that night, while Adam and Victoria put Emilia to bed, I stayed to help with the dishes. Even though they had a dishwasher, I enjoyed washing them by hand. Something about the rhythmic task soothed me, letting me work through all the chaos in my mind. Cam was somewhere in the house, but he'd left the room right after Victoria and Adam. For all I knew, he went to bed without saying a word to me. *Not like I expected him to.* As I ran the sponge over a bowl, I tried to push him out of my mind, still unsure about what happened earlier.

I'd apologized—to Cam.

And I meant every word.

Lots of things irked me about Cam. He used to be so arrogant and rigid, it made my head hurt. But that was back in college, and even I had to admit, he had changed a lot over the years. Emilia had brought out a lot of his better qualities, and he was the best dad I ever met. He doted on his little girl and was a great co-parent with Victoria. It was also getting harder to hold on to my resentment about

Victoria leaving school now that she was doing so well. Maybe this was always her path. Why did I question it?

Beyond that, so many of my issues with Cam were out of his control, resentment over our situations instead of his actions. Thinking about when that professor had refused to change my grade, it brought up all the feelings I tried to bury—feelings of inadequacy and shame. It was like being thrust back into my childhood. Everyone had judged me because of my circumstances, rather than trying to get to know me better. God, every time I thought I'd moved on past these problems, they loved to rear their ugly heads.

But no matter the reason, I'd still pushed off those feelings onto Cam. Easier to target someone else than try to deal with the root cause. And now, I'd done the same thing to Cam other people had done to me: I'd judged him unfairly.

"Fuck," I whispered as I placed the dish on the rack. Did I really feel guilty about how I'd treated Cam over the years? When Victoria told me to cut Cam some slack, I thought it meant we'd get through a conversation without taking swipes at each other—not me apologizing to him.

As if he knew he was occupying all my thoughts, Cam strode into the kitchen and opened the fridge. He grabbed a bottle of water, and I was sure he'd head back to his room without acknowledging me. Instead, he walked over to my side, placed the bottle down, then held out the towel.

"Let me dry."

I shook my head. "I've got it."

"Let me help, menace." He reached out and took the dish from my hand.

We moved in silence for a few moments, working together to clear the rest of the sink. It was weird. Cam's presence always created tension, like I was waiting for him to say something annoying. But that same hum wasn't in the air tonight, like we'd both laid down our armor inside these walls.

Despite all the dishes being clean and on the rack, I didn't move, instead toying with the towel in my hands. I should have just left, gotten away from Cam as soon as possible—but I didn't.

From the way he stood there, tapping his fingers on the counter, Cam didn't seem in any hurry to leave either.

"How's the team shaping up?" I asked.

"It's, uh, different." Cam smirked, and my insides turned to jelly. When he smiled like that, there was that small dimple on the left side of his face. It made him look almost charming. He shifted so his hip leaned on the counter. "We're trying to feel each other out, but it's going to take time. Hopefully, we can get it together so we can get into the playoffs."

"And when's that?"

Cam chuckled. "You really know nothing about baseball, do you, menace?"

"You swing the bat and then run around in a giant circle? That's about the extent of my knowledge," I said as I turned toward him, shocked to find Cam smiling back at me. It was probably the longest we'd been cordial in, well, ever.

"That's the basics," he said. "But that's when we're up at bat. Otherwise, we're on the field, and we need to depend on each other. You've gotta be able to trust your teammate to complete the play correctly. And when you haven't played together that long..."

"That trust is hard to come by," I finished for him.

"Yeah," he sighed. "But we've got to get there fast. Got a big series at the end of the week."

"Damn, you don't get any downtime, do you?"

"Not really," he said. "The season is hectic and exhausting, but it's also the best kind of high. We don't really get a solid break until the season is over."

I nodded, still toying with the towel in my hand. Cam took a step closer to me, and my breath hitched in my throat, suddenly overwhelmed by his presence. Cam wasn't the most imposing guy, practically a human-sized teddy bear, but he still eclipsed me in size and height. He was easily a foot taller than me, especially when I was barefoot. As I looked up into his clear eyes, I tried to keep my breathing steady. *He dated your best friend.* The sharp reminder made me edge backward, stopping when my hip jammed into the edge of the countertop.

Cam's face twisted into a grin, making that damn dimple pop again. "Why did you apologize to me, Hadley?"

"Because I was wrong." I inhaled sharply. "And...I know what it's like to be judged because of your position in life. Even unintentionally, I did that to you. And I am sorry."

"I know you are," he said. "That's the thing about you, Hadley. You tell the truth, even when it hurts. It's admirable."

"It is?"

"Yeah." He smirked. "You're an open book, and that's a good thing. Always honest to a fault, even if you're busting my balls."

"I thought you hated when I did that." My voice turned meek, barely above a whisper, as if raising it would break this moment between us. As much as I tried to tell myself this was Cam—someone I'd spent the better part of seven years hating—I didn't want this to end. I liked this little bubble when we weren't a menace and a drill sergeant—just

Cam and Hadley, two people who might have been friends if things had worked out differently.

He smiled, but it differed from his usual cocky grin. This one was slight, almost vulnerable. "Not as much as I should," he whispered. The hushed confession clung to the air between us, and I stared up at Cam, studying the serene expression on his face. His admiration, his respect, it was all there. I'd just never taken the time to look before.

"I don't hate you as much as I should either." The words rushed out of my mouth before I could think better of it.

Cam's eyes crinkled in delight as he reached out and carefully took the towel from my hands. He placed it on the counter and then traced my palm with his thumb. Lightning lingered on my skin where he touched, and my mouth went dry. My body erupted in butterflies, tumbling out from the places he traced. It was jarring, the sudden shift from disdain to desire, but the need for him to keep touching me was overwhelming.

"Hadley—"

Just as my name left his lips, Adam burst into the kitchen, breaking the quiet stalemate between us. "Which stuffy is Peanut Butter?" he huffed as he searched the dining room. "Emilia doesn't want to go to sleep without it."

"Yeah," Cam said, jumping away from me to join Adam on the hunt. "She's that purple elephant Calla and Theo got for her last month. I saw her in the living room earlier."

With that, both men left the kitchen. But when he reached the doorway, Cam stopped, giving me one last, secret smile. "You good, menace?"

I rolled my eyes. "Better than you, sarge."

TEN

Hadley

As the last car pulled away from the curb, I let out a long breath. Another week over. It was almost bittersweet, watching the weeks tick by on the calendar. On the one hand, teaching could be exhausting, more than I ever realized. Rewarding for sure, but exhausting. I looked forward to the weekend but also dreaded striking the days from my calendar. Each day down meant another day closer to this assignment being finished. I should've been excited about that, especially considering I'd planned out the next few months already. I'd be traveling north, trying to get in as many as the colder states before the weather shifted.

But each day I spent with these kids, the harder it was to think about leaving them behind. Watching them grow and learn new things was intoxicating, making me smile for days on end.

A few of my colleagues bustled through the door, breaking me out of my thoughts. On Friday afternoons, everyone left the school in a rush. In another life, I'd be right there with them, excitedly chattering about all the fun things we'd planned.

Not me.

Tonight, I had a date with my Netflix account and my couch.

I'd avoided the main house for most of the week. After that strange moment between Cam and me in the kitchen, I wanted to stay off his radar. I still didn't know what passed over us. How did we end up so close, closer than we'd ever been before? And why, days later, did I have zero clue how I felt about it?

Okay, the second part was a lie. It was intoxicating, being the sole focus of Cam's attention, like being trapped in the hurricane's eye, a calm serenity surrounded by overwhelming forces. But it also made an uncomfortable guilt settle in my stomach, like reaching for something that wasn't mine to take. No matter how settled Victoria and Adam became, Cam would always be her first love, her daughter's father. I couldn't allow myself to forget that, no matter what my stupid hormones wanted me to think.

I walked back inside and headed into my classroom, just in time to wave Brianna off for the weekend. I'd tried to ask her to hang out, and she said something about spending time with her husband before evading the question.

As I prepped my lessons for the following week, my mind kept wandering, wondering what would be next for me. While most people needed to have a plan, I was the opposite. I hated the idea of settling for something so routine. It was probably because of my childhood. What most people don't tell you about living with chaotic parents? You learn to thrive in the unknown. To resist change only led to heartache. Complacency and comfort made me itch, like wearing a sweater that was too tight. In the past, things going well meant more room for disappointment. Now that I was an adult, I'd always chosen the road less taken, the more challenging one, but it was worthwhile to me.

I refused to always play it safe.

I wanted the adventure.

"Ms. McKay," the principal, Mr. Cutler, greeted as he knocked on my classroom door. "Can you stop by my office before you head home?"

My heart instantly beat faster. It didn't matter how old you were; when you got called to the principal's office, your pulse raced—especially considering I was only a temporary hire.

My anxiety only rose as I followed him into his office, and he shut the door behind us. "So, Ms. McKay, I've gotten numerous phone calls from the parents of your students."

"Oh?" I asked, trying to make my voice calm.

"Yes, they're very impressed. I agree with them. You're doing an excellent job running the classroom."

"Oh!" I said, ducking to hide the color on my cheeks. Even though this job was only for another couple of months, it felt good he'd noticed my hard work. "Thank you, sir. It's been a pleasure to work here. I've loved getting to know the teachers and students."

"I'm pleased we've made a good impression." Mr. Cutler smiled at me. Just as I was about to stand, he said, "I spoke to Mrs. Noltings last week. She's one of our fourth-grade teachers. She's going to have a baby in September, and we need someone to cover her leave. Before I posted the position, I wanted to ask if you would be interested in joining us next year. You would begin right in September alongside Mrs. Noltings and then take over when she went on maternity leave. And who knows," he chuckled. "Perhaps we'll find a permanent position for you when this wraps up."

Oh, shit. This was the last thing I expected when I walked into his office. I loved this school, loved the purpose it gave me. This should have been the dream. But agreeing to this job meant my dream of opening a daycare center was dead. The thought zapped all the breath from my lungs.

As if he read the panic on my face, Mr. Cutler continued, "You have some time to think about it. I'll post the position, and we'll hold interviews at the beginning of August. If you decide you'd like the job, please let me know. We'd love to have you."

"I'll do that," I said as I stood, not waiting to be dismissed. As soon as I shut the office door, I leaned against the wall. My heart thumped an erratic beat, unable to handle the weight of the decision now resting on my shoulders.

It should have been a simple answer. *No, thanks.* I had other dreams, ones I was determined to see through. It would also put a hold on dreams of travelling, determined to see more of the world before I tried to find my place in it.

Then again, this job offered stability, probably something I should have put more stock into. But on the other hand, I knew myself. If I stayed at this school, it would pull me in even more, and then I'd never want to leave. Finding a home was always the goal—a place to grow old with four solid walls and a strong foundation. The call was so strong, a large part of me wanted to grab this opportunity with both hands.

The offer was tempting, much more than I even wanted to admit. I meant every word I said—I loved working at this school. The kids were incredible, and I loved my teaching team. Maybe I'd even get to work with Brianna again.

"No," I spluttered as I pushed myself off the wall. I had a plan, one I owed to myself. I wasn't ready to give up on my dreams yet. Teaching and everything else would wait. It wouldn't be this school, but I'd find a job I loved again.

After stopping in my room to grab my things, I jumped into my car, needing the distance to clear my mind. When I got back, I needed to talk to Tori about what happened. She was always the voice of reason, the calm and collected one between the two of us. While I was impulsive, Tori weighed her choices before she ever leaped. It helped us balance the other out. If anyone could help me dissect the competing thoughts in my mind, it would be her.

Honestly, we needed to sit down and discuss our business plans. We'd both skated around it, neither willing to drive that final nail into the coffin. Maybe I could open the place on my own, but we'd developed based on our strengths. Victoria was the level-headed one while I was the dreamer. I'd need someone else to take on her role, someone who had the financial background to make sense of the books and any other fiscal situations. Not my strong suit. But having someone else come in would be hard, especially finding someone to trust and depend on. If that wasn't Victoria, I didn't know where I'd look.

As I pulled into the driveway, my smile fell away, not seeing her car parked in its usual spot. I pulled out my phone to text her, but I saw a message already waiting for me.

VICTORIA

Adam got the part! We're going out tonight to celebrate. Cole and Alex have Emilia, so enjoy the quiet. I'll fill you in tomorrow.

Normally, I'd be over the moon for her and Adam. She gave everything and more to Emilia, and Tori deserved some time for herself. I forced a smile as I sent her a message back, telling her to have fun and to pass my congratulations to Adam. As soon as I hit send, I dropped my head back, trying to keep the tears at bay.

God, I was being so damn selfish. Tori had her own life, and I was crying because she didn't have time for me. But I couldn't help it. I needed my best friend—my person. While I was ecstatic she'd found love, it also made a knot form in my chest.

It was fine. I'd be fine. It wasn't the first time I'd had to pivot my dreams. And look how that turned out—I found my best friend and so many more amazing things. Perhaps the universe was signaling to embrace my wandering spirit more.

I leaned back in my seat, trying to force my tears away. I hadn't lost Victoria, but I'd been pushed aside a little. Would this rift continue to grow between us until it became a chasm? Would I be stuck here, waiting for my dreams to come to fruition, while everyone else grew around me?

That was a depressing thought.

As I tried to talk myself out of my spiral, a knock came from the window. I turned my head, meeting Cam's disapproving frown.

"What are you doing in there, menace?

ELEVEN

Cameron

What the hell was I doing?

I should have been in my truck, heading back to the field for our game tonight. I'd already pushed my luck by sneaking out of practice, hoping to get back before our manager realized I'd ducked out. But I'd forgotten one of my good luck charms, and there was no way I could play knowing it sat on my end table. Damien covered for me as I rushed back to the house. The rest of the guys would be relaxing in the clubhouse anyway, trying to get their heads together before we had to take the field.

I should have hopped right back into my truck and slammed on the gas, should have already been on the highway, praying a trooper didn't pull me over. Instead, when I left the house, my feet faltered when I saw Hadley unraveling in her car.

It was jarring. The girl never got rattled and always seemed to be in an annoyingly good mood. She was all smiles and rays of light. So, seeing her close to tears brought an uncomfortable ache to my chest.

Before I questioned my actions, I stepped to the driver's

side of her car and rapped my knuckles on her window. Her blue eyes darted to mine, and I sucked in a breath, almost losing the ability to speak when she looked at me like that. Shit, had I ever really looked at Hadley? Sure, I'd spent time with her, knew the girl was beautiful. But now that we were so close, I couldn't help but take in the little details I'd over-looked before. The deep blue of her eyes, the color like the deepest trenches of the ocean. The dusting of freckles that covered the bridge of her nose. How her lips pouted so perfectly when she was surprised.

"What are you doing in there, menace?" I called out, unable to ignore the feeling in my chest. The longer I stared at Hadley, the more I noticed, which was a fucking prob-lem. I needed her to piss me off and remind me why she irritated me so much.

She shoved open the car door, almost taking me out in the process. "Didn't anyone ever teach you it's rude to spy on people?"

"Don't flatter yourself," I scoffed. "You're having a melt-down in the middle of the driveway. I'd have to be a dick to ignore that."

"Never stopped you before."

But her words didn't hold their usual level of snark, and when I looked down at her, it seemed like she was doing everything to keep herself standing tall. It softened the walls in my chest, wanting to take that look off her face. "You wanna talk about it?"

Hadley's eyes darted up to me, her brow furrowing in confusion. "You want to talk? To me?"

"If you want." I shrugged. "You seem like you could use someone right now."

It was the absolute last thing I should do right now. Every minute I stood here was a minute I missed from my pre-game ritual. I'd be cutting it close, and now, there was an even bigger risk of Benny catching me sneaking back into the stadium.

Hadley shook her head, "No. Thank you, but the last thing I want to do is talk right now. Honestly..." She chewed on her lower lip, looking over to the carriage house, then back over to me. "I need to get out of my head, find something to do for the night that doesn't require me to think."

"Come with me."

The words came out before I realized it, flying out with some sort of need to help. I should've taken them back, said anything else to get Hadley out of my space. I was playing with fire, and God knows she loved to burn me. Seeing her so defeated fucked with my head, and for some damn reason, I wanted to be the one to fix it.

I nodded over to my truck. "Come to the game with me. I can hook you up with a ticket, and you can sit with some of the other families and friends."

"You want me to come to your game?" Hadley repeated slowly.

I shrugged. "If you want to. No thinking required, just some overpriced beer and cheering for our team."

"If I decide to come, do I have to cheer for you?" Hadley asked, some of that familiar spark coming back into her voice.

I just shook my head and held out my hand for her stuff. "Come on, menace. Get your ass in the truck."

***

HOME GAMES WERE A DIFFERENT BEAST. Tension hung in the air, almost as if the stadium was waiting to see what the team would pull together. With our newer team breaking even in losses and wins, fans filled the seats, cautiously optimistic about our season so far. Even though the Hawks were new to the city, it had embraced the team, and people came out in droves to experience the stadium for the very first time.

Now, if only I felt the same way. Becoming part of the team was a change, one I appreciated and didn't take lightly. I'd found my stride in the outfield, but the whole thing seemed like an audition. One wrong move, and they'd kick me right back down to the minors.

I stared at the phone in my hand, desperately waiting for it to ring. My eyes darted up to the clock, knowing it was now or never. Just as I started to lose faith, my phone rang out, Victoria's brother on the other side of the line.

"Hey, man. Sorry about that," Cole huffed out. "We walked down to the lake, and I left my phone at the house. Here's your girl."

All the tension left my shoulders when Emilia got on the screen, her toothy smile wide as she looked at me. "Is it time for your game, Daddy?"

"Almost, baby. You ready?"

"Yup." She smiled back at me. "Love you."

"Love you more," I said into the phone.

"Love you forever and ever," we both said at the same time. It was a simple tradition we'd started, way back when Emilia's words were more like babbles. We'd said the same phrases, and I had one of the best games of my career—the one that got me picked up by our local minor league team. Ever since, I needed to hear her voice before I headed out onto the field. Call it superstition, call it luck, but whenever I heard my daughter's voice before the game, I always played better.

We said a quick goodbye, and I got back into my pre-game ritual, taking the time to get my head right before we got started. I was usually good at tuning out the rest of the world, but tonight, it was harder to focus. Maybe it was the pressure of wanting to do well.

Or maybe it had something to do with Hadley being out in the crowd.

When we got to the stadium earlier, I asked one of the guest services reps to help her find her seat while I went to the locker room, watching a little too long as she walked away. Sadness still clung to her, but it wasn't as strong as before. Hopefully, the game would help her escape her worries for a while. I wished she'd tell me what had upset her. My fists clenched at the image of her in that car, defeat coming off her in waves. But I wasn't someone she'd ever confide in. That was Victoria's role.

My phone dinged, and an alert from a cash-sharing app awaited me. Hadley had sent me money for the seat. I chuckled, automatically sending it right back to her.

As soon as I moved down here, I bought three season tickets, hoping Victoria, Adam, and Emilia could attend some of my home games. They wouldn't be able to make all of them, but I didn't want them to have to worry about seats if they wanted to come. I liked that someone was using them, even if it was Hadley.

My phone pinged again, and there was the same amount, with Hadley sending a follow-up text.

> MENACE
>
> Accept the damn payment, sarge.

> ME
>
> Nope. I asked you here. Seat's my treat.

I stared at my phone, waiting for a response. When it

finally came through, I couldn't help the wide grin that spread across my face.

MENACE

Fine. But I will make it up to you somehow.

ME

Stop giving Emilia glitter, and we'll call it even.

Never gonna happen.

Have a good game, Cam. You've got this.

"Fuck, man," Damien said from my side, breaking my focus from my phone. "Must be texting someone good. You've got that goofy grin."

"Nah," I said, trying to fix my face. "Nothing like that. Just getting my head in the game."

Damien nodded, fidgeting with the chain around his neck. He touched each of the pendants before tucking it under his jersey and patted it twice. As he turned back toward me, I ducked my head, not wanting him to know I was watching. Baseball players were notoriously superstitious about their pre-game routines, and I didn't want to be the one to throw him off.

Damien grabbed the towel from the top of his locker and twisted it in his hands. "How do you think we're looking?"

"Pretty good," I said. I truly believed it. Our team might be new and untested, but we'd walked away from our last series as the victors. Despite Weber's comments, we'd done well in practice. At least, most of us had. I jutted my chin across the locker room to where another group of players gathered. "You might have to have words with Jace."

"Still refusing to pass the ball?"

"Yup," I bit out. In the outfield, it was my job to end runs. It meant I had to work closely with the infield players and needed to trust they'd be where they were supposed to be. But our second baseman had an attitude, one that had steadily grown since I joined the team. Jace was a lot like me, drafted up from the minors and looking to make a name for himself. What he hadn't realized? Teams hate selfish players, especially the kind who would screw over other players to get the headlines.

Damien shook his head. "Don't worry about him. If Coach doesn't talk some sense into him, Gray will. He's got no patience for that shit."

I turned, studying the expression on Damien's face. "Is that weird for you? Going from him being your teammate to your coach?"

"Nah, Anders always had it in him. And that last season, his heart wasn't in it. He seems happier now, so I'm happy for him. Makes me think there might be life after retirement."

My jaw locked up. "Are you thinking about calling it?"

"Nah, man," Damien chuckled. "You'll have to drag my old ass off the field. I'm here as long as my body will let me."

"Good to know," I said right as the coaches shuffled in. With a few quick words and reminders about what we were playing for, we all headed off, ready to show our fans what we had under the lights.

TWELVE

Hadley

Holy hell. The air was electric in the stadium. I'd never been to a professional baseball game, and I understood the appeal. A Hawks fan filled almost every seat, many ripping the tags off their brand-new jerseys, purchased from one of the many gift shops inside. There were a ton of Ramos ones in the surrounding space; from what I'd gathered, he was one of the most senior players.

"The Rebels traded him to the Hawks," Ollie said from the seat next to me. She'd introduced herself right away, noticing the shell-shocked look in my eyes. "Damien's got the most impressive stats coming into the season, so a lot of fans are here to see him." She scrunched her nose as she scanned the crowd, then pointed across the seats with a wide smile on her face. "There's also some with the other guys' names. Don't worry—with the way your guy's been performing, he'll be selling out in no time." Ollie elbowed me. "In fact, there's one now."

I smiled as I spotted the guy wearing number eight, Seda embroidered across their back. It had nothing to do with me, yet I felt a huge amount of pride for Cam, knowing how hard he worked to get to this moment. But as I tried to school my smile, Ollie's words came back to me. "Wait, Cam's not my guy. We're..."

What even were we? Reluctant friends? Mutually parasitic houseguests? Cam didn't fit in any of the usual assigned categories, so I picked the one that required the least amount of explanation. "We're friends."

Ollie shook her head. "Trust me, I get that." She scanned the audience again and pointed out another last name on the back of a jersey. But this one said Drobrek in all caps. "That's Parker. He's been my best friend since we could walk." She lifted her can of beer and clinked it against mine. "Welcome to the platonic baseball besties' fan club."

"Is that a thing?"

"Nope," Ollie said. "But I'm making it one. All the other women in these seats are wives and girlfriends. They give you strange looks if you say you're friends with one of the guys. At least, that's how it was with Parker's old team. They never believed me when I said we're only friends."

I'd never say this to Ollie, but I got where the question came from. The girl was objectively gorgeous. She had a chin length, bleach blonde bob and a smile that lit up the entire stadium. Her green eyes were wide and welcoming, and insecurity washed over me in her presence. Hell, I hadn't even met Parker, and here I questioned his decision to stay in the friend zone.

Before I could ask more questions, music blared from the speaker. Ollie grabbed my arm. "Ahh, I love this part. Get ready to scream for your guy!"

As intros started, I whooped and yelled with the rest of the crowd. All the other names were unfamiliar to me, but the excitement built as they each stepped out onto the field. Ollie screamed when the announcer called out Parker's name. He rushed out to the field, and his eyes darted to the stands. When he spotted Ollie, he smiled widely, making some sort of signal with his hands. Ollie returned the gesture, then turned toward me.

"What was that?"

"Nothing." She blushed. "It's this thing we've done since grade school."

I was dying to find out more about her past with Parker, but when the announcers introduced number eight, I couldn't help but jump up to my feet. My eyes darted to the screen, where a large picture of Cam's close-up smiled back at me.

The crowd went wild as he ran out onto the field, a ridiculously wide grin filling his face. It was so different from the Cam I knew—rigid about rules and always looking to put me in my place. Victoria always said he came to life on the field, but I never knew what she meant until now.

The announcers kept calling out other names, but my attention remained fixed on Cam. I watched as he stretched, as he joked with his teammates. He was magnetic, and I kept being pulled into his world, helpless to fight the attraction. Cam only made it worse when his eyes scanned the crowd and he found me sitting in the seat he'd gifted me. I half-expected the smile to fade when he caught me watching him. Instead, he just kept grinning, and then he winked at me.

What the fuck was that?

And worse—why did I like it so much?

It was like there was a secret between us, a connection neither of us had ever acknowledged. Was this what it would be like if Cam and I were actually friends? Would I be in this seat more often, cheering him on at each of his home games? The idea appealed to me, much more than I wanted to admit.

As I leaned back, my smile still etched on my face, Ollie leaned into my side. "You sure you're just friends?"

* * *

MY BASEBALL KNOWLEDGE might have been minimal when I walked into the stadium, but that was no longer the case. Through each inning, Ollie explained the rules and all the calls from the umpire—a term I'd learned after I called him a referee during the first inning.

When the final score filled the board, the Hawks had won their first game by a couple of runs, and I had a new friend to add to my roster. Ollie gave me her phone number and made me promise I'd come to plenty more games this season.

After the team left the field, we hung back for a bit, finishing the last of our beers and the pretzel we'd shared. I had to admit—I loved the vibe of being at the field. Sitting among the fans, we were all a part of the team, rooting for our boys to bring home the win.

When we demolished the last couple of bites, Ollie's phone rang. "The guys are almost done with press and showers. We should get going."

"Where?" I asked, my mouth still stuffed with dough.

"The friends and family area," she said. "Man, Cam needs to give you the tour before the next game."

"You're telling me," I muttered as I climbed to my feet, tossing our trash in the garbage before following Ollie. She grasped my hand as we went straight toward the elevators. She showed them our badges, which, luckily, the attendant had given me before the game started. I hadn't asked what it was for, but apparently, select friends and family got them so they could wait for the team outside the locker rooms.

As we climbed off the elevators, Ollie burst into the crowd, jumping into the arms of one of the waiting players. He didn't even flinch as she launched herself, catching her with a practiced ease. I recognized Parker from the image on the big screen earlier. Now that he was off the field, he was wearing glasses that made him look like a blond version of Superman. He held Ollie tight for a long moment, then pulled back.

He placed her back on the ground but stayed close. "What did you think, Oleander?"

"I loved it!" she squeaked. She turned around, finding me waiting behind her. "And I met a new friend. This is Hadley. She came with Cam."

"Nice to meet you," Parker said as he extended his hand. "He'll be right out. Coach just wanted a word with him."

I nodded, too distracted by the rest of the group to listen to his words. Excitement radiated through everyone in the crowd, an intoxicating mix of pride and relief. It was exactly how I felt, and suddenly, I was beyond excited to see Cam.

When he came out of the locker room only moments later, it took everything in me to stay in place, to not launch myself into his arms like Ollie had done with Parker. We were friends. At least, sort of. And friends hugged during moments like this, didn't they?

As I overanalyzed my next move, Cam stepped closer to me, his eyes almost glassy with happiness. "Hey, menace," he said as he pulled me into a hug without pause. I relaxed in his arms before placing my own around his waist. My head rested against his chest for a beat, taking in the subtle scent that would always belong to Cam.

I cleared my throat, then shifted away from him. "Good game, sarge. You killed it out there."

"I did alright," he said. "Gotta say, never thought I'd see you cheering for me in the stands."

"You invited me," I bit out, embarrassed by my enthusiasm. My cheeks flooded with heat, and all I wanted was for it to fade away before Cam noticed.

Cam shook his head. "Didn't say it was a bad thing, Hadley. I liked seeing you up there."

"You did?" I asked, my mouth dropping open at the insinuation.

He shook his head, taking my hand and leading me through the crowd. I looked down at our joined palms. Why did this seem so natural? After everything we'd been through, Cam should be the last person whose hand I held.

So why didn't I want to let go?

THIRTEEN

Cameron

The drive back to the house was drastically different from our ride out to the stadium. Hadley animatedly asked me everything about the game, wanting to understand every single play. It made me smile, knowing she not only enjoyed herself but was getting invested in baseball.

Victoria was the same way, taking in each game and always wanting to debrief afterward. But Hadley brought her usual spark to the conversation, and it made me smile. I used to pray Hadley had an off-switch, that she'd keep quiet for five seconds, but when she'd gone quiet on me during the ride out to the stadium, I hated it.

Hadley's fire brought out my own, making me even more proud of the game I played. It was a close one. We'd given up a few too many runs, and there were a couple of plays that should've gone smoother, but we were starting the weekend off on a good note, and that was all I wanted.

The majors had been my dream for so long. I still had to pinch myself every time I walked out onto the field. But now that I was starting to make a name for myself, it was even better. When the announcer called my name and I walked out onto the field with thousands of fans shouting my name? That was a highlight of my life. There was no better feeling than the fans' support.

At least, until I found Hadley in the stands, screaming for me. I usually tried to ignore the crowd, knowing it would only add to the mounting pressure resting on my shoulders. Yet, every time I took my position, my eyes instantly found her.

She looked like she was having the time of her life, even making friends with the other family members cheering us on. Not that it surprised me—no one was immune to Hadley's charms.

Apparently, not even me.

"And that last catch?" Hadley said. "Pure fucking magic, Cam. I didn't even see the ball! How the hell did you do that?"

"Practice," I smirked. "It's a lot of muscle memory. That, and the coaches make us do drills all day."

She rolled her eyes. "This whole humble thing doesn't work for you, Cam. You were incredible on that field. Own that shit."

"Own that shit?" I shook my head. "Always poetry out of your mouth, menace."

She laughed as she settled back into the passenger seat. Her legs curled underneath her, and for a moment, I wanted to yell at her. It wasn't safe to sit like that. But then, the hem of her dress drifted a little higher, exposing a swatch of her smooth, toned thigh. My mouth went dry, and I had to squeeze the steering wheel a little tighter to resist reaching out.

It was the oddest shift in my brain. For years, I couldn't stand this girl, trying to spend as little time with her as possible. But was that even true? Could I not stand being around her, or did I like it a little too much? Looking back, Hadley always made me laugh, pulling me in with her spirit and determination. She wasn't just beautiful—she was ferocious and used her voice to help others. There was a lot to admire about Hadley McKay's spirit, but this was the first time I was letting myself admit it.

Fuck. I couldn't think about Hadley like this. There were plenty of other girls out in the world—ones who weren't best friends with my ex. Even if Hadley felt the same way, there was no way we'd ever cross that line. Victoria might not have cared, but I would. Too many strings tied us together, and with one wrong move, I would burn all of them to dust. I couldn't do that to Victoria or Emilia.

My daughter loved Hadley, thought of her like an aunt. I'd never be able to live with myself if I put that relationship at risk.

No, any simmering feelings for Hadley were just because we spent time together, nothing more. I had to get my head together, to shove Hadley back into that friends column.

"Hey Cam, are you alright?" Hadley asked, reaching out to place her hand on my forearm.

"Yeah," I pushed out gruffly. "Just thinking about tomorrow's game."

"Okay..." she said. "Because you parked the car five minutes ago but haven't moved at all."

Shit. I looked out of the windshield. We'd made it back to the farmhouse, and I'd barely realized it, too preoccupied by the spitfire next to me. I shook my head and hopped out of the truck, moving over to open Hadley's door. She tried to open it, but I cut her off. "Let me."

She wrinkled her brow as I held out my hand and

helped her down. "Look at you, sarge. Didn't know you had this side of you."

"My dad had a lot of rules about how to treat a woman," I said. "Number one, always hold the door open and help her out of the car."

"I think I'd like your dad." She smiled up at me. "Although, what would he say about you calling me a menace for almost a decade?"

I let out a loud laugh, and Hadley's eyes brightened with delight. "He'd understand after spending ten minutes with you, Hadley. He talks less than anyone else on the planet and has more rules than I can count."

"Ahh," she said as she leaned against the passenger door. "That's where you get the whole rigid thing."

My jaw tightened. "What do you mean?"

She shrugged. "I guess you've always seemed like you need control, need order. Like you have no tolerance for anyone who throws you off your routine."

I leaned in closer, unable to resist the spark in Hadley's eyes as she pressed against my truck. "Like you, Hadley?" She swallowed as she nodded. I shifted closer and lowered my voice. "I don't need control, menace. No one else tests me like you."

Her blue eyes widened as they met mine. "Why is that?"

My fingers lifted to her soft blonde hair and ran through the front strands. "I've been asking myself that same fucking question since the day we met."

"Cam..." My name was a breath against my skin, and it took everything not to pull her in closer, to hear that same low tone, but this time, I wanted to be holding her, making her eyes brighten for an entirely different reason. I had so many mixed emotions wrapped up in this woman. Frustration. Longing. Anger. Desire. They all jumbled in my mind, making it impossible to move away from her. My hand shifted, and my thumb traced her lower lip, tugging it lightly. I cursed at the first touch of her lips to my skin, wishing more than anything to kiss her for real.

Why couldn't I?

All common sense left my mind when Hadley lifted on to her toes, bringing her face closer to mine. This woman had me in tailspin, and I didn't care what would happen if we crossed the line anymore. I would give almost anything for a taste of her lips, to have her moving against me.

Just as my hands dropped to her hips, determined to make her mine for a moment, headlights flashed from the end of the driveway. Hadley let out a little shriek, darting away from me with a furious flush over her cheeks.

I stared at the space where she just stood, finally letting my mind snap back into place. What the fuck happened? Was I seriously about to kiss *Hadley*? Fuck. It had to be exhaustion, the adrenaline, something that made me lose my damned mind for a moment. She was the forbidden fruit, way too fucking tempting but lethal all the same.

Nights like this couldn't happen again. I needed to get some space from her, go back to our old routine of avoiding each other at all costs.

Adam's truck pulled up next to mine, and Victoria hopped out of the passenger seat. She bounced over and wrapped me in a tight hug. "You played so well, Cam. You should celebrate!"

"I will," I said. "With a long shower and a good night's sleep."

"Boring, but I get it." She smiled as Adam joined us and clapped me on the back.

"Sorry we weren't there," he said as he wrapped an arm

around Victoria's shoulders. "Hope you had a good number of fans cheering for you."

"Yeah," Victoria added. "Did you find someone to take our seats?"

My jaw tensed, and I resisted the urge to look at Hadley. I didn't know if she'd want Victoria to know she'd gone to the game tonight, so I shook my head. "Nah, but it's all good. We had a lot of fans cheering us on."

"I'm sure you did." She beamed at me before looking over my shoulder. "Oh my God, Hads! I'm sorry, I didn't even see you behind Cam. How's your night going?"

I glanced over my shoulder, and the moment I did, I regretted my lie. Hadley's smile was tight as she looked at Victoria. "Fine. Nothing special."

"Well, this actually works out." Victoria smiled up at Adam. "We have something we wanted to talk to both of you about." She walked over to the porch, Adam's arm still around her shoulders. "Come on, I'll make some coffee."

As they walked inside, Hadley stormed past me, not even sparing a glance in my direction. Guilt gnawed in my chest as I watched her walk through the doors, trying to remember the oath I just made.

I needed to stay away from Hadley McKay.

No matter what happened next.

FOURTEEN

Hadley

"So..." I asked. I shifted uncomfortably on the living room couch. Victoria rushed us inside, saying we needed to talk about something. Annoyingly vague. "Are you going to tell us what's going on?"

Victoria glanced at her boyfriend as she snuggled next to him on the couch. I did everything in my power not to glance over at Cam, who sat on the other side of me. I was still trying to figure out what happened outside, how we ended up pressed against his truck, half a second away from jumping each other's bones.

Did we suddenly slip into an alternate dimension? One where Cam and I not only got along, but actually wanted each other? Don't get me wrong—I appreciated a handsome man with the best of them, but Cam had never been an option. I'd never let my mind wander too far, knowing we'd never be more than passing acquaintances.

At least, until today.

From him helping me during my meltdown to the way he tugged on my lower lip, Cam had planted himself at the forefront of my mind, and I couldn't pry him out of it, even when he'd lied to Victoria about me going to the game.

I understood why he didn't tell her—it was probably the same reason I hadn't told her when we were texting earlier. Still, it stung when he lied. He seemed embarrassed about spending time with me.

Victoria's voice snapped me back into the present. "So I told both of you earlier that Adam got a part in this new movie."

"Congrats again," I said. Adam took a step away from acting a couple of years ago, after an incident with a stalker left him reeling. It took a lot to get him to even look at a script again, much less audition for a role. He'd finally stepped back in front of the camera last year, taking on a smaller part that required him to only be gone for a couple of weeks. Despite being a smaller, independent film, it had done well and brought a lot of attention back on Adam. Last we spoke, he had a ton of project offers, but nothing seemed to interest him. I was thrilled he found something interesting.

"Thanks, Hadley." Adam clasped her hand in his. "I'm really excited. It's more of an action role than I originally expected, but it's got a really strong script. There's just one problem."

"It's filming in Australia," Victoria finished for him.

If there had been a single cricket outside, you would have heard it chirping. Cam and I both stared at the couple in silence, unsure of what to even say. My silence broke first. "Australia like the continent?"

"I think it's a country," Cam whispered at my side.

"It's both," I bit back, holding my hand to quiet him. "And no one was talking to you."

Victoria chewed on her lower lip, glancing over at Adam. "This might not be such a great idea."

Adam squeezed her hand. "Yes, that Australia. And normally, I would say no. I hate the idea of being away from home for that long, but I've always dreamed about working with this director, and the script is pretty great. I can't pass that up."

"No, of course not," I said. "When do you leave?"

"Next week," Adam answered. "I have to go to LA for a month for rehearsals and coordinating the stunts with the team, and then I'll leave from there to head to set."

"How long is filming?" Cam asked.

"At least six weeks."

"Six weeks?" I gasped. I looked over at my best friend. She was trying to hold back tears, but I saw how much she was dreading this. While Victoria knew traveling was part of the deal when she started dating Adam, it didn't make these long stretches any easier. But she would never stand in the way of his dreams, supporting him every step of the way. I moved over to her side and wrapped my arms around her shoulders. "What are you going to do, Tori?"

"I'll be okay," she said. "It's not that long, and luckily, we're going to FaceTime every day. But three months is a long time to be apart, which is why we wanted to talk to both of you."

My spine instantly stiffened as I peeked over at Cam, who looked at Victoria with the same uneasy expression.

She inhaled slowly. "Adam asked if I'd visit him in Australia, maybe meet him in LA, and then I'd be there for the first couple weeks of filming."

"Of course you should go!" I said as I squeezed her tightly. "You've always wanted to go to Australia, and you deserve a fun trip."

But Victoria's eyes stayed fixed on Cam. A silent conversation brewed between them, and I couldn't help the pang of jealousy that struck my gut. I had no right to feel that way. They were each other's first loves, and even if it hadn't worked out, there would always be a connection between them.

Cam nodded. "I'm here for Emilia. Go, Vic. You need to go."

"I know, but it's in the middle of your season—"

"I'll figure something out."

"I can help," I blurted. Everyone in the room turned to face me, all with different expressions etched on their faces. I didn't dare glance over at Cam, instead focusing on my best friend, who gave me an appreciative smile. "It's not like it's out of the way for me. I can help Cam when he's traveling or if he has a game."

"Are you sure?" Victoria asked. "I know you love Emilia, but she can be a lot, and this would put a ton on your shoulders."

"Please." I rolled my eyes. "First—don't disparage the good name of my niece. She is a precious baby angel who does nothing wrong. And second—I've helped before. Between Cam, me, and your brother, we have plenty of people to keep her happy and safe."

She chewed on her lower lip, looking over at Cam, then back at me. "Are you sure? Obviously, I would be more comfortable with both of you keeping an eye on her, but this is a big ask, Hadley. If you aren't sure—"

"It'll be fine," I said. "Cam and I can work together to figure out a plan. We'll make it work." Adam and Victoria shared a look. "Okay, I saw that. We survived each other before, and we'll survive each other again. Right, Cam?"

I finally forced myself to glance in his direction, and I

wished I hadn't. Cam was staring at me with the same intensity as he had outside, except this time, I couldn't read what he was thinking. Had I crossed some line by offering to help? Did he not want me around? Had we flown too close to the sun, and now, he wanted to get as far away from me as possible?

While all those thoughts stung, none of it really mattered, not when Victoria needed me. We might have had a passing moment, but she was my everything. If my best friend needed me, I would step up, no questions asked. I'd handle anything for Victoria, even dealing with her annoyingly handsome ex.

"Cam?" Victoria called out. "Are you okay with Hadley helping?"

He never broke his stare, keeping his dark eyes trained on me. If I could melt into the couch, I would have. There was an intensity there, one that rivaled what I noticed on the field. It made me want to squirm, but I refused, not wanting Cam to realize he affected me.

After a long, drawn out silence, he finally nodded. "Fine. Let's see how this goes."

FIFTEEN

Hadley

I'd always been impulsive as a child. Need someone to dive into the lake? I was your girl. Want to try out a new hair color? Sure, I'll be your test subject. Maybe it was luck, but I'd been fortunate enough to not get hurt by any of my reckless choices. I'd skated by on luck and adrenaline, making me never bother to doubt my choices. After all, what did I really have to lose?

I'd tried to tame that side as I grew up, but it never quite died. My gut never seemed to falter, and I leaned on it to lead me down the right path.

At least, until today.

I sat on Victoria's bed as she packed her stuff for her three-week trip to visit Adam. While I watched her pull out her suitcases, a knot formed in my stomach. When she first talked about going, it was a simple choice. I'd do anything for my best friend, and Lord knows she needed to see her man. Adam had already been in LA for almost four weeks, and even though she tried to be strong for Emilia, his absence weighed on her. She'd even resorted to sleeping in his shirts, needing to feel a little closer to him.

"You're sure that you're okay with doing this?" Victoria asked as she loaded the folded clothes into her bag.

I leaned down, reaching into her basket of shoes and holding up two pairs of sandals for her to pick from. As she pointed to the pair in my left hand, I answered, "Of course I'm okay with this, Tori. I'm excited to get to spend some time with Emilia. We'll be fine—great, even. You have nothing to worry about."

Okay, that was an overstatement. But even though I had doubts about this whole situation, I wasn't about to tell her, not while she was already struggling with her choice to leave her daughter.

"I know," Victoria sighed, holding her hand to her stomach. "I just hate leaving Emilia. It's that double-edged sword—I'm excited about going, but I hate leaving her behind. What kind of mother leaves her daughter because she wants to spend more time with her boyfriend?"

"One with healthy boundaries, who is setting a good example for her kid," I said. "Seriously, Tori. Emilia needs to see that her life doesn't end the moment she becomes a mother. You're incredible with her, and everyone can see your world revolves around her. You don't have to feel guilty for wanting a little time for you and Adam."

She chuckled, brushing tears away from her lash line. "When did you become the voice of reason?"

"I've always been the wise one." I smirked. "Now, are we packing lingerie, or is Adam more of an au natural kinda guy?"

"Hadley Rose!"

"What?" I gave her my most innocent smile. "Just trying to help my bestie. I need to live a little vicariously through you."

Victoria rolled her eyes as she stepped back into her

closet, throwing out some more clothes I dutifully folded. "No luck on the dating apps?" she called out, her voice a little muffled.

"Nope," I said, letting the "p" sound pop. Not that I'd even opened them. I was still trying to forget about that moment with Cam, when he pressed me up against his truck and ran his thumb over my lip. It was a sign of how pathetic my love life had become lately. We hadn't even kissed, and yet, he was all I could think about. How his eyes darkened when he leaned into me, the fresh, subtle scent that clung to his clothes after his shower. The callouses that lined his thumb, making my insides clench.

However, there was a freeze between us now, worse than it had ever been. At least, in the past, Cam and I would verbally spar, neither of us willing to back down to the other. Now, it was complete radio silence. He was busy with the team, but that was only a part of the equation. He was avoiding me. Literally. If I walked into a room, he'd find an excuse to leave it. Beyond a mumbled hello, he hadn't said a word to me since Victoria and Adam interrupted our moment.

It bothered me, and I *hated* that it bothered me. A month ago, I would have been delighted if Cam avoided me. Now, it left a pit in my stomach, one I couldn't soothe, no matter how much I tried.

I missed our arguments, missed that teasing glint in his eyes, missed the friendship that had been developing between us. It was worse than before, when I thought Cam hated me. At least then, I knew where we stood, and I was good with our mutual loathing.

But after seeing the other side of him—the one that was warm, funny, and attractive—it would never be enough for me. It was like flying too close to the sun. There was a risk you'd get burned, but you were willing to take it for a few moments in its warm embrace.

Victoria slammed her suitcase closed with a loud thud, breaking me out of my head. She sighed as she looked around the room. "I think that's it." Her wide eyes met mine. "It's really happening. I'm leaving."

I stood, wrapping my arms around her in a tight hug. "Yup. And you are going to have the best time ever."

"Thanks, Hads," Victoria said as she dropped her head to my shoulder. "How am I ever going to repay you for this?"

"You don't have to," I said as I leaned back. "It's what we do for each other. I have your back, Tori. But..." I smirked at her. "If you stumble across any of Adam's co-stars in spandex, I wouldn't be opposed to a photo or two."

"Hadley Rose!"

"What?" I said in mock innocence. "Nothing indecent, just enough to get my imagination running."

Victoria grabbed her suitcase, muttering under her breath as she walked out of her bedroom. "You're going to get me kicked out of Australia."

SIXTEEN

Hadley

Only twenty minutes after Victoria left for the airport, my apprehension had grown into an immovable knot in my stomach. And the biggest reason was sitting right across from me, looking like he'd rather get an enema than sit at the same table as me.

I should have taken the win. At least Cam was actually staying in the room with me—though he was on the complete opposite side of the dining room table, a large calendar between us. He'd barely said anything, just mumbling under his breath every time I suggested a plan for the next three weeks.

"This is ridiculous," I said. "How are we supposed to get through this if you won't even talk to me?"

"We're not," Cam bit out. "You can go, Hadley. I've got this handled."

"Oh, really?" I leaned forward in my chair. "Because you're going to take Emilia to school, make sure her lunches are packed, *and* go to all your away games?" I smirked as his face fell. "Yeah, that's what I thought."

"I don't need some goddamn babysitter."

"Then it's a good thing I'm not here for you," I bit back. I sighed, running my hand over my face. This was not working. Cam and I had proven in the past that we could go back and forth for hours, neither of us willing to concede, but that wouldn't help us now. Emilia wouldn't suffer because we refused to communicate. Not to mention, Tori said the tension between us was taxing on her. For my best friend's sake, I'd suck it up and play nice with her baby daddy, even if he was behaving like an unbearable ass.

"Then why are we having this conversation?"

Sorry, Tori. Can't say I didn't try.

I pressed my palms into the table, standing up to glare in his direction. "You know, you really had me fooled there for a moment. I thought maybe you weren't a cocky dick with a permanent stick lodged up your ass. Thank you for reminding me who you really are."

I turned, ready to stomp away to my carriage house, when something stopped me. Cam had his hand on my arm, turning me so I was facing his direction. The bitter sting of tears hit the corners of my eyes, but I refused to give him the satisfaction of seeing me upset.

"You're right," Cam sighed. I waited for him to let go of my arm, to keep up this distance he'd placed between us. Instead, his hand lowered until he reached my hand, and he wrapped his fingers around mine. "I'm sorry. Joining the Hawks has put a fucking ton of pressure on my back, and I'm still learning how to navigate it."

"I thought you wanted to play in the majors."

Cam shook his head. "It's been my dream for most of my life, but now that I'm finally here, it feels like one mistake, and it all could be ripped away from me. I need to be at the top of my game, but I also need to be there for Emilia. If it's a choice, she always comes first, but if I lost this chance, I'd regret it for the rest of my life." He sighed, his thumb stroking my bare skin. "It doesn't help that Victoria thinks I can't handle my daughter alone."

"What are you talking about?" I asked, shifting to face him fully.

He gave me a dry smile. "C'mon, Hadley. You think I haven't noticed? Every time Victoria leaves me alone with Emilia for a couple of days, she calls in reinforcements. Like I can't take care of Emilia. But that little girl is my world."

"She knows that." The words came out like a whisper, but it was enough to remove some of the doubt in Cam's eyes. "Look, I might not know anything about baseball., or the pressure you're under, but I know this. You are an amazing dad, Cam. One of the best. And Victoria knows that too. She didn't ask me to help. I offered because we all want you to achieve your dreams. Everyone needs a little help sometimes, sarge."

He stared down at me, his dark eyes shimmering with something that looked a lot like appreciation. "Thank you, Hadley. I, uh..." He cleared his throat. "I needed to hear that."

"Don't get used to it," I threw back at him.

But Cam's face didn't shift, didn't contort into his usual annoyed scowl. Instead, he brought his fingers up to my face, stroking the underside of my jaw. "I don't know how to do this, Hadley."

"Do what?" My words were breathless, almost low enough for him to miss them.

"Be around you," he quietly admitted. "I...I don't know how to navigate it. You're Vic's best friend, and you're the last person I should want..." His dark brown eyes lifted, and I saw what he'd been trying to hide. Desire. Longing. It was all there, reflected at me.

"It can never happen," I finished for him. "It's too complicated, and if we crossed that line, it wouldn't end well for any of us."

"Right," Cam said. He cleared his throat and dropped my hand. My skin instantly ran cold, and it took everything to keep up the distance between us. He wasn't the only one who felt the pull between us, it seemed. It felt like there was a rope around my chest, tying me to him. "I'm sorry for acting like an ass, Hadley. I've been stressed, and I took it out on you." The corner of his mouth ticked up. "I won't make that mistake again."

"No, you won't," I said, keeping my eyes trained on him. We might be working through this delicate dance, trying to figure out how to move forward in each other's lives, but I wouldn't stand for being treated that way.

Cam nodded his head, and I saw the sincerity in his words. In all our time together, I couldn't remember a time Cam had apologized to me. Between my apology last month and this one, it was feeling like hell really did freeze over.

As he walked back to the table, I finally saw what I missed before—the dark circles under his eyes, the sallower color of his skin. Even his shoulders seemed to droop further than they ever did before. I walked over and took a seat next to him. "Do you want to talk about it?"

"You don't need to take on anymore of my worries, Hadley."

He'd used my name so many times in this conversation, and as much as I enjoyed hearing it, I almost missed the menace name he'd gifted me. It was almost like our private joke now that we were working on mending fences. I placed my hand on top of his before realizing what I'd done and yanking it away. "Although things might be complicated between us, I want us to be friends. At least until Victoria gets back."

"And after?" Cam asked.

"Then..." I slowly smirked up at him. "Prepare for the torture to resume. I promise to play nice for three entire weeks. I can't promise anything more than that."

"Oh, menace," Cam said, his voice lowering several octaves. "I don't think you'd know how to play nice if you tried."

Cam leaned forward, resting his elbows on the table. I swallowed, hating how the sight of his brawny forearms made my heart beat faster. Why was that so fucking hot? I might be a slut for some forearm porn, but we needed to establish some boundaries. It was the only way we'd make this work. His dark eyes cut right through my soul, and his full lips curled at the edges. "You think we can do it, menace?"

"I can," I bit back. "But considering you'd rather act like a toddler than a grown adult most of the time, I have my doubts about you."

He leaned back in his chair and, thank God, he lowered his arms into his lap. Cam glanced up, and I swore there was a rare hint of vulnerability in his eyes. "You're right." I bit my tongue, not wanting to interrupt. "Look, I'm under a ton of pressure this season. Playing for the Hawks...this is my fucking dream, Hadley. But Emilia is everything to me. I can't—I won't let her down." He ran his hand over his face. "So if you're willing to help me out..." His eyes leaped up and met mine. "Then I could really fucking use it."

I smiled back at him. "See, was that so hard?"

"You have no idea," he said. "We'll work something out, a schedule or something that works for both of us and keeps us from getting annoyed. But we might need some kind of secret code for when we're at our limit."

My eyes widened. "Like a safe word?"

"Jesus, menace," he chuckled. "No, not like a safe word. Just a word we use when we need a break."

"So...a safe word."

Cam cursed under his breath, then turned his head up to the ceiling. I couldn't help my smirk at his forlorn expression, loving how easy it was to get under his skin. I held up my hands. "Just messing with you, Cam. I think it's a good idea. You and I are going to butt heads, and I don't want it to affect Emilia. So if we need a break, we'll say something like..."

"Porcupine."

My eyes widened as I looked across the table. "Seriously, sarge?"

He shrugged. "First word that popped into my head."

"Fine." I rolled my eyes. "If either of us says porcupine, we have to retreat and try again the next day. It's our line in the sand."

Cam nodded as he smiled back at me. "You've got a deal, menace."

SEVENTEEN

Hadley

As I hit the blinker to turn onto Main Street, I let out a small breath of relief, loving that I was on time for my first morning drop-off. It had been three days since Victoria left for Australia with Adam, and I was still finding my footing. Cam and I had worked out a tentative agreement to try out these first few days. We'd alternate staying at the main house. When he played home games or had practice, Emilia would stay with him, and I'd keep to the carriage house. But when his games were away, or if he needed to be at the stadium at night, I'd be on Emilia duty.

Which had started right away. After dinner on Thursday, Cam left, and his team would travel for six consecutive games. So, for now, it was just Emilia and me. I'd spent plenty of time with her in the past, but this was the first time we'd been alone for more than a day. I was used to being around kids—hello, education degree and dream job—but being the lone responsible adult for a while chafed a little.

"Auntie Hadley, are you sure you know where my school is?" Emilia asked from her booster in my back seat.

"Of course, Emilia Bedelia. We'll be there soon." My little bestie just nodded, frowning as she stared out the window. Come to think of it, she'd been a little extra quiet all morning. Emilia was a spit-fire, taking after her Aunt Hadley on that one, but today, she looked like she was on the verge of tears. When we hit a red light, I peeked up at her in the rearview mirror. "What's on your mind, babe?"

"Nothing," she sighed.

"Nah, not buying it," I said. "You can tell me anything, Ems. And trust me, when you have big worries, it's always better to talk them out."

"You promise?"

"Promise, babe." A car honked behind me, alerting me to the changing traffic signal. We drove down the next two blocks in silence. I wanted to wait out Emilia, to let her form her own thoughts and worries and realize she'd be safe to express them to me. Growing up, I learned to bite my tongue, not knowing what would trigger my mom into a rage. If I ever became a parent, I'd hate for my kids to experience that, and I extended the same courtesy to Emilia. Tori would feel the same way and would want Emilia comfortable enough to express herself. So, we kept driving in silence until a little voice popped up from the backseat.

"I just miss my mommy." Emilia sniffled. "I'm trying to be brave, but I miss her a lot. She takes me to school every day."

"And now it's me," I finished for her, watching as she nodded in the mirror. "It's okay to miss your mom, kiddo. She misses you too."

"She does?"

"Of course she does," I said. "You're her favorite person in the whole wide world. But sometimes, we need to try new things, even if it takes us away from home."

"Like you?" Emilia asked. "Mommy says you like to go 'sploring. Do you miss us when you're gone?"

"More than anything. I miss your mom right now." We'd talked twice on the phone over the past two days, but it was hard to connect with the different time zones. Victoria took care of me when I got stressed or overwhelmed, but I couldn't confide in her when I was watching her kid. She needed me to succeed at this, and I'd die before I ever let anything happen to Emilia.

For a moment, I worried I was failing at this whole pseudo-parenting thing, but then, Emilia beamed back at me, all the storm clouds gone from her expression. She leaned forward in her booster seat. "Is my mommy your best friend?"

"She is." I smiled. "You know I met your mommy on the first day of college?"

"You did?" She blinked back at me, her voice full of curiosity, even though she had no idea about higher education. "Did you meet my daddy too?"

"Yup," I said. I smiled forcefully to hide my groan. As I turned into the line of cars for drop-off, I glanced at Emilia in the rearview mirror. "So that means I've known your mom a long time, Em. Trust me—she misses you just as much and can't wait to be home with you again. But until she gets back, when we're both missing your mom, we'll tell each other, 'kay?"

She nodded, but her smile dropped. I looked up, and the parking officer ushered us ahead. "How about this? As soon as we get home from school, we'll call her. I'll even text her to make sure it's a good time."

A big, beautiful smile covered her face, and I turned around, giving myself a silent pat on the back. There were going to be a lot of learning curves over the next three weeks, so I was going to take my wins when they came. I'd take any chance to make sure Emilia felt comforted and seen.

The teacher called our car to the front of the line, and I hit the unlock button, letting Emilia out of the back seat. She hopped over to her friends, already forgetting our conversation. One thing I loved about working with kids— they were resilient. Most adults couldn't handle the slightest amount of change, but kids were little warriors.

As soon as I pulled away from the school, my phone rang through the speakers, the word SARGE covering the screen. My throat instantly dried, hating how the sight of his name made my pulse race. While he called Emilia multiple times a day, we'd only texted. Simple messages. He wanted to check on things at home, and I'd send him photos throughout the day.

As hard as it was to believe, I missed him—missed his sleepy smile in the morning, missed the way he was with Emilia. Hell, I even missed the teasing tone of his voice, the way my stomach swept up when he grinned at me.

"God, Hadley," I said to myself as I pulled away from the school. "You need to get a fucking grip." Without further thought, I hit the green answer button. "To what do I owe this displeasure this early in the morning?"

"Hilarious, menace," Cam chuckled. "I just want to make sure my kid's still in one piece."

"She is." Another burst of pride washed over me. It might not seem like much, but I'd tackled the morning routine all by myself. "Just dropped her off at school. She was a little sad this morning because she misses Tori, but she was all smiles by the time she saw her friends."

"Good. And Vic's house is still in one piece?"

"Eh, relatively," I teased. "We might have made a craft

project with every type of paint available. You weren't partial to any of your shirts, right?"

"I'll take that as a yes." He paused for a moment before his voice lowered. "Fuck, this is harder than I thought it'd be. You're sure she's okay?"

"Yeah, she's doing great," I said, stripping my voice of its usual tease. There was a lot about Cam that irked me, but his devotion to his daughter was unmatched. He loved Emilia more than anything else in the world. I'd been around enough to know his career and parenthood were a constant juggling act, and he often beat himself up trying to balance the two. But now that I saw them up close, it was even more clear: their pre-game ritual, how his face lit up when she entered the frame of the phone, his knowledge of every aspect of her life, asking for more and more details like it was the most interesting thing in the world. "She's missing Tori a lot. We talked a little about it, and I promised her we'd try to call after school."

"That's a good idea," Cam answered. "I'll be back on Thursday, and then we should sit down and try to hash out a plan for next week."

"Wow, that's very adult of you. Willing to have another entire conversation with me? I'm flattered, sarge."

"There's a lot I'll do for the sake of my kid," he chuckled. "Even deal with your stubborn ass."

I barked out a laugh. "And we were getting along so well."

"Don't push your luck," he said. I could picture him running his hand down his face, trying to hide his smirk. Cam cleared his throat. "Seriously, Hadley—thank you for being there for Emilia. The next few weeks are going to be hard without her mom, and I'm..." he swallowed. "I'm glad you're there with her."

My heart stuttered in my chest, committing this moment to memory. In the past, Cam treated my presence as a burden, as if he wanted me as far from his daughter as possible. Bad influence. I'd overheard him call me that once, and it almost killed me. So hearing differently now, his words sure and sincere, soothed a long-standing wound. "Th-thank you," I spluttered. "You've got a great kid."

"Damn right, I do," Cam said before hanging up without so much as a goodbye. But even as the call cut out, I still stared straight ahead, my brain short-circuiting after that brief conversation. My heart still thudded in my chest, a constant reaction to Cam's praise and attention. And the worst part? If this was how I reacted to him over the phone, what the hell would happen when he came home?

EIGHTEEN

Cameron

"Fuck," I groaned, leaning back into my chair. Every muscle ached after two brutal, back-to-back series. The first three games were easy wins. The other team deserved their bottom ranking in the national league. We'd swept through them with little effort, ending the series with three wins to their zero.

But the second set was against our west coast rivals. As two of the four new teams in the major leagues, both groups were determined to get the win. We'd gone into game three tied, but they'd taken us in the last game. Even with the loss, I was pretty proud. We left nothing on the field tonight, and my body was going to be sore for days.

At least the seat was pretty fucking comfortable.

When I played on the minor league team back home, I hated travel days. It always meant piling into a coach bus, listening to the guys snore and talk shit for hours on end. Don't get me wrong—I loved the team aspect. Nothing bonded you like dealing with a broken bus bathroom during an eight-hour ride.

If only those guys saw me now.

I leaned back in my seat, still trying to wrap my head around the fact that I was on the team *plane*. A fucking chartered plane, all to ourselves. It was one of the most surreal moments of my career.

There were a lot of similarities about playing in the major and minor leagues. The team aspect, the game itself. But the pressure weighed on my shoulders. With the bigger paycheck came higher expectations, for the entire team but even more for us new guys who'd just made the move up the ladder. While it happened often, no one wanted to get sent back down to the minors. Teams changed constantly, especially with the trade deadline in the middle of the summer. Every manager and owner wanted to secure the best line-up to get a shot at the playoffs. Have one off-game? You could come back from that. But if you let the pressure build and got into a slump, that was it—the end of the road for your major league career.

And shit, was that a heavy burden to carry.

So far, we'd gotten off to a decent start, but we had a ways to go if we wanted to make it into the playoffs. Even with our losses in California, we had more ticks in the win column than the loss one. Still, we could do better. We'd yet to face some of the more established teams, legacies that ran deep. It made my teeth clench, knowing we had so much fucking potential on our side. We'd make it all the way if we got on the same page.

I glanced to the back of the plane, watching as Jace pounded shots with the outfielders. He was a wildcard, and you never knew what energy he'd bring onto the field. The games when he acted like a teammate, we made magic on the field. But on other nights, when he had an axe to grind, it was like wading through sludge, sloppy moves and unco-ordinated plays. Even with Drobrek on first and Damien on third, I needed Jace to stop the other team from scoring runs.

I looked over at Anders, huddled with Coach as they played back the last game footage. I watched what they saw, not remembering half the plays. Instincts took over when I was on the field. I played well, determined to go home with the win.

All because of one fucking text.

I pulled my phone out of my pocket, staring at my background photo. Emilia smirked over her shoulder, her back covered in one of my old tee-ball jerseys, our last name displayed across her back. And then, there was Hadley's message.

MENACE

Rooting for you back home. Knock 'em dead, sarge.

I pushed the phone back into my pocket, forcing my mind away from the blonde who infiltrated every aspect of my life. I'd left the day after Victoria, hoping the space would help me clear my head. It was a complete failure. If anything, the distance between us made me want her even more. I couldn't escape her. In my thoughts, on my phone, everywhere I went, my mind turned to Hadley.

"You okay over there, man?" Damien asked. He pulled out an earbud as he leaned across the aisle to check on me.

"Yeah," I huffed, trying to push Hadley out of my mind. "Just thinking about the games this weekend. Made a couple of rookie mistakes last night, and I need to make sure they don't happen again."

Damien grinned while he leaned against the headrest. "You and me both, brother. But all we can do is focus on the next one, right? We always get our shit together at home.

Try focusing on something other than the game for the night, man."

"Fucking hope so," I grumbled. Easy for him to say. But then again, he wasn't fixated on his ex's best friend. Baseball was the safe topic—the one thing in my control.

He turned over to me. "You coming out with us when we get back? Some of the guys are hitting up this new bar downtown."

"Nah," I said. "Gotta get home to my kid. Missed her like crazy." I looked over at my new teammate who'd become my friend. "But have fun, man. Looking to meet someone?"

"Nah, not for me." He shook his head. "That shit's too hard during the season. Gotta give everything to the game, you know? No one's going to get in the way of that."

"I get it."

"So no to the bar?"

"Not tonight," I said as I closed my eyes. "Maybe next time."

IT WAS ALMOST dawn by the time I walked through the front door. Maybe getting an apartment in the city wouldn't be the worst idea. I'd have to wait until Victoria got back, but it wouldn't hurt to look, find a place to spend my nights when I didn't have Emilia. My ultimate plan was to get a house a little closer to her, but a smaller crash-pad in the city for late nights like this one wouldn't hurt.

The house was silent as I crept through the hallways, stopping when I saw the television on in the living room. I walked over and grabbed the remote, hitting the off button before I found Hadley curled up on the couch. Test papers laid scattered all around her, some graded in a pink, sparkly pen, others still blank.

I smirked as I leaned down and gathered the ones that had fallen to the floor. Hadley made sense as a teacher. When she first mentioned it, I didn't know if it would be a good fit. She was too wild, too unpredictable. But after watching her with Emilia for years, I'd learned that was only one side of her. Hadley had this way about her, a graceful patience I'd never emulate. She'd always show Emilia how to do things on her own, guiding and correcting her but letting my daughter discover new skills for herself. It helped Emilia when she got to school. She wasn't afraid to take risks or try something outside her comfort zone.

All because of Hadley.

The fearless, willful woman who was becoming my obsession. After dropping the papers on the table, I ran my hand over my face. I was not this guy. I didn't get obsessed—especially about a woman. Emilia and baseball. Those were the only things that mattered. I barely had enough time for those two things, much less a relationship.

Hadley shuddered in her sleep, her face scrunching up. She shivered, and for a moment, I thought about draping a blanket over her and leaving her on the couch, but she squirmed against the cushions like she couldn't get comfortable enough. Fuck it. I reached down and pulled her gently into my arms, letting her head settle against my chest. A soft hint of her shampoo hit my nose, the smell soft and intriguing. Floral, fresh. It reminded me of opening days and quiet spring mornings. When I took a step toward the stairs, Hadley stirred in my arms. Her brow furrowed with confusion as she looked up at me, her eyes out of focus, like she still slept.

"Cam?" Her voice crackled. "What are you doing?"

"Putting you to bed," I said. "Close your eyes, Hadley. I've got you."

Normally, something like that would have caused her to lash out, reminding me she didn't need anyone to take care of her. Instead, Hadley just nodded, her head returning to the crook of my neck. Her soft breaths graced my skin, and I had to shake my head to still the images crashing into my mind.

Holding Hadley was a mistake. Her body was too soft, the curves that always called to me too close. She'd made plenty of comments about her body before, especially how she filled out clothes, but I loved her curves, such a contrast to her sharp personality. It was an intoxicating combination that made my head spin. Lately, I'd been obsessed with wondering what it'd be like to guide her full hips as she rode me, my fingers soft enough not to hurt but tight enough to leave marks on her skin.

I pushed open Victoria's bedroom door and placed Hadley down on the bed. She'd stayed here plenty of nights, but the room held none of Hadley's stuff. It was all mementos of Victoria and Adam's life together. Emilia was a frequent addition in the photos, but most were just the two of them. Looking around the room, I expected to feel a pang of nostalgia, longing for what might have been. Instead, the woman lying on the bedspread drew me in, consuming all my thoughts.

I walked over to the bed and grabbed the blanket at the foot, then draped it over Hadley. She smiled in her sleep. I put that image away for later, wanting to remember the content smile when she hated me tomorrow. Without thinking, I reached down, brushed a couple of her blonde waves away from her face, and kissed her forehead. Don't ask me why I did it. I had no fucking idea. But I couldn't stop myself.

When Hadley got settled, I went upstairs and peeked my head inside my daughter's room. She slept in her bed, clutching another stuffy in her little arms. I sat on the edge of her mattress and ran my fingers through her hair. She must have sensed me, because she opened a sleepy eye. When she realized it was me, she bolted up and smiled. "Daddy, you're home!"

"Yeah, baby. Sorry I woke you up."

"It's okay," she yawned. "I missed you."

"Missed you more, kiddo. Did you have fun with Auntie Hadley?"

"So much fun," Emilia said as she leaned back against her pillows. "We made a present for Mommy and Adam. Hadley let me use the grown-up markers and everything."

"Glad you had fun, Em." As her eyes fluttered closed, I leaned down and kissed her forehead. No matter how much I wanted to crawl to my bed, I wasn't ready to leave her side. Five more minutes. That was all I needed. After almost a week without my daughter, I wanted a couple more minutes to hold her as she slept.

At least, that's what I told myself before my eyes closed as well.

NINETEEN

Hadley

I woke up the next morning wrapped up in a blanket. It took me a minute to realize where I'd fallen asleep. The last thing I remembered was trying to keep my eyes open until Cam got home, wanting to see him for some unknown reason. Apparently, I must have forced myself up here. *Thank God.* That couch might be comfortable for sitting, but now that I was getting older, I couldn't crash like I used to.

Wait—what time was it? I fumbled for my phone, unable to find it in the mess of pillows. I glanced over at the alarm clock. 6:35. Shit, shit, shit. I'd overslept by an hour, and now, my whole morning routine was fucked. Most days, I was an early riser, trying to get my morning yoga session done before I got ready for school. I'd let it slip this week, too busy trying to get Emilia presentable and out the door.

I jumped out of the bed and dashed down the stairs. If I didn't rush, we'd be late for drop-off, and Laila had to be starving. Okay, feed the cat, then get the kid out the door.

When I rushed into the kitchen, trying to figure out where I'd left my phone, I instantly stopped in my tracks.

My cat laid on the floor by the sink, purring contentedly as she basked in the sunlight. She barely even looked up as I walked over and scratched her head. "How did you get over here?"

"I grabbed her this morning."

Cam's voice made me jump out of my skin. I held my hand to my chest as I turned to face him. "Oh my God, Cam."

His eyes darkened for a moment before he gave me his usual careful grin. "Careful, menace. Keep looking at me like that, and I'll think you're happy to see me."

"In your dreams, sarge." Laila batted my hand away, lying back to soak up more warm rays. I leaned against the edge of the counter. "How did you get her here? She hates almost everyone, including me most days."

Cam smirked. "Not me. The moment I opened the door, she purred at my feet."

"Traitor," I mumbled under my breath. Cam turned back to the stove, scrambling eggs in the pan. The smell of bacon permeated the air, and my mouth drooled on instinct. Breakfast had always been my favorite meal, but I rarely made it myself. Usually, I grabbed a protein bar or shake as I ran out the door.

Cam turned back over his shoulder. "Sit, Hadley. I made enough for all of us."

As I contemplated his offer, Emilia came crashing into the room, throwing her arms around my legs. "Auntie Hadley, Daddy's back!"

"I see that, kiddo," I said as I leaned down and kissed the top of her head. Her perfectly braided hair. Seriously, what the fuck had I walked into? Was I still asleep, trapped in some weird dimension where Cam was this domestic guru, capable of making a mouth-watering breakfast and getting his daughter dressed like she was going to the senior prom?

Cam turned, giving me a stern look. "Breathe, Hadley. You've got an hour before you have to hit the road." He motioned to the set place next to Emilia. "Sit. Eat."

I dropped into the chair, still staring at Cam. His plain white tee stretched over the ample planes of his shoulders and back, and his gray joggers clung to his ass. God, what was it with baseball players and their glutes? Yes, I had looked when I was at the game. I was only human, after all. I'd concluded there must be some sort of correlation with the sport and the way all the players filled out their pants. It was the best kind of treat for my eyes, especially first thing in the morning.

Cam set down a plate for me, then returned a second time with a cup of coffee. Just as I opened my mouth to protest, he shook his head, "Oat milk, two sugars. I got you, menace."

My jaw hung open as he walked away. How the hell had he learned how I liked my coffee? I couldn't remember us ever sitting down for a cup, not since college. There were only group project sessions we'd had at the local shop, but I didn't think he even noticed I was there, much less paid attention to my coffee order.

Warmth sizzled in my chest as I took the first sip, letting myself enjoy this simple pleasure. I drank little coffee—it made my insides jitter too much—but I allowed myself one in the morning, just enough to match the energy of my second graders when they burst through the door.

Cam grabbed a plate and settled down next to me. Emilia abandoned her spot at the table and climbed into his lap. God, my ovaries wanted to explode at the sight. I'd always thought Emilia was a clone of her mother, but seeing her with Cam now made their similarities stand out more. They had the same smile, same shape of their eyes. As he nuzzled into his daughter's neck, Cam smiled, soft and serene. He missed her. Obviously, I knew he said he missed her, but it was different seeing them together after a week apart. I wasn't used to public displays of affection after growing up with my mom. The most I ever got were awkward sideways hugs.

Seeing Cam so open and honest with his affection for his daughter made my heart pound a little faster.

As Emilia stole a couple of pieces of bacon from his plate, Cam turned to me. "Busy day today?"

I shrugged, taking a large bite of my eggs. Holy shit. Add this into the unfair column. The man wasn't only ridiculously attractive and incredibly athletic, but he cooked? It had to be the worst kind of cosmic joke. I quickly scooped up another pile and shoved it into my mouth. An appreciative groan slipped out of my mouth, and my eyes snapped up to Cam. He was smirking back at me, almost like he knew exactly what that sound meant. *Bastard.* He was already smug enough. I didn't need to help him in that department.

He arched a brow. "That good?"

I shrugged. "I've had better."

"Oh, I doubt that, menace." He pressed a kiss to Emilia's chubby cheek. "Why don't you go color before school, Em? Daddy's going to drop you off today."

Emilia let out a loud cheer as she rushed off into the playroom. As soon as she turned the corner, tension crackled through the room, almost like a live wire flicked on whenever Cam and I were alone together. God, this stupid crush was getting frustrating. I couldn't help but squirm under his intense stare.

I brushed the corner of my mouth, wondering if I'd left crumbs on my lips. "What?" I asked.

"Nothing," Cam said as he kept studying my face. "Don't think I've ever seen you first thing in the morning."

"Yeah," I chuckled. "Usually, I try to look a little more presentable before facing you, sarge. But I passed out last night and was way too tired to do my usual routine." When Cam wasn't here, I'd been sleeping in Victoria's house, at her request. Between the two of us, I moved easier than Emilia. After we visited Laila during the afternoons and evenings, we came back to the main house to tuck Emilia in. I brushed a couple of errant hairs away from my face. "Sorry if my morning face doesn't live up to your standards."

Cam chuckled as he scooped up our plates and walked over to the sink. I took that as my cue to leave, so I raced to the side door, ready to hide out in my house until work.

"For what it's worth," Cam called out as my hand hit the doorknob, "I think you look beautiful all the time—early in the morning or not."

His words washed over me, and for a moment, I debated turning around and telling him just how much I'd missed him, how this house hadn't seemed right until he walked back inside of it. That his grin was the best thing I'd ever seen at this hour, and I wanted to start all my mornings that way.

Instead, I walked outside, letting the fresh morning air wash all those words away.

TWENTY

Cameron

"We need to talk."

Hadley's spine instantly stiffened as she put down the dish she was drying and slowly turned to face me. Fuck. Her blue eyes were wide and wild, making me almost lose my nerve. I'd been back at the house for three days, and even though I'd had a game yesterday, I spent my limited free time with Hadley and Emilia. It wasn't enough. I didn't know if it would ever be enough. Not only with my daughter, but the vixen in front of me.

Hadley had crawled her way underneath my skin years ago, but for the first time, I didn't mind it. I wanted more of her, wanted to soak in every moment of her warmth. Seeing her with my daughter had softened my heart, but so much of it was just her. She brought out the best in the world, and I wanted to be surrounded by her. When we were apart, I felt like the air was colder, as if I wasn't complete until I was back with the two of them.

She cocked her head. "Okay, those are the four most brutal words in the English language. Speak fast, sarge, or you're going to get sprayed with the sink hose."

I let out a gruff chuckle, scratching the stubble on my chin. Coach was a stickler for us being clean shaven, but I had gotten lazy this morning, wanting to spend a bit more time with Emilia before I headed out for the day.

I cleared my throat. "Tomorrow's family day at the stadium. All the kids come out, and we've got special giveaways and everything. I would like Emilia to come out to watch me play."

Hadley beamed back at me. "Yeah? That would be so much fun. Ollie's been texting me nonstop about coming to another game, so I'd be happy to take her—"

"Cole asked to take her." The moment the words left my mouth, I regretted them. Victoria's brother seemed like the natural choice to take Emilia to my game. While we'd never been close, I wanted to get to know him more, and this seemed like a good opportunity. Cole was a good guy, and he and his wife doted on Emilia like she was their own. When he stopped by earlier in the evening, I'd mentioned the game, and he offered to take Emilia. I didn't second guess it, happy I'd have people cheering me on.

But the forlorn look on Hadley's face instantly broke my heart. I never dreamed she'd want to go, much less be looking forward to it. She forced a smile and then turned back to the dishes. "Oh, okay. Good to know. I'll find something to do around here. It'll be a good time for them."

"Hadley..."

"It's fine," she said, reaching out to grab the dish towel. She dried her hands, then started toward the side door. "Guess I'll see you on Monday."

Without thinking, I rushed behind her. As she tried to pull the door open, I pressed my palm against the surface, keeping it closed. My chest brushed against her back, and her subtle scent overwhelmed me. A current rushed through my veins, the reaction so visceral, I swore the shift was visible for all to see. She turned slowly, and my eyes raked over her confused features. I wanted to touch her. Fuck, I wanted to do so much more than that. But right now, what I wanted most was for her not to step out that door. "Don't walk away from me, Hadley."

Her face contorted into a glare, a familiar fire and fury reflecting in her eyes. "And don't tell me what to do, Cameron. I'm here for Emilia, so if you don't need me, I'm going back to my house."

"Not like this," I bit out. "We've come too far to let a simple conversation derail us. Now, if you're done being a brat, you need to let me finish."

Hadley's eyes flared as she stared at me. This close, I could see every emotion flicker across her face. The flush of her cheeks. The heavy pulse in her neck. Everything called to me, but I had to keep my needs locked down. We'd agreed it was too complicated. Nothing could ever happen between us. But, fuck, I wanted to give in.

"I wasn't sure you'd want to come," I said. "I was hoping you would. A bunch of us rented out a box for our friends and families. I told them I was bringing three people, just in case you did."

"Really?" she asked, in disbelief at my words.

"Yeah, menace." I leaned closer, brushing my fingers over her blonde waves. "I mentioned the game to Cole, and he asked to take Emilia, but I still want you there. I want to hear you cheering my name."

"Why?"

It was one word, one simple question, yet it broke the last wall inside me. My hand slipped to the back of her neck, and I pulled her forward, finally claiming the kiss I'd been dreaming about. Hadley stiffened against me, and for one dreaded moment, I thought she was going to push me away. Instead, she melted into the kiss, her hands fisting my shirt, anchoring me to her.

Her lips pressed to mine, and a deep growl echoed from the back of my throat. My hands found her hips, bringing her flush against me. Her taste, the weight of her lips on mine—everything was fucking perfect. This kiss was everything I imagined it to be and more.

But just as quickly as we'd come together, we broke apart, the silence heavy. Fuck, I wanted to kiss her again. That was too brief, not nearly long enough to get my fill of Hadley. I wanted to taste that sweetness that coated her lips. She tasted like sunshine and honey—a flavor I'd never get out of my head.

She searched my expression. "You never answered my question."

"I think I did." I smirked. "I want to see you up in those stands, Hadley. I want you. When you cheer my name..." I shook my head. "It feels like I could take on the fucking world."

I leaned down and kissed her one more time, softer than before. It was more of a promise of things to come—a sign I didn't regret what was happening between us. If anything, this moment cemented in my mind that I wanted this woman, wanted her in every way possible. But I needed her to want it too.

As we broke apart, she leaned her forehead against my chest. "Okay, I'll be there."

TWENTY-ONE

Hadley

"Girl, you are rocking that jersey!"

My cheeks brightened at Ollie's words. Her voice radiated through the room, and everyone turned and looked in my direction. When Cam said a couple of guys rented out the box, I thought five, maybe six people at the most, but there were easily twenty-five people hanging out with us, other players' family members and the occasional girlfriend.

I toyed with the hem of the jersey draped over my sweater. I wasn't sure about wearing Cam's number, but it seemed something friends would do. Almost everyone in the box was wearing one, so it would have been weirder if I didn't wear it, right? Especially when Ollie went out of her way to get it for me. Cam's jersey hadn't hit most of the markets yet, but she had a hook-up in one of the stadium shops, and they found three for Cole, Emilia, and me.

It felt odd, like trying to claim someone who didn't belong to me—especially after last night. We kissed. Pretty sure it was the best kiss of my life, but I refused to say that out loud, refused to inflate Cam's ego any further.

Also, I had no idea where we stood after that stolen moment in the kitchen. As soon as we backed away, Emilia had called out for Cam upstairs, and he dashed off to tend to her, leaving without us discussing what the kiss meant— not that I had any idea what I wanted it to mean.

I expected a million other things to happen before kissing Cam. Pigs flying? Yup, that seemed more probable. But now, not only had my lips collided with Cam's, but I wanted to do it again. Ever since we parted last night, all I could think about was him.

My hand flew to my mouth, tracing the lines with my thumb. Out of all the people in the world to make me feel this way, why did it have to be him? Cam had awoken something in me with his touch, as if I'd been sleeping for years, coasting by and never realizing what the world offered until his lips touched mine.

No, not going to happen. I was already the usurper in Victoria's life, spending time with *her* kid and living in *her* guest house. The last thing I should ever add to that list was lusting after her baby daddy. It was a moment, nothing more. Plenty of people had kissed and nothing ever came of it. Shit, I had met plenty of guys in college, kissed them once or twice, and walked away with no hurt feelings. Who said that couldn't be true for Cam and me?

Ollie elbowed me and gave me a curious smile. "You okay over there?"

"Yeah," I lied. "I'm great. Just excited to watch the game."

"Uh huh," she drawled. "Okay, if we're going to play Lie to Ollie, let's change the subject. Who is that adorable little peanut I saw you come in with?"

"That's Emilia." I waved at her as she excitedly bounced on her uncle's lap. The jersey eclipsed her petite body, and it was desperate for some extra bedazzling, but she was adorable nestled in her uncle's protective arms. My smile softened as she looked over at me and waved. "Cam's daughter."

"She might be the cutest kid on this planet."

"Agreed," I said. "But I'm also biased. She's my mini-bestie, so I love her more than words. It also helps that she's an amazing kid."

"I love that," she said. "And the hottie she's hanging out with. Please tell me he's single."

"Not even a little," I chuckled. "That's her uncle, and he's disgustingly devoted to his wife. If she wasn't eight months pregnant, she'd be here with him."

"Damn, the good ones are always taken."

"What about Parker?" I asked. "Nothing between the two of you?"

"Not you too," Ollie said. "Parker and I...it's complicated. We're more than best friends—we're family. I'd never jeopardize that." She sighed and glanced down at her hands. "Besides, there's a window, you know? If something was going to happen, it would have happened years ago. He's shown no interest in anything more than friendship, and I've got to respect his wishes."

I nodded, wanting to ask so many more questions but also knowing it wasn't any of my business. Besides, with my own complicated love life, I had no right to give anyone else advice.

As Ollie turned to talk to the person on her other side, the scoreboard lit up, and the announcer started calling out names. As each player rushed out onto the field, I held my breath, waiting until I saw Cam dash out onto the field. The same country song blared through the stadium, amping up the excited crowd. Just the familiar rhythm made my heart beat a little faster, building anticipation for things to come. I mouthed along with the lyrics, watching as the players rushed onto the field.

The heavy bass line clicked on, and Cam's face lit up the giant scoreboard directly across from us. I hated the way my stomach somersaulted at his image. His grin locked, as if he was staring through me. It was a cheap imitation of his genuine smile, the one that only came out with Emilia. His picture made him look handsome, someone who would catch everyone's eye. But the real Cam? The one whose eyes sparkled when he looked at his daughter?

Downright devastating.

Cam ran out on the field, clapping his teammates' shoulders as he passed. His eyes scanned the boxes, not stopping until he found ours. He held up his hands in a heart before pointing to Emilia. Her entire face lit up as she screamed out for her dad.

I waited for him to turn back to the game, but he frowned, continuing to scan the box until he caught my eyes. A wide grin filled his face as he winked up at me, just like he had during that first game. For that moment, I forgot about why I shouldn't want him, forgot about the complications, forgot about my best friend who had loved him first.

All I could think about was how good it felt when his eyes met mine.

At least until Cole turned, his brow furrowing as he stared at me in confusion. *Oh, God.* What was he thinking? With just one look, Cole had drowned all the excited little butterflies in my gut, crushing them until they turned to dust, souring my stomach.

What the hell was I doing? It was one thing to daydream about Cam; it was another beast to act on these impulses. By kissing him back, I'd broken every cardinal rule of friendship. *Thou shall not covet thy best friend's ex.* And while I knew in my heart Victoria would give us her blessing, I didn't think I could ever bring myself to ask.

I glanced down at Cam as he stretched on the field, and an ache echoed through my body. There was something here, wasn't there? Something more than a couple of stolen moments? It was complicated—messy—and I didn't do that well. I was much more of a *get out before anyone gets too attached* kind of girl. After all, I'd already formed my world around a boy once, and all that earned me was heartache.

However, when the guest of honor—some country singer—belted out the national anthem, my eyes stayed trained on Cam, unable to turn away, no matter how many times I told myself I should. The crowd erupted into cheers, and I half-heartedly clapped along, not sure if I heard a single word.

TWENTY-TWO

Cameron

The dugout radiated with tension as we stared at the scoreboard. At the top of the fifth inning, Denver led us by four runs, and our outfield had gifted almost all of them. Benny cursed as he watched two players fumble over a ball, tossing it to Jace to end the player's run. His catch was just as sloppy, letting the ball fly past his mitt toward the pitcher's mound. Robbins, the runner from the other team, seized the opportunity and dashed to third.

"A motherfucking triple," Benny cursed, his fist clenching like he wanted to strangle the entire outfield. He signaled for a time-out, then pulled over the bench coach. They whispered for a second, and then Benny met my eye. "Seda, get your ass out there. Don't let them score another goddamn run."

Gray slapped me on the back as I ran out onto the field, passing by Jace. He scowled when I dashed past him. Part of me felt bad for the guy. We were in the same position, both fighting an uphill battle to stay at the top, but while I was getting comfortable on the team, Jace seemed to be the opposite. It was like the pressure made him even surlier, his temper rearing its head too often. There'd been rumbling from some vets—talk about him going back down to the minors if he didn't get his shit together.

As much as I hated to admit it, I was relieved it wasn't me. Not that I wanted the guy to fail, but I'd hate to be the subject of that negative talk.

The stands called behind me as I found my position in left field. They chanted my name, but I tuned them out, only focusing on the game in front of me.

Well, that, and my family up in the crowd. While a lot of coaches thought having family in the stands distracted players, for me, it was the opposite. I performed better when I knew they came to the games, when I heard them cheering me on. Everything I did was to make my little girl proud, and I wanted to show her how hard work paid off.

But as much as I wanted to show off for Emilia, it also helped that Hadley was up there too. I'd spotted her when we first ran out to the field, and she looked so damn good, especially when I saw her Hawks jersey. With her long, blonde hair sticking out of a baseball cap and a cold beer in her hand, she looked like she belonged here.

Like she belonged with me.

"Yo, Seda," Manny, our center-fielder, called out to me. "Get your head in the game."

"Talking a lot of shit after missing that fly ball," I said. Manny flipped me off under his glove so the cameras couldn't see him. I flashed him a smirk, knowing the guy could take some shit talk. After that bullshit play, he deserved it.

The next two batters struck out, leaving only one more needed to turn over the field. Better to have players strike out rather than risk another run, but I was bored with waiting. As I stretched my legs, I squinted toward the opposing team's dugout, wondering who was next in their line-up.

My answer came only seconds later. Hernandez, one of the best right-handed batters in the league, stepped up to the plate. A deep samba rumbled through the stadium speakers, and his confident swagger matched the vibe. We all went silent as he pulled the bat over his shoulder, eying down our pitcher. The scoreboard behind me lit up, and I knew if I tilted my head, all his stats would be visible. But I wasn't that kind of player, one who analyzed every stat before I walked onto the field. No, I read the player in front of me. Stats only told part of the story, and one night could change them. But this guy? I read the fire in his eyes from all the way back here. He was dying to beat us, but there's no fucking way I'd let him, not without a hell of fight.

Our pitcher, Mitchell, wound up, but the batter didn't move. "Ball!" the ump screamed out. Not a shock there. The entire team seemed to skip the first pitch, even this late in the game. Mitchell dusted the ball on his leg, then slammed it into his glove. He wound up and released the ball at an incredible speed. His fastball was a goddamn masterpiece.

But it didn't matter, not when the ball collided with the player's bat, sending it ricocheting in my direction. Instinct took over as I watched it fly past the bases. The thing was high—too high for me to grab easily. My feet moved backward, and I jumped right as it started to pass over the wall. I leaped up, nothing in my brain but the ball.

My arms stretched more than I thought possible, and right as I thought I'd missed, the ball collided with my glove.

When my feet hit the ground, I glanced down at my hand, where the ball rested. Holy fuck. No time to celebrate, I sent the ball back to Mitchell, giving him a nod. I'd caught the one ball, but there'd be others, and we needed to keep blocking runs if we wanted a chance at the win.

But when I looked up at the screen, the cameras focused on my family, Emilia and Hadley, hugging tightly, like I'd just won the World Series. They cheered, and Hadley yelled out, "Get 'em, sarge!"

We might not win the game tonight, but when she screamed for me, it sure as hell seemed like I did.

***

WE ENDED up losing the game, unable to fill the gap Denver had created. After that one save, I played the rest of the game. Some assists, nothing crazy, but I did my best. Part of this job was always going over every play, wondering what you could have done with a little more time and a little more effort.

"Good game out there tonight, Cam." Damien saddled up next to me, freshly showered and looking like he was ready to let off some steam. I just nodded as I leaned down to tie my sneakers. Damien sat down next to me. "Can't win them all. Remember, it's a long season. Get in your head now, and you're doomed. Learn from the losses and ride the high of the wins."

"Talking as my buddy, or as the team captain?" I said. He just shook his head. Benny had left the captain's seat open for the first part of the season. He wanted to make sure the right man was leading us before he made that call, and I respected that. But Damien had been the unofficial leader before I even stepped onto the team. It only made sense for him to take charge.

"Nah, man," Damien said. "If I was talking to you as

your captain, you'd know it. This is just me giving my buddy an 'atta boy. You did good tonight, Cam. Keep it up, and you'll be on the starting line soon."

My jaw clenched, trying to hide my smile. That was the goal, what I came here to do. While I was trying to show up every day and do my best, it was good to hear it from someone else, especially someone I respected as much as Damien.

He clapped me on the shoulder as he stood. "You're coming out with us tonight."

"Nah, man." I shook my head. "Can't do it. Gotta get my daughter home and into bed. She's exhausted."

"Right," he said. "The kid. And what about that girl hanging out in the box? Hadley, right? My sister said she was watching you the whole game."

"It's not like that." At least, it shouldn't be like that, not with so many strings binding us together. Still, no matter what I tried, Hadley was at the center of my mind, even when she shouldn't be. As Damien argued with me, Benny popped out of his office, scanning the room until his eyes met mine. Fuck. He crooked his fingers, beckoning me into his office.

"Shit," I hissed. "This can't be good."

"You're fine," Damien said. "Benny's a good guy. He knows talent when he sees it. Like I said—get out of your head."

Easy for him to say. He earned his place on this team. Hell, he'd earn a place in the Hall of Fame before the end of his career. As I walked over to Benny's office, all I could think about was how much I'd enjoyed this ride, and that I'd fight like hell to keep my place on the Hawks.

TWENTY-THREE

Hadley

"She's getting heavy," Cole chuckled as he adjusted a sleeping Emilia on his shoulder. "Gonna have to start lifting with Gray if I'm going to keep carrying her."

"Tell me about it," I said. "My back's still killing me after trying to carry her to bed earlier this week."

We stood at the edge of the family and friends' zone outside the team locker room, waiting for Cam to join us. He'd played a great game, especially with that one stellar catch in the fifth inning. My throat still scratched from how loud I screamed in disbelief he'd made the catch.

I monitored the door as the other players trickled out, hugging the people waiting for them. Ollie and Parker had already left, stopping at her place to grab some things before they went out for the night.

Where was Cam? Many players had already left, and the crowd was thinning, leaving only a few of us still standing. Every moment that ticked by, anxiety thrummed in my chest, unsure how I'd handle seeing Cam after the game. If I thought the wink was a one-off, I was wrong. Every time he made a play, Cam looked right up to the box, giving Emilia a wave before finding me again. There'd been a couple of comments about keeping his head in the game, but Cam proved them all wrong. It was easy to see why the coaches pulled him up from the minors. Not even halfway through the season, and he was making a name for himself.

I toyed with my nails, unable to stand still with all the tension racing through my bloodstream. Cole must have noticed, because he turned and smiled softly down at me. "Don't think I've ever said thank you to you, Hadley."

My eyes widened as I blinked at him in surprise. "For what?"

Cole gave me a knowing look. "We both know Tori's not good at putting herself first. Without you, she never would have had the courage to take this trip." He placed his free hand on my shoulder. "So thank you for being there for my sister, especially when I couldn't be. She's lucky to have a friend like you."

I nodded, unable to form words. Guilt almost made my knees buckle. Oh yeah, Tori's *so* lucky. I'm supposed to be watching her kid. Instead I'm sucking face with her ex. *Go me.*

Cole stared at me, probably able to read my crestfallen expression. I tried to fix my face, forcing my lips to curl into a half-smile. Luckily, he dropped it, but my chest still pounded, needing to clear the air with Tori. As much as I wanted to convince myself otherwise, last night did not seem like a one time thing. Instead, it was an eruption, years of built-up tension igniting both Cam and me. Now that we'd unlatched the box, there was no shoving our feelings back inside.

We needed to stop before this got any more complicated. At least, that's what I wanted to say. I wanted to bury these feelings deep in the back of my mind and never reveal them again. But there was a block there, one that wouldn't let me slam the door closed, no matter how hard I tried.

Cam only made it worse when he strode out of the locker room, and his dark eyes instantly met mine. Every fiber of my body called to him, wanting him to hold me and make me forget about the guilt knotting my stomach.

He walked up to Cole first, running his hand over Emilia's back. "She's really out, huh?"

"She tried to fight it," Cole answered. "She was cheering her little heart out, but the moment the game was done, she passed out in my arms."

"I'll take her."

As Cole handed Emilia over, one of the other players walked over to Cam and clapped him on the shoulder. Damien, I think, was his name. His sister and her wife joined us in the box tonight. Mariana was a character, full of life and hilarious, while Angie was much quieter. I couldn't blame her for soaking it in. They had five girls, all under the age of ten, which made their house wonderfully chaotic. Mariana joked the stadium was their "quiet" night out.

Damien chuckled as he looked at Emilia curled up in her dad's arms. He rubbed her back before turning to Cam. "Got the good news?"

"Yeah. You knew, didn't you?"

Damien shook his head. "Not for sure, but Benny's smart. He'll make moves if something's not working."

I glanced between the two men, my brow furrowing. "Is everything okay?

Cam nodded his head, then shifted to face me. "Yeah, it's good news. Benny wants me to start next game. Keeping me in left field for now, but he might switch up the infield."

"Told you, kid!" Damien whooped. "You're going to be a goddamn all-star if you keep this up. Now you *have* to come out to celebrate." He turned toward me. "Help me out here, Hadley. Tell this guy he's gotta go out and celebrate tonight."

"Nah, man. Gotta get my girls home."

My heart stalled at his words, unsure if Cam realized what he said. Girls. *Plural.* Was he including me in this little group? When his eyes met mine with a sly smirk, though, I knew it wasn't a mistake. "Ready to get out of here, menace?"

My blood heated at his deepened tone, his insinuation clear only to me. We'd made no promises last night that we'd continue what we started, but the look in his eyes left little room for argument. There was a part of me that expected him to shut down this simmering tension, for him to throw back up those walls between us and pretend nothing occurred. But from the way his eyes kept darting to my lips, Cam was clearly not going to let this go. *Good,* a little voice called out in the back of my mind. I wanted this —wanted him.

"I can take her," Cole said from our sides. We both jumped apart, forgetting we had an audience, one that included my best friend's brother. How could I get so swept away? Had Cam done some sort of magic on my libido, making me impervious to everyone but him?

"I can't ask you to do that, Cole."

"I'm offering," he insisted. "We haven't gotten Emilia for an overnight in a while, and I know Alex is dying to see her. I'll bring her back tomorrow." He nodded over to me. "I can drop you off at the house if you want, Hadley."

"Oh..." I glanced over at Cam for an answer. The smart move would have been to go with Cole, to leave this confusion in the stadium and away from our everyday lives. But before I agreed, Damien interrupted my thoughts.

"She's coming out with us," Damien said. "I insist."

My mouth dropped open, unsure if it was a good idea. But when I looked at Cam, he beamed back at me, as if he wanted me there with him. "Yeah, Hadley, come. It'll be a lot of fun, and the guys have been asking about you."

My heart pumped an unfamiliar rhythm. This was a bad idea. A *colossally* bad idea. I should get as far away from Cam as possible, especially tonight. I couldn't trust my judgment, not after a full day of studying him on the field. His body was a machine, finally honed through years of dedication and practice. It was the biggest aphrodisiac—him mastering his game. Every single cell in my brain screamed, begging me to go home before I did something I couldn't take back.

"Okay," I whispered. My voice was barely audible over the surrounding crowd. I didn't miss how Cam's eyes lit up, like he hoped that would be my answer.

We both stood there as Cole walked away, Emilia snoring on his shoulder. When the stadium cleared out, and the rest of the players headed to their cars, Cam held his hand out to me. "You ready to get out of here, menace?"

I placed my fingers in his, trying to ignore the voice in the back of my mind that warned of consequences and loyalties.

All I could think about was how Cam kissed me.

And how much I wanted to do it again.

TWENTY-FOUR

Cameron

Erie City couldn't have been more different from Victoria's adopted home, Saint Stephen's Lake. The sleepy little town reminded me of our hometown, with the peaceful ambiance and natural elements. It was relaxing compared to the city. I preferred the quiet, enjoyed the slow mornings, the way everyone knew your name.

Though, to be fair, everyone seemed to know my name tonight. The club blared with the heavy thumps of bass, and the spotlights swayed, illuminating the sleek lines of the building. Shadows cloaked every inch of the club, yet everyone seemed to find our team partying in the VIP lounge. Some guys were eating up the attention, soaking up the free drinks and female attention. I couldn't blame them. After a tense first half of the season, we all needed to blow off some steam.

Although I hated to admit it, it was good to get out for the night. Having a kid so young messed with my internal clock, and I always felt older than I really was. At twenty-five, I was still on the younger end of the team, but I had more in common with the veteran players than the other rookies.

Most of us stuck to the VIP section, up a level from the rest of the club. The seats were more obscured by gauze curtains and low lighting, but there was a balcony that jutted out so you could see the throngs of people dancing below. As I toyed with the beer in my hands, I leaned over the metal railing, watching the party unfold below me.

Scanning the crowd, I searched through the sea of faces until I found who I was looking for. Hadley was in the middle of the dance floor, laughing with Parker's friend Ollie. She looked like a fucking beacon in the darkness, calling straight to my soul. Her body rolled with the pulse of the music, her movements almost hypnotic. I couldn't have looked away from her if I tried. My fingers tightened on the railing, as if the cold metal was the only thing keeping me from rushing to her side. It was getting ridiculous, this need to be as close to her as possible.

As if she sensed my eyes on her, Hadley looked up and winked at me, just like I had done on the field today. *Fuck.* Just the thought of seeing her in that box, knowing she wore my fucking jersey, was enough to get me hard.

I'd stolen a taste of her last night, but I wasn't done, not by a long-shot. As I brought my overpriced beer to my lips, someone joined me on the balcony.

"Damn, Seda," Jace chuckled. "Please tell me you're fucking her."

A low growl emanated from the back of my throat. I used my free hand and shoved him away from me. "Talk about her like that again, and I'll break your goddamn arm."

"Shit," Jace said, his voice a little wobbly after too many shots at the bar. He bee-lined to it the moment we got to the club and showed no signs of slowing down. He stumbled again, and I reached out to steady him.

"You should slow down, man," I said. "Order water."

"Fuck off, boy scout."

I brought my beer up to my lips and took a long pull. As soon as I finished it, I turned away from Jace. But before I could get too far, he called out. "How do you handle it?"

His voice was quiet, almost vulnerable. It surprised the hell out of me. Jace and I never saw eye-to-eye, on or off the field, but we were in the same situation, both fighting like hell to hold on to our dreams.

I shifted toward him. "What do you mean?"

"The pressure." He dropped his elbows on the railing and ran a hand over his face. "Every time I walk out onto that field, I keep thinking *this is it*. I've fucked up my one shot." Jace shook his head. "Hell, maybe I want it to be my last moment. Can't stand hearing the fans scream at me for fucking up another play."

I nodded, knowing exactly what he meant. While the fans seemed to be in our corner most of the time, when we fucked up, they had no problem letting us know. Between social media and the news outlets, everyone had an opinion about our performance. I'd learned early to tune it out, to not let others define my expectations, but Jace seemed to struggle with letting it go.

"We're doing the best we can," I said. "And when you're on, you're fucking lightning, Jace. Keep your head down. Keep fighting. If you need to talk, I'm around."

Jace nodded before his usual cocky grin slid back into place. "Yeah, Seda. Might do that." He took a step back and motioned toward the dance floor. "Now, let me give you some advice. You've got a chick that hot waiting for you—

what the fuck are you doing sulking up here?" He nodded to the stairs. "Better get your ass down there before I do."

As he took another step back, he knocked into a server, spilling her entire tray of drinks. I rushed over, trying to help her, but Jace lowered to his knees first, trying to pick up the shards of broken glass. "I'm so fucking sorry," he mumbled, but the server just shook her head.

"It's fine. Work at a club long enough, and you're bound to get some drinks spilled on you." When she lowered to help, Jace let out a low hiss of pain. I rushed over just in time to see a red streak of blood cascading down his hand. The server grabbed his hand and pulled him up to stand. "Crap. This isn't deep, but you might need stitches. Come around back with me, and we'll get it cleaned up."

She made a hand motion to one of the other bartenders before she led Jace down a barely lit hall, still holding his bleeding palm. I was tempted to follow them, to make sure Jace was alright. Hopefully, he didn't do too much damage, and the cut just needed a bandage. I frowned as I replayed his words, hating that Jace thought I'd had it so easy. The pressure got to me, but it seemed to drown him. Hopefully, he'd get it together soon, but it was hard to tell what was going through Jace's mind on any night.

But he was right about one thing: I was done waiting for Hadley to come to me. After dropping my bottle on our table, I headed down the stairs, pushing through the dance floor as I made my way to Hadley. Ollie caught my eye and gave me a slow, knowing smirk. She whispered something in Hadley's ear, then disappeared into the crowd. Hadley turned around, her eyes widening at me as I approached her.

"Cam—" she started to say when I stopped in front of her, her tone almost questioning.

I'd spent nearly a whole day away from her, and I desperately craved her presence. My hands found her neck, and I pulled her closer. Then, I kissed her, right in the middle of the dance floor, not caring who saw us.

All day, all I'd wanted was to claim her, to show the world what this girl meant to me. But she wasn't ready for that, too busy making excuses for this intense connection between us. Right now, though, none of it mattered, not when her moves matched my intensity, like she'd been dying for this, just like me.

I pulled back, and she stared up at me, confusion and desire coloring her eyes. We didn't speak as I brought my hands to her hips, dragging her closer. I let out a low, guttural curse as she twisted so her ass pressed against my straining cock. One arm looped around my neck, and the other found my hand on her hip, pressing it further into her skin. Every sway of her hips only made me harder, almost to the point of pain with the need for release, but I didn't dare move away. At least I'd changed into jeans before coming out tonight. Between the way she swiveled her hips against me and my name still draped across her back, I was helpless against her. She was the hurricane, and I was done trying to resist her pull.

"Feel that, menace?" I said in her ear as my fingers tightened against her skin. "Feel how hard you make me in a room full of people?" Her lip tucked between her teeth as she nodded. "You like that? Like teasing me when you know there's nothing I can do about it?"

She shivered as I pressed my lips to the apex of her neck and shoulder. "God, Cam," she moaned. "What are you doing to me?"

"The same thing you're doing to me, Hadley." My fingers traced the smooth line of her stomach where her shirt had ridden up. She hissed as I pressed into her bare skin, needing to savor every part of her. My pinky traced the underside of her jeans, and she squirmed against me. "You see what you're doing to me, baby. But what if I slid my hand lower? What if I touched you right in the middle of this crowd? I bet you're fucking soaked for me."

Her head fell against my chest, almost daring me to keep going. *Fuck.* I could. Between the loud, pulsing bass and the couples grinding around us, no one would even notice. Plenty of other people had paired off. Hands trailed various body parts like there was no one else in the room, but I'd waited a long time to hear my name fall from Hadley's lips, and I didn't want to share the experience with anyone else.

Without warning, I snatched her hand and dragged her off the dance floor. "Cam?" she asked, her voice a little more uncertain than before. When we got to the edge of the club where the shadows covered us from head to toe, I dragged her forward, pressing her back against the wall. She looked up at me with surprise before her eyes lit up, almost in a dare.

"Fuck, Hadley," I groaned as I pressed myself against her. "You've got my head so messed up, all I can think about is you."

"And that's a bad thing?"

"The fucking worst," I ground out. "Especially when I've been hard all goddamn day and haven't gotten a moment alone with you."

"We're alone now." She smirked. "What are you going to do about it?"

My hand reached up, and I grasped her chin, forcing her to meet my eyes. My thumb rubbed against her plump lower lip. Shit, I wanted to see my cock in her mouth, sliding through her gorgeous lips. Wanted to experience her falling apart underneath me. Wanted everything Hadley offered, leaving no doubts about how much I needed her.

My lips slammed down onto hers, almost bruising with my need to have her again. She moaned as I ground against her, loving the way she went so pliant when I held her. Hadley was strong—the kind of woman who never backed down from a fight. So it was even more intoxicating when she let me take control like this, when she let me claim her body like it was made for me.

"Are you gonna be good for me, menace?" I whispered in her ear. "Are you gonna let me touch this sweet little pussy until you come on my fingers?"

"Yes," she moaned.

"Not good enough," I said, wrapping my hand around her hair and pulling her head back to nip at her neck. "Use your words, baby. You've got more to say than that."

"God, are you going to touch me or just keep fucking talking?"

I bit her earlobe, and Hadley's back arched, trying to close the space between us. "Just for that, I should leave you like this, all needy and desperate for me."

"What?" she snapped. "Don't you—"

I silenced her when I undid the button of her jeans, tracing the bare patch of skin right above where she wanted me. "Let's try that again." My fingers inched a little lower. "Tell me what you want, and ask nicely, Hadley."

"Please, Cam. Please, touch me," she whined. "I want you to make me come."

"That's it, baby," I said as I pressed a trail of kisses down her neck. "Keep asking nicely, and you'll get rewarded."

Hadley almost bit out another comment, but I silenced her as I dragged her panties to the side and traced her soaked core. She wasn't kidding about needing me. She was as desperate for this as I was. As I lazily stroked her, she writhed against me, almost looking like she was still moving to the music. Good—not that I would let anyone else get eyes on her at this moment. Her orgasm was mine alone to witness.

I circled her clit with my thumb and then lowered my hand, arching my fingers to dip inside her core. Shit. She was so tight, it was almost hard to fit more than one inside her. We'd have to work on that if she was going to take me. And there was no question in my mind that we'd be doing that—soon.

As my thumb and fingers worked in tandem against her, Hadley stiffened in my arms before her walls pulled me in more. She gripped my wrist, holding me tightly in place as her orgasm ripped through her. With her head thrown back and her mouth parted in ecstasy, she was the most beautiful thing I'd ever seen in my life.

When she came down from her high, Hadley went limp in my arms, almost shuddering as I pulled my fingers out of her. I brought them to her lips, and she smiled up at me before flicking out her tongue and licking them slowly. I growled before snapping them away, needing to see if she was as sweet as I'd imagined. Sunshine and honey. That was my girl's flavor, and I was already addicted.

As my fingers fell away from my lips, Hadley stared up at me with a sultry, satiated smile. I couldn't resist kissing her, letting her taste tangle on our tongues.

When the kiss broke, I dropped my forehead to hers, wanting to hold on to this moment a little longer. I could live here forever, loving how much Hadley had opened up to me. I leaned back and brushed the hair away from her eyes. "Want to get out here?"

She paused, and my heart pounded in my chest. It was as painful as it had been at the end of the game, when we were so close to winning but we let it slip through our fingers. After a long moment, she finally smirked up at me. "I thought you'd never ask."

TWENTY-FIVE

Hadley

Cameron Seda just made me come on his fingers.

In the middle of a fucking club, with hundreds of people around us. Anyone could have looked over and saw us, but I didn't care. I'd never added exhibitionism to my list of kinks, but I might have to after tonight.

Cam's hand wrapped around mine, pulling me out of the club like a man on a mission. The same fingers that had just been inside me, wringing out every drop of my pleasure, the ones that had held me as though I was precious to him. And God, it was everything. From his commanding words and the powerful strokes against my skin, Cam was sure about what he wanted, and for some reason, that was me.

As soon as the cool, early spring air hit us, Cam turned and pushed me back against the wall. The man had a thing for shoving me against surfaces, and I was not complaining. I loved the way he commanded my body, almost submitting it to his mercy. It was so fucking hot, my panties instantly dampened. I'd barely recovered from my last orgasm, and I was already dying for his touch.

My back collided with the cold exterior of the building, and Cam captured my lips in a brutal kiss. His hands moved to my neck, shifting me so he could deepen our embrace. He tasted like imported beer and impulsive choices, and it was the sexiest thing in the world. Cam was expanding my mind, bringing beauty into the banality of everyday life.

"Damn it, Hadley." He pulled back, resting his forehead against mine. "Why do you feel so fucking good?"

"You're one to talk." I smirked, letting my hand dip down to the front of his jeans. As my palm worked down his length, he groaned, shifting further into my touch. "I want you in my mouth," I said, my voice taking on an unfamiliar, sultry tone. I was no stranger to sex, but this connection was stronger, more alive than anything I'd ever experienced. It made me bolder. I wanted to please him, wanted to see what he looked like when I made him fall apart.

Without warning, Cam reached down and ripped my hand away, dragging us to his parked truck. "Oooh," I chuckled as we moved through the parking lot. "Are we going to defile your baby? I know how much you love this car."

"Don't tempt me, menace," he ground out. "I'm so close to busting in my jeans that even your smart mouth is turning me on." As we reached the passenger side door, he turned and brushed a finger along my jaw. "But the first time I fuck you, I want to see you. Every single inch. So we're going to go back to my hotel, where I can spread you out and lick your pussy until you scream my name."

"H-hotel?" I stammered.

Cam nodded. "I booked it before we left the stadium. I didn't want to risk driving home too late." His hand dropped to his side. "Is that okay?"

"Awfully presumptuous of you, sarge. You just assumed I'd want to fuck you?"

"Nope." He leaned in closer. "But I fucking hoped you would. You're all I can think about, Hadley. During the game, I kept thinking how badly I wanted to fuck you in my jersey." His voice lowered. "But the room doesn't mean anything. Nothing has to happen if you don't want it to. You're in control here."

My lips rolled together, loving that he was being so open and honest with me. But then again, hadn't Cam always told me the truth—even if it wasn't what I wanted to hear? I trusted him—he was a man of his word. If I said no right now, he'd probably offer to book me a separate room.

Lucky for him, I wanted him just as badly. I reached over to toy with the collar of his shirt. "I like the sound of that—being in charge. Does that mean you'll get on your knees if I asked you to?"

"Hadley, I'd crawl on my fucking hands and knees if it meant I got to have you."

"Tempting." I tapped my finger on my lips. "But not my kink. However, the part about you going down on me until I scream—that, I can get on board with." I pulled open the door and hopped in the truck, smirking at him over my shoulder. "Come on, sarge. You've got promises to fulfill."

THANKFULLY, the hotel was only minutes from the club. If I had to wait any longer, I would have died from the tension. The air between us bristled with unspoken desires and an understanding about what was going to happen next. It was enough time to heighten my anticipation, but not enough for the nerves to kick in.

At least, not until we entered the lobby. The hotel was nothing fancy, what you would expect from a mid-range tier of hotels. If the front desk clerk recognized Cam, they said nothing. But then again, considering it was only minutes from the baseball and football stadiums, they were most likely numb to athletes traipsing in and out of here. After he checked in, Cam took my hand and led me to the elevators without saying a word. Each step only amplified the pounding of my heart, recognizing this was one of those moments that was going to change everything.

I was about to sleep with Cam Seda.

That was a sentence I never thought I'd string together.

When we stepped into the elevator together, Cam turned toward me, studying my face like it held all the answers. "Are you having second thoughts?"

"What?" I snapped. "No. Why would you think that?"

He held up our joined hands. "You're squeezing the life out of me, menace. If you want to go home, I'll drive you. I only had one beer."

"Don't you dare." I turned toward him, lifted onto the tips of my toes, and kissed him. Cam cursed as my fingers found their way to his hair, tugging on the disheveled strands. "In case that's not clear—no, I haven't changed my mind. But we need to talk about what happens after tonight."

Cam's jaw tensed as he leaned forward. "What do you mean?"

"I mean—this is only a onetime thing, Cam. We're just trying to douse the tension between us. I'm not looking for anything more than that."

"And if I don't agree?"

My eyes narrowed. "Then this can't happen, and I'm going home."

A terse silence filled the elevator, as if we were both waiting to see if the other would break first. I meant what I said—I wouldn't commit to anything more than one night. But then again, did I have the willpower to walk away? Or was this always where we were going to end up?

"Fine, menace. We'll have it your way. Tonight only. No other expectations."

Cam smiled and rubbed his thumb over my cheek. It was soft and gentle, a sharp contrast to how he held me at the club. I was learning to embrace all sides of Cam, but this softer, sweeter side was becoming my new addiction. He lowered his lips down to the curve of my neck, leaving feather-light kisses until he got to my ear. "Tell me what you like, Hadley."

"Like?"

"In bed," he said. "Do you want me to be gentle with you? Hold you tight until you shatter on my cock?" I shook my head, too nervous to use my voice for the first time in my life. His hand trailed down to my hip, taking a firm hold of my skin. "Or do you want me to take control? To bend and break you until you can't take one more second without me inside you?"

"Option two, please," I mumbled as his thumb traced the bare skin of my neck.

Cam chuckled against my neck. "I knew you were made for this, baby. Made for me. You're going to look so fucking pretty when you're dripping with my cum."

I sucked in a sharp breath. Was that what I wanted? To be honest, all my past sexual encounters seemed tame, almost timid, in the face of Cam's words, muttered curses and fumbling around in the dark. I never dreamed a man would speak to me like this, and yet, it snapped something inside me, a craving that had never been satisfied until this exact moment.

While the elevator continued to climb, Cam pulled away and searched my eyes. "Are you on birth control?" I nodded. "If you want us to use a condom, I'll do it. But I can't lie, Hadley, the idea of filling you up is making me so fucking hard, I can't see straight." A brush against my pulse point. "Are you okay with that? I had to get tested before the season, and everything came back clear."

"Same here," I swallowed, studying his eyes. I wanted to take a picture of his expression—wanted to remember this feeling forever. One day, when I was in the nursing home, my only company my memories, I needed to remember being so wanted, like Cam couldn't take another breath without my touch. "I want you bare, Cam. Nothing between us."

"Nothing between us," he repeated, leaning in for one last kiss before the elevator doors parted. We walked toward our room, every step heavy with the desire coursing through our veins. As soon as the door closed behind us, I moved to the middle of the space, not taking in any of the sights in front of me. Cam's stare weighed on my back, as if he wanted me to speak first.

I turned around and arched my brow, but he leaned against the door. As he crossed his arms over his chest, a heavy lust filled his dark eyes. I smirked at him. "Getting cold feet, sarge?"

He laughed, the sound dark and full of mirth. "Keep sassing me, menace, and I'll find a better use for that bratty little mouth. Now..." He paused and took a step toward me. "Strip."

"What?"

He reached out and cupped my jaw, brushing his thumb along my lower lip. "You heard me, baby. Strip. I told you I wanted to see every fucking inch of you, and I meant it. So take off your clothes and get your ass on that bed so I can admire the view."

TWENTY-SIX

Cameron

Hadley stared at me, her pouty lips forming an almost perfect circle. Just as I was about to change my tone, she reached down to the button of her jeans and flicked it open. My eyes traced every single inch of skin she bared, wanting to follow the same path with my tongue. I'd buried my fingers in her pussy only an hour ago, but I'd yet to see her naked, and I couldn't wait another fucking second.

I stepped forward, ready to tear the rest of her clothing to shreds, when she held up her hand. "You want me bare, right, sarge?" she asked, the same teasing flicker in her eyes. "Then you need to let me take my time. I want to savor the way you're watching me."

"I'm always watching you, Hadley." My hands clenched at my side. "Always wanting you. You're a fucking goddess, baby. All I want to do is worship at your feet."

"Oh, there will be plenty of time for that later." She kicked over her jeans. "But for right now, with the way you're staring at me? I've never felt sexier in my life." She pointed to the armchair in the corner. "Sit, Cam. I spent hours watching you today, wanting you. You can wait a couple more minutes."

"Doubt that," I grumbled under my breath, but I complied with her request. My need to touch her—taste her, fuck her—was strong, but I couldn't help but smile at the dare in her eyes. She was baiting me, wanting me to fight her. This push and pull between us had taken a dark, lust-soaked turn, and I had to admit—it was working for me. I'd never been with a woman who pushed me like Hadley, and I was craving her brand of torture.

She turned around, and my jersey hung from her shoulders, slowly slipping down to reveal her bare skin underneath. Fuck. My name on her back was hot, but seeing my jersey laying at her feet was even better. When Hadley shifted back toward me, I sucked in a sharp breath, and my eyes took in every inch of her thin white tank top and lace panties. She wasn't wearing a bra, and her nipples peaked through the fabric, desperate for my tongue to mark them as mine.

And she was mine.

Even if Hadley didn't know it yet. Even if she would fight me every step of the way. From the moment she walked into this room, she was only ever going to be mine. Fuck her one time rule.

She stepped closer, letting her hips swing as she came into my space. Her eyes met mine, and for a moment, a rare flash of vulnerability crossed her expression. That wouldn't do. I lifted my hand and crooked a finger toward her. "Come here."

Hadley crawled into my lap, her legs spreading on both sides of mine. I reached up, tracing her ribs until I met the curve of her breasts. My eyes leaped to hers. "Is it okay if I touch you?" She nodded, so I pulled my hands away. "Words, Hadley. I need you to tell me what you want."

She rolled her eyes, so I grabbed her chin, forcing her to meet my gaze. "You want to act like a brat, Hadley? I have ways to tame that side of you. But nothing else is going to happen tonight if you don't tell me what you want." I softened my grip, brushing the hair away from her eyes. "You have all the control here, baby. Now use your words and tell me exactly where you want me to touch you."

"Everywhere. My breasts, my ass. My pussy's so empty without your fingers inside it," she breathed, her eyes wide, lost to her desire. "God, I want you so badly, Cam. Touch me and show me what I've been missing."

My hands moved to her ass, kneading the soft skin like I'd dreamed of doing a million times. All the fights, all the barbs—they'd all been leading to this moment when I got to hold Hadley close. As her head fell back, I freed one hand, pulling down her tank top to expose her breasts. Her petal pink nipples tightened with the rush of cool air, and I traced them with my tongue. She was so soft, and all I wanted was to memorize every inch of her. When she let out a soft moan, I couldn't hold back another second. I stood with her in my arms, dropping her in the middle of the bed.

"Wait," Hadley called out, lifting her sapphire eyes to mine. "I said I wanted to taste you too."

"Too fucking bad, menace." I grabbed her ankles and pulled her closer to me. When her clothed center hit my straining cock, she let out a soft gasp, like a single touch was going to shatter her. "Right now, I need to bury myself in your cunt, need you squeezing my cock like you'd die without it." I reached up, brushing her plush lower lip. "And then, after I've painted you with my cum, you're going to use that poison tongue of yours to clean me up. Do you understand?"

Hadley's whole body blushed crimson, like she didn't believe what was spilling out of my mouth—and neither did I. Perhaps it was because Hadley's anger was a familiar foe, and knowing what it was like to be on the other end of her vitriol unleashed this side of me. I'd felt the weight of her glare, knew how her hands tensed when she was on the edge of exploding. None of those happened now. Instead, her sapphire eyes stared directly into my soul, like she craved this just as much as I did.

She looked up at me like I was her undoing.

Right back at you, baby.

I wrenched her panties down her legs, tossing them to the other side of the room. Those were mine now as well, a reminder of the first time I got to have her. Hadley shivered as I unbuckled my jeans and pulled my shirt off, leaving me almost as bare as her.

I leaned down above her, kissing and licking my way from her navel to her neck. She squirmed underneath me, so I reached around to her ass, kneading hard enough that there would be marks tomorrow. *Good*, a primal part of my brain called out. I wanted her to wear my marks on her skin.

My fingers trailed down to her center, testing and teasing her. Holy hell, she was soaked, ready and waiting impatiently for me to fuck her. I lined my cock up with her entrance, searching her expression as I pushed inside her. Her mouth flew open as I pressed in, already meeting resistance, although I'd barely started.

"Relax for me, baby," I cooed as I pressed kisses to her collarbone. "Need you to relax so I can get all the way inside you."

"I'm trying," she sighed, her hands tightening against my skin. "You're so big, Cam."

"Oh yeah?" I shifted to get another inch closer. "You like my big cock inside you, menace?"

"God, you're going to be even more insufferable now, aren't you?" She chuckled, and her body relaxed, letting me slide further into her.

I pulled out, and my whole body clenched. Holding back was fucking killing me, but I refused to hurt her. Not like this. With each thrust, she opened a little more, until finally, I bottomed out. Once we connected, I leaned down and brushed the hair away from her eyes. "Hadley, are you..."

"Full," she said. "So full. Please move, Cam. I need you to move."

"Good girl." I brushed my lips along her collarbone. "I love when you tell me what you need."

After giving Hadley a moment to get used to the intrusion, I started shifting, watching for any signs of discomfort. But her expression was pure bliss, relishing everything I gave her. "Yeah, baby," I groaned as I raised onto my haunches, pulling her closer by her hips. "I'm going to be so damn smug when you shatter on my cock. But it's what you get for denying me this perfect little pussy for so long."

"Cam..." she gasped as she tried to grab me, but instead, I took her wrists in one hand and lifted them above her head.

"I was going to take it easy on you, but then you had to run that sexy little mouth," I said as my thrusts quickened. "Told me I could only fuck you once. Now, I'm going to give you everything, Hadley. Every single inch. If that's not what you want, tell me now, baby."

"Yes," she cried as I slammed into her, the rhythmic

movements making her walls tighten. "Give me all of it, Cam. Don't hold back. I don't want you to hold back."

I reached down and lifted her, depositing her into my lap. Hadley's eyes widened as she sunk down onto my cock, relishing every single inch. God, this was everything. Every move, every moan, every flush of her cheeks branded itself on my psyche. I'd had good sex before—amazing, even. Nothing like this, though. Nothing compared to being inside Hadley. Our bodies instinctively knew each other. This woman was made for me, designed to tempt and enthrall me until all I saw was her.

When her walls strangled my cock and she screamed my name, I couldn't help but follow over the edge, helpless to stop my cum from coating her. When she breathed a little easier, Hadley pulled back, searching my expression as if to ask, *what the hell was that?*

I had no idea, no answers to give her.

But one thing was for sure—we were going to do that again.

TWENTY-SEVEN

Hadley

My hand flew to my chest, trying to calm my erratic heartbeat. I'd expected good sex with Cam, but it wasn't supposed to be this life-altering. The way he moved inside me, the way he spoke so filthily while holding me like I was the most precious thing in the world to him, it all combined into the most mind-blowing experience in my life. There was no way I'd ever be able to wipe it from my memories.

Which only meant one thing—we could *not* do that again.

Not because I didn't want to. No, something monumental had shifted inside me, like the pieces of a puzzle fitting together for the first time. Nothing in my life had ever been so good—so right. All I wanted was to crawl into his arms and never let him go.

Maybe it was naïve, but a small part of me hoped the sex would be terrible so I could push Cam out of my mind, convince myself this whole thing was nothing more than a misguided crush, fueled by our proximity and the way he filled out his baseball pants. We'd fuck, then move on, and life would go on like before.

Now that I'd known his touch? Heard his gravelly voice commanding my body like he knew what I wanted? I'd never erase his impact on me. He would be forever etched inside me.

Which was why it could not happen again.

Cam must have read the panic crashing through my mind, because he made no attempt to fulfill the other half of his promise. Instead, as soon as we were finished, Cam retreated into the bathroom, giving me a moment to clear my mind. However, he could have stayed out of the room for a thousand years, and it still wouldn't have been enough time to compose my racing thoughts.

My pulse thundered when Cam walked out of the bathroom, holding a washcloth in his grip. He brushed the terrycloth material between my tender thighs. It was gentle, such a stark contrast from how he fucked me, it almost made me weep. I loved the sex, but how he took care of me now was almost better. More intimate. He kissed my quaking thighs, moving up my body until he cradled me in his arms.

Cam searched my expression and must have noted the uncertainty still lurking in my eyes. "Don't pull away from me now, menace," he whispered as he leaned down to kiss me. I shook my head, not trusting my words. My emotions were so jumbled, as likely to hand over my heart as I was to tell him off. When he pulled back, he frowned. "What's going on, Hadley?"

I bit my lip, trying to put my thoughts into concrete words. Nothing seemed to tie down my emotions, as if they were just wisps in the wind. Cam just waited, not moving away from me but giving me time to plan my next words. "I feel guilty," I finally said. "Victoria—"

"Has nothing to do with this." Cam rolled away from me. It hurt, knowing he'd just begged me not to pull away, only for him to do moments later. Tension radiated off him, decimating the quiet peace we'd had moments earlier. I hated it. The moment he backed away, I wanted to rush to him, already missing the warmth of his skin. I forced myself to stay in one place, watching him as I bunched the sheets in my fist. He climbed off the bed and started pacing. "This is about us, Hadley. No one else."

"There is no us." I sat up on my knees. "There can't be, Cam. Not with all the history between you and Tori."

"So she can move on, but I'm supposed to stay tethered to her?" he bit out. Pain laced his words, and my heart stuttered in my chest. Oh my God, had I gotten it all wrong? I could have sworn Cam was over Victoria. What if he held out hope, only biding his time until Victoria and Adam either made things official or fell apart?

I clutched the sheet over my bare chest, feeling sick to my stomach. Sleeping with my best friend's ex was bad enough. I'd only crossed that line because there was a deep connection between us. If it meant nothing to him—

"Don't, Hadley." Cam moved back to the side of the bed and brushed his fingers over my cheek. I hadn't realized I'd started crying until his fingers came away damp. "Don't question what happened between us. If you think this has anything to do with Vic, you're wrong."

I shook my head. "If you're not over her—"

"I want *you*, Hadley. *Only* you." He brought my hand up to his chest. "I loved Vic, and part of me always will because she gave me Emilia. But we're family. I haven't looked at her like that in years." He shook his head. "And now, with you..."

The small, insecure girl in my mind called out. "What about me?"

Cam's umber eyes searched mine, everything I didn't

want to give a voice to reflected in his expression. This connection, no matter what I tried to tell myself, was not a one-sided thing. I'd embedded myself inside him, like he'd done to me. He pulled my hand away and kissed my open palm, then placed it on his chest. "You're different, Hadley. Whatever this is, it's not going away after one night together. If anything, having you made it worse." He pulled back, his expression pleading. "Tell me you feel this too."

I wanted to. God, I wanted to. I wanted to leap into his arms and tell him to never let me go. For so long, I'd been searching for a place to belong, convinced some magical spot in the world would cure my restless heart. After years of searching, I found a family, a job I loved, and even a small, borrowed place to call my own—almost all thanks to Victoria.

"I do," I whispered. "But it doesn't matter. You might be over her, but she is still my best friend. No matter how you two feel about each other now, I betrayed her tonight. It can't happen again, Cam. I won't hurt her like this."

"And if she's okay with us?"

"Doesn't matter," I answered. "I'm not okay with it. Yes, there's something between us, Cam, but we need to let it go. Tonight can't happen again."

Cam just stared at me, fierce determination filling his expression. I expected him to fight, to push me into admitting my fears. God help me, part of me wanted that, wanted him to refuse to let me go without a fight.

Instead, Cam just nodded and started grabbing his clothes. "If that's what you want, Hadley, I'll respect it." After he pulled his shirt over his head, he stepped closer and pressed his thumb under my chin. "But don't waste your time lying to yourself. This wasn't a one-time thing.

There's a connection between us, and it's not going away, no matter how much you want to deny it. When you're done fighting us, I'll be here, waiting for you to catch up."

With a featherlight kiss to my lips, Cam left the room, leaving me alone to wonder what I'd done.

TWENTY-EIGHT

Hadley

Days since last sleeping with Cam Seda: *Three*.

Times I've *thought* about sleeping with Cam Seda: *Infinite*.

I stared out at the main house through my kitchen window. How had it only been three days since Cam and I hooked up? It felt like a lifetime and yesterday at the same time. It'd be so easy to sneak over there and give in to the desire coursing through my bloodstream.

No. Do not pass go. Do not collect two hundred dollars.

Do not give in to a moment of weakness and hop back on Cam Seda's dick.

The torrential downpour outside was an unexpected blessing. At least with the heavy rain, I had no excuse to leave my house, especially not to pop in across the yard.

Laila meowed at my feet, reminding me I'd been neglecting her in my Cam-induced haze. I'd been like this since Cam drove me back from the hotel, unbridled tension filled the space between us, the knowledge of what could happen if we both let go. He stayed true to his word, acting like he had before we crossed that line. However, the moment Emilia left the room, he'd find reasons to touch me, to inch closer than appropriate. I should have stopped it, but I basked in those stolen moments, wanting to hold on to him and never let go.

But no matter how much I wanted Cam, there was a wall there, at least for me. The sharp reminder had me walking away from the window, smacking myself on the forehead as I headed into the kitchen. *Tori. Tori is your best friend. Sleeping with her ex once was a mistake. Any more than that is a pattern, which would place you in the shittiest best friend column.*

I turned back toward the couch and turned on the television, hoping to maybe find anything else to focus on. Just as I found a show to watch, my phone rang, Tori's name scrolling at the top. *Fuck.* I should've sent it to voicemail, unsure of how I'd hide what I'd done. But no matter the circumstances, I missed my best friend. I slid the bar over, and her smiling face filled the screen.

"Hey!" Tori said.

"Uggh," I groaned. "Not only are you in paradise, but you look so happy, I might cry. If I didn't love you, I'd probably hate you."

Tori tucked her lip between her teeth. "It's pretty amazing here. Adam rented us this bungalow by the water, so when he's filming, I get to just relax and enjoy being somewhere new. You'd love it, Hads."

"I'll add it to my travel list." I settled more on my couch. "Tell me everything! What's it like there? How's the movie going?"

Tori filled me in on all the details of her trip, sharing all her favorite places in Sydney. I sat back and soaked in every detail, wishing I could be there with her. She sounded so peaceful. This time with Adam had done wonders for her, and she looked more tranquil than I'd ever seen her. Even though she was only half-way through her trip, there was a fresh air about her, a calm serenity that had been missing before she left. Tori loved being a mom, no question about that. Her entire life revolved around her family, but it was great to see her take some time for herself.

Her voice suddenly cut out, and I realized she'd asked me a question. "Huh?"

Tori rolled her eyes. "I asked how things were going with Cam? Have you two killed each other yet?"

Nope, not unless you're counting orgasms. In that case, yes, he almost murdered me.

"Not yet," I said. "We've been getting along, actually."

I was desperate to add on more, to tell my best friend about the conflict rushing through my heart. There was a line, and I was pretty sure talking about my carnal desire for her ex crossed it.

Her brow furrowed, almost as if she read the words I refused to say. Each unspoken moment made my pulse thunder a little harder, unsure what to do with myself when she studied me. Finally, she sighed, "Wait, you aren't being sarcastic?"

"No," I said. "I can be serious from time to time. Adds to my mystique."

"You two are actually getting along?" I nodded. She beamed back at me. "That's amazing! I always hoped you guys would become friends, but I didn't think it would ever happen."

"Don't get too crazy," I said. "This is a temporary cease-fire. When you get back, we'll go back to hating each other."

She went silent again, looking off into the distance beyond the phone. When she finally turned back to me, she sighed, "Why?"

"What do you mean?"

"Why does it have to be temporary? Why are you so determined to hate Cam?" She shook her head. "You two are both too stubborn for your own good, I swear."

"I am nothing like Cam," I protested.

"Bullshit," Tori said. "You two are opposite sides of the same coin. You're more free-spirited, but you're both two of the most stubborn, infuriating, loyal people I've ever met." She shook her head. "Is this because of school? Hadley, it was my choice."

My jaw clenched, remembering that conversation all too well. I was the first one to find out Tori was pregnant, holding her hand while we counted down the minutes until she checked that stick. When two lines appeared, she broke down, convinced her life was over. I'd held her through her tears and convinced her it didn't have to change her life. We'd made a plan to get an apartment off campus, and I'd help with the baby. She was too smart, too determined to let this derail her goals. When we finished talking, she was actually smiling, excited about the prospect of becoming a mom and staying in school.

At least, until she talked to Cam.

Then, everything changed.

"Hadley, I love you. I love that you're so protective over me." She paused, and my pulse instantly quickened. "But I'm not your mom. And Cam—he's not your dad."

"Ouch," I said. "Way to dive right into my daddy issues. Anything else you want to bring up? Want to dive deep into my childhood bullying problems?"

"I'm serious, Hads. I can't imagine what it must be like, hearing your mom complain constantly about how her life turned out, especially with her as your only parent." Tori shook her head. "It's not the same with Cam and me. I'm happy with the way my life's turned out. If I stayed in school, who knows what it would look like right now? I might not have Emilia, and she's the best thing that ever happened to me." She smiled at me. "Cam has been there every step of the way, and every single decision, we've made together. We might not be perfect, but we're trying hard for Emilia. He's a good guy. The very best."

My entire face flushed with shame. Was I really that transparent? Listen, I might have spent years working with a therapist to work through my family issues, but they always lurked under the surface, waiting for the right moment to rear their ugly heads.

"He is." I swallowed and forced my eyes away from the phone. "At the same time—you lost yourself, Tori. Even after you guys broke up, you limited your world to only Emilia. Easier to blame him than look too at why it bothered me. I should have realized I was holding onto my stuff about my parents."

She nodded in understanding. "I get it. I'd be more concerned if it didn't trigger you. However, it might be time to face what's really bothering you."

I exhaled, trying to force away my tears, but it was useless. They broke free, trailing along my cheeks. "I don't know how to do this, Tori—how to let other people in and trust they'll stick around."

"You've done pretty well with me."

"You're different."

"That might be true," she said, "but you're not giving yourself enough credit, Hads. You're the best, and if other people don't see that, it's on them, not you. Give Cam a chance. Let him in."

God, she made it sound so easy. Could I really just let

Cam in and trust he'd stick around? If I let down my walls, threw away all my defenses, would it be worth the risk?

Who was I kidding? Cam had already decimated them. Every moment we spent together, he proved worthy of my trust.

As much as I tried to deny it, I'd spent years hiding. After all, it was easier to keep everyone at a distance than risk getting my heart broken again, worried someone would see the real me and deem me unworthy. Or worse—squash my spirit and bend me to their will.

Even when we hated each other, Cam had never done that. He took my comments, understood my teasing nature. He might have pushed back, but he knew when to turn that off. Cam was steady, a force that rattled against my nature, but I needed it at my back.

"Okay," I whispered. "I'll try. Who knows? Being friends with Cam might not be the worst thing."

I left off the end of my sentence, the one that screamed I wanted so much more than friendship with Cam. After a few hours of pleasure, I wanted to spend more nights wrapped up in his sheets, to wake up in his arms, to cheer him on in the crowd and see that adorable wink he saved just for me.

For a moment, I thought about telling Victoria that exact sentiment. *Not over the phone.* This was an in-person conversation, with alcohol and chocolate on standby. Victoria had every right to be upset with me. After all, this was the biggest secret I'd ever kept from her, but I doubted she would be. I knew my best friend's heart, almost better than my own. If Cam and I had something real, she'd give us her blessing.

At least, I was pretty sure she would.

A rock dropped into the pit of my stomach. That was, if

Cam hadn't changed his mind. Our last conversation echoed in my mind, and I cringed, thinking about how I'd slammed the door on our burgeoning relationship. I hid the truth behind Victoria, using her as an excuse to keep Cam at arm's length.

As we said our goodbyes and I hung up the phone, I walked over to the window and watched the sky open. Thunder and lightning crackled in the darkness, illuminating the shadows of the main house. It felt like a sign from the universe, encouraging me to wait until morning, to make sure that this was the right path. Maybe I wanted more with Cam, but life wasn't that simple. Just because I willed something to happen didn't mean it would all work out like I wanted.

I was the girl who leaped first, never worrying about where I might land. With Cam, for the first time in my life, the fear of falling held me back.

Because to jump and miss this time wouldn't risk only my heart—it could tear apart this little family I'd grown to love as my own. As I imagined life without Emilia or Victoria at my side, my heart ached, deep confusion rotting through my determination.

With another crackle of lightning, I forced myself back to bed. Even though I blamed the weather, I knew there was another reason I couldn't keep my eyes closed.

TWENTY-NINE

Cameron

"Daddy?"

At the sound of Emilia's frightened voice, I instantly sat up in bed, pulled from a deep sleep. The sky was still dark, so it must have been the middle of the night, but my daughter was curled up at my side, shaking with fear.

I wrapped my arms around her and pulled her close. "What's going on, Em?"

"The storm," she said. Her voice sounded high, like when she was younger. While she was only six, there were days when it felt like she was growing up too fast. I loved watching her grow and change—seeing glimpses of the woman she'd become one day. She was bold, fearless, and kind, a force I hoped would only grow with time. But time passing pulled at my heartstrings, knowing that, soon enough, she wouldn't need her dad to be her hero, rushing into the night to slay her dragons. Time was the ultimate thief. No matter how hard I tried to hold on, the days passed faster and faster each year.

Warmth filled my chest when she snuggled closer, her

breathing steadier than it was moments ago. "I don't like the thunder." Her words were little more than a shaky whisper in the dark.

"Me either, Em," I lied, savoring having my daughter safe in my arms. I ran my hand over her hair. "What does Mommy do when you're scared?"

"She sings me a song."

I chuckled. "Trust me, little bug, that won't help much. My voice isn't nice like Mommy's."

"I know. Hadley says it sounds like you're stepping on Laila's tail."

"Oh, does she?" I couldn't help but smirk. Of course, the woman had to give me grief even when I wasn't in the room. "What else does Hadley tell you about me?"

"That you're the best daddy in the world." Emilia yawned and nuzzled into the pillow. "That you're strong and kind, and that you're always there for me, even when I don't see you."

Heat rushed through my veins. The words weren't ones I'd ever thought I'd hear Hadley say about me, which made them matter even more. She saw me, saw how much love I wanted to give my daughter. I wasn't a perfect dad by any stretch of the imagination, but Emilia was my greatest gift— the number one priority in my world. If she felt safe and loved, I considered my job well done.

Emilia toyed with my arm like she often did with her stuffed animals when she was trying to fall asleep. "Did you know Hadley doesn't have a daddy?"

My eyes blinked open, searching through all our past conversations. There had been plenty over the years, mostly with Victoria or Emilia as the glue. Even so, I knew little about Hadley's home life. Shit, I didn't even know where she was from. When we first met, she said Massachusetts, which made me picture luxury homes along the coast of Cape Cod. That could have still been true, but my gut told me it wasn't. Hadley rarely talked about her family, and the one time I got the nerve to ask Victoria, she told me I'd have to talk to Hadley, that it was her story to tell.

I glanced toward the window, where a tendril of lightning lit up the backyard with violent hues of violet and silver. It was just enough that I could see the carriage house in the distance, where Hadley slept.

For years, I'd assumed I knew her, that there was nothing hidden under Hadley's surface. But after the last few weeks, she'd opened up to me, and there was so much I'd missed. Now that I knew what it was like to have her in my arms, there was no erasing the impact Hadley had on me.

Last week, I'd let her push me away, knowing her issues had less to do with me and more to do with her loyalty to Victoria. It was difficult to walk away from her, especially after what we'd just shared. But I was willing to—for a time.

Emilia's breathing evened out as she laid in my arms, but I just stared out at the storm, watching for those brief glimpses of the house in the distance. When I finally closed my eyes, Hadley was the last thing on my mind, wondering what secrets hid behind her infectious smile.

THE NEXT MORNING, my whole body ached—not just from the grueling practices and games, but from the physical assault my daughter launched in her sleep. I didn't know what the fuck she dreamed about, but the girl landed some serious hits in the middle of the night. There were going to be bruises I didn't want to explain to the guys.

Rubbing my hand over my face, I sat in bed, finding

Emilia laying sideways, her feet resting against my chest. At least it was the weekend, and she could sleep a little longer.

Don't get me wrong—we'd gotten really lucky with this kid. She was well-tempered and kind most of the time. But mess with her sleep, and she became a grizzly bear no amount of sugar and glitter would soothe. With my game tonight, I wasn't in the right frame of mind to cage that beast.

After kissing Emilia's forehead, I headed down the stairs. Fuck, I needed a strong cup of coffee. Give me an injection of the stuff at this point. Nothing else would erase the exhaustion fogging up my brain.

I dug through the cabinets, making myself right at home in Victoria's kitchen, but there was a voice in the back of my head, reminding me not to get too comfortable. As much as I appreciated her hospitality, this would all be ending soon. While I wouldn't miss the house itself, I would miss seeing Emilia every day. The last year had been tough, going from seeing my kid every day to having her only on the weekends.

We'd figure something out, especially for the off season. I'd love to have more time with her, and if finding a place in town was what it took, I'd do it without hesitation.

When the coffee machine pumped out my drink, I shifted over to the sink, looking over the damage left by last night's storm. It raged into the early morning hours, long after Emilia and I fell back to sleep. Luckily, the property looked like it was in good shape. A few trees lost their branches, and water covered the driveway, but everything seemed to be in working order.

At least, until I spotted Hadley rushing up the yard, her pajamas drenched and her cat clutched in her arms. My blood ran cold. I dropped the cup down on the counter and ran outside. When I got close enough to touch her, I scanned her over, checking for any injuries, something to make sense of her appearance.

Hadley glared at me, but I couldn't feel her usual anger in it. It was more like she was internally seething, and I was the closest target.

"Are you okay?"

"I'm fine." Her face fell. "The carriage house...not so much."

"I don't give a fuck about that," I said, moving closer to her. "You sure you're okay? You're not hurt?"

Her sapphire eyes jumped up to meet mine, and for a moment, I saw a flicker of emotion lurking under the surface. She might hate that she wanted me, but she wanted me all the same. But as fast as it came, it faded. "I promise. The storm must have damaged the roof last night. I thought I left a faucet on because there was the annoying dripping sound, but when I got up to check it out, the roof above my bed collapsed."

"Shit, Hadley!" I ran my hand over my hair. "You could've been killed!"

"I'm fine," she said. "I'm more mad than anything. Not only is Tori and Adam's hard work ruined, but the leak ruined most of my stuff."

"It's just stuff." I moved closer and took the pissed-off cat from her arms. "You can replace it."

"Easy for you to say," she scoffed under her breath. Hadley's eyes tracked her cat as she settled in my arms, purring contently, like this was her plan all along. "Okay, seriously. How did you get Laila to like you? She hates everyone except me, and I'm barely tolerated."

I shrugged, petting the back of Laila's head. "Might have had something to do with the tuna I fed her last time she came up." I turned, walking over to the main house. Hadley grumbled as she followed me, muttering traitor or something similar under her breath.

THIRTY

Hadley

So much for avoiding Cam while I tried to sort out my feelings. Standing in the wreckage of my former bedroom, it was hard to see much of a silver lining. I'd spent all morning on the phone with Victoria and Adam, profusely apologizing for what happened to their hard work. They insisted it wasn't my fault, but the guilt overwhelmed me. It was like the house knew I didn't belong here, and it wanted to force me out against my will.

At least we were safe. Laila already made herself at home in the main house, napping in the dining room, when I left to see what I could salvage. It wasn't much. The water had destroyed most of my room, especially my closet. Hopefully, I could get some pieces cleaned up, but I'd have to go shopping if I didn't want to live in pajamas for the foreseeable future.

There went my road trip fund. Probably for the best. I'd avoided setting down roots for a long time, and maybe the universe was showing me it was time. Most of my friends had started their own grown-up lives. The dream of traveling around the country might be just that—a dream. One I pictured but would never quite grasp.

"What else do you need?" Cam asked from my side. I sucked in a sharp breath, unsure of what to say. Tears were dying to come, but I pushed them back, trying to remind myself it was just stuff. I was okay. My cat was okay. That was all that mattered in the end. It still stung, knowing I'd be throwing away so many pieces of my home. Yes, it had been temporary, but for a while, this space was mine. I'd decorated it, made it cozy, done all the things I'd dreamed of doing since I was a kid. Now, all of it was gone, thanks to one fucking storm.

Cam moved through the destruction, grabbing whatever he found and putting it into a box for me. He'd called the team manager and told him what happened, insisting on staying home with me, which meant he'd miss his game. I hated that he'd done that for me, especially during his rookie season. He'd worked so damn hard to get there. Every game offered a chance to prove himself, especially now that he was a starter.

I held out my arms, motioning for me to hand over the box. "You should go," I said solemnly. "If you leave now, you can get a warm-up in before the game. I've got this."

Cam placed the box at his feet and shifted toward me. "No. I'm not going anywhere, Hadley. Stop telling me to leave."

"This is ridiculous," I shouted. "There's nothing we can do right now! You shouldn't have to miss out on your life because of my issues. You should be on that field, not digging through all my crap."

Cam frowned, narrowing his umber eyes at me. For a moment, my heartbeat pulsed wildly in my chest, knowing we were treading a dangerous line. This was too much—I'd already come to rely on Cam, his strength, his warmth, all things that made me feel safer without him even trying. It was the kind of support I'd barely even noticed until I spent a few days without him. The more time we spent together, the more he chopped down my walls, and soon, I'd be helpless to stop falling for him.

He moved in front of me in two long strides, cupping my face with a familiarity I didn't expect. His touch brought some much needed heat to my skin as his thumb swiped along my cheek. "Listen to me, Hadley. You think you have to be strong and handle this on your own, but I'm here, and fuck, I want to be here with you. When life gets hard, when everything goes to shit, I want to be the one you call. Nothing else matters if you need me."

"But your career—"

"Is just that," Cam finished for me. "It's a job. It'll never come before the people who matter most to me." His eyes searched mine, and I swore, his words patched up the worn spots in my soul. "Now, let's get your stuff and head back to the house. Cole's got Emilia for another couple of hours, and you should get settled before she gets back."

I nodded, but Cam didn't release me, instead pressing his thumb along my bottom lip. He swore under his breath, as if I was his biggest blessing and curse. "You're making this hard for me, menace."

"What do you mean?" I asked, although I knew damn well.

"Being around you, not touching you, it's fucking torture, especially now that I've seen what you look like when you come." My cheeks blushed, and I tried to avert my eyes, but Cam's grip on my chin wouldn't let me. "Don't hide from me, Hadley. You are so fucking gorgeous all the time, but when you come..." He sighed. "You're everything. Never in my life have I seen anything as beautiful."

I swallowed, trying to keep my rising emotions at bay, but it was useless, like sandbags trying to hold back a tsunami. Victoria's words from last night echoed in my mind, reminding me how much I'd already missed out with Cam. Perhaps we were meant to take this path, both too jaded by our experiences to let go sooner.

Without letting myself think of anything else, I lifted onto the tips of my toes and pressed a soft kiss to Cam's lips. He stilled under my touch, barely breathing when I leaned away from him. If not for his expression, I would have thought I'd made a mistake, but the look in his eyes left no room for misinterpretation.

When I backed away, Cam's hands found my hips, pulling me flush against him. "Don't you run away from me, Hadley. If we're going to start this again, I need to know you're not going anywhere. I walked away from you once, and I'm man enough to admit I don't have the strength to do it twice. If you want this, you better be fucking sure you're all in."

His words should have terrified me, should have had me running in the opposite direction. For so long, the idea of commitment had frozen me, but now, I craved belonging. Not to anyone else—just Cam. This bond between us had been simmering for so long, disguised under layers of misunderstandings and distrust. Now that it had finally been exposed, we couldn't escape its pull.

I didn't speak, not sure how to articulate what I felt around Cam. Was this what it felt like to fall for someone? It was fast—too fast. Then again, we'd been dancing around each other for years, and now that we'd connected, my heart didn't want to waste time.

So instead of saying words I couldn't quite get out, I kissed him again. And this time, I had no doubts about what I wanted.

THIRTY-ONE

Hadley

As soon as my lips touched Cam's, he transformed. His hands gripped my hips, lifting me until my legs wrapped around his center. He was already hard, his thick cock evident even through his jeans. God, I wanted him inside me. My mouth, my pussy—any part of me he wanted to take, I'd gladly hand over.

He pushed through my bedroom door and shoved me onto my couch, which was luckily spared from any damage. As I flopped onto the cushions, Cam stared down at me, his eyes wild, like a man possessed. He lifted his hand to the back of his neck, pulling his shirt off with one tug. Why was that the hottest thing I'd ever seen in my life? My hand reached out, tracing every line and indentation on his chest, savoring every inch of his bare skin. When my hand reached for the button of his jeans, he grabbed it and brought my fingertips to his lips.

"Not yet, menace," he said. "Do you have any idea how insane you make me? You put your hands on my cock right now, and I'm going to explode. I'm not ready to be done with you yet."

"Lots of talk," I smirked up at him, "and no action. Maybe I want you to explode. Have you ever thought of that?"

Cam leaned down to kiss me again. "Oh, Hadley. One of these days, I'm going to fuck that sweet little mouth, fuck the back of your throat, so every time you think about getting mouthy with me, you remember who you belong to."

I arched my brow. "And who is that?"

Cam practically growled as he lowered down to his knees and ripped my pajamas shorts off my legs, leaving me exposed in front of him. He stared at my pussy, as if I was a piece of art designed just for him. His first touch was soft, just enough to make my hips buck, seeking more.

"Look at you, baby," he breathed, his eyes not leaving the apex of my thighs. "So fucking wet for me. So needy. You want me to touch you?"

"Yes," I bit out, shifting to get him closer.

"Not yet." Cam tsked his tongue. "Not until you tell me you're mine, Hadley."

"This is extortion," I groaned, dropping my head to the back of the couch, only to pop up again when his tongue traced my heat. Light, too light, like the beginning of a song when all you wanted was to hear the bridge.

"Say it, Hadley. We both already know it's true. And before you start, yes, I'm possessive as fuck. I don't care. I want you—all of you. I *crave* all of you. Other guys might have settled for only parts of you, but not me. I need every last part. So tell me you're mine, just as much as I'm yours."

My breath stuttered at his admission. "Y-you're mine?"

Cam chuckled as he pressed a kiss to my pussy. "If you even have to question that, you haven't been paying attention." Another long lick of his tongue. "I'm all yours, Hadley." He circled my clit, making me cry out. "All of me belongs to you." Cam lifted his fingers, using them to explore the parts his tongue left behind. As pleasure built in my core, he leaned back. I screamed out in protest, and Cam reached out to grip the back of my neck. "Anything you ask of me, I'd happily do—but only if you say you're mine."

"I'm yours," I whispered, tears coming to my eyes as I searched his expression. His resulting grin was almost unbearable, like looking directly into the sun. Cam kissed me, my taste coating his tongue. But before my mind could catch up, he shifted us, turning me so I faced the back of the couch. His warmth faded away as he lowered himself behind me, continuing what he had already started.

But there was nothing gentle about his tongue or his touch now. No, instead, he feasted on me like a man starved. Every touch made my insides turn to lava, my fingers digging into the couch with each flick of his coaxing tongue.

"Cam..." I moaned as he pressed against me. White spots filled my vision when his mouth found my clit and sucked. When I came, it was like a part of me unleashed, unable to hold back from the torrent of pleasure Cam provided. My body tensed and folded under its waves, and all I could do was hold on, especially when he kept licking and caressing me through my release.

When my vision started to re-align, he'd undressed, positioned himself at my entrance, and was pushing inside me inch by inch. Despite my orgasm, there was still a slight burn, but the pleasure that accompanied the pain was the most exquisite torture.

"Fuck, Hadley," Cam ground out as he fully sheathed himself inside me. "This is going to be fast, baby. Hold on to that couch and don't let go."

I did as he said, not bothering to fight him. Not when he was promising me more of this pleasure, like I didn't know where he ended and I began. Each thrust of his cock lit me up from the inside. His pace was rough, almost punishing, but I loved every second. Cam's hand gripped my hips, his fingers digging into my sweat-soaked skin.

Despite the ruin surrounding us, I'd never felt more alive, never more at peace. It terrified me to let go, to allow someone to get close, in case they decided I wasn't worth the effort. But it terrified me more that I'd almost missed out on this. Cam wrecked me, body and soul, until I was helpless to resist. My orgasm cascaded through my veins, building higher until I couldn't hold back anymore.

But just as I was about to crash over the edge, Cam's hand found my throat, gripping softly. Pulling me up, he pressed my back against his chest. His thumb stroked my pulse point. "Don't you dare come yet, baby. You come when I say you do."

"Cam, I can't—"

"Yes, you can. Just a little longer."

I tried to hold back the current, to fight against the release my body needed. All I wanted was to let go, to defy Cam like I'd done so many times in my life. But there was another part, a much larger part, that loved to comply with his orders, knowing it would make the reward so much sweeter. Cam's thrusts became harder, slamming into me with reckless abandon.

With his hand still gripping my neck, he nipped at my ear. "Now, Hadley. Come for me."

My body didn't hold back for one more second. My orgasm ripped through me, devastating every inch of my soul. If I didn't belong to Cam before, I definitely did now.

He had marked me as his completely, a fundamental shift right down to my core.

Cam roared his own release right after me, screaming my name like an oath. As he came down, he rolled to the side, shifting to look me over. His thumb grazed my neck where he'd held me. "Did I hurt you?"

"No." I smiled up at him. "I loved every second of it."

"God," he muttered as he shook his head. "You're fucking perfect, Hadley. Such a good fucking girl."

I basked in his praise, letting him hold me close as our pulses slowed. As we sat on the couch in my ruined carriage house, I couldn't help but think about what Cam declared. I'd never wanted to be claimed. I always thought it was akin to being caged. But knowing Cam and I belonged to each other had the opposite effect—it made me feel free.

THIRTY-TWO

Cameron

After we came back down to Earth, Hadley and I dressed and carried her salvageable things up to the main house. She stayed behind as I grabbed Emilia, sorting through her remaining belongings. When we got back to the house, stacks of Hadley's belongings covered the living room. Musty, damp boxes sat stacked against the far wall, some she had labeled for the trash and others for storage. Next to them was the laundry hamper stuffed full with clothes waiting to be cleaned and stripped of the residual dust and debris from the ceiling cave in.

When we returned home, I tried to help her, but Hadley was insistent she wanted to handle all this change on her own. Seeing her stuff destroyed was hard for me—I couldn't imagine how she was holding up. Besides those few minutes in the carriage house, Hadley closed off all her emotions, back to hiding behind her practiced smile and insisting she was fine. It was on the tip of my tongue to offer to help replace what she'd lost, but Hadley was proud, and any offer of money right now would appear pitying. Still, I wanted to take care of her, wanted to erase that lost expression on her face.

I wanted to keep her safe in my arms for as long as she'd let me.

Unable to watch and not help, I headed into the kitchen, grabbing some groceries out of the refrigerator to make dinner. Through the chopping and dicing, I kept an ear out on the other room, wanting to stay close enough if Hadley needed me but far enough to give her space.

Emilia had no such concerns and made herself right at home in all the chaos. She prattled on about helping her aunt and uncle at their lodge while Hadley kept going through her things. Yet, despite her divided focus, Hadley followed along with all Emilia's stories. When Hadley reached one box, piled high with photos and other mementos, Emilia dropped into her lap. Her little hands grabbed a photo album and scanned through the pages.

"Who's this?" Emilia asked.

I tried to stay in the kitchen and give them some space, but my need to learn more about Hadley got the best of me. I knew Hadley as a person—her personality and her core values. Her past, however, was a mystery I hadn't dared to ask about before.

"Fuck it," I muttered, turning the burner down to simmer. When I walked into the living room, Hadley sat on the floor with Emilia in her lap, staring at the pictures with a soft smile. In between them laid the photo album, opened to a photo of a woman standing in front of a dilapidated home. The siding sagged, and mismatched shingles lined the roof —a poor attempt to patch some of the weaker spots, if I had to guess.

"That's my mom," Hadley answered.

"Really?" Emilia stared at the picture. "You look like her!"

"Thanks." Hadley pressed a kiss to the top of my daughter's head. Emotion clawed at my chest as I watched them, loving how comfortable my daughter felt around Hadley. When I'd dated women in the past, that was always the first question I asked myself. How would they do around Emilia? All too often, I couldn't see it, unable to imagine my date meeting her, much less spending real time with her. After way too many first dates that led nowhere, I stopped trying, convinced I wasn't supposed to have a partner.

Baseball and Emilia were all I needed.

But Hadley changed all that. With her, I saw it all. Quiet mornings, future sports events we'd have to drag ourselves out of bed to attend. Holidays with all of us together, celebrating with our own mismatched family. We worked, despite all our imperfections. She supported my career while also showing me there was more to life than the game, balancing me when I got in my head too much.

When Emilia spotted me approaching, she held up the album. "Daddy! This is Hadley's mommy."

"I heard, bug," I said as I took a seat at their side. "What else do you have in there, Hadley?"

Her eyes softened as she looked over at me, almost relieved to tell more of her story. This woman didn't get it, did she? I was already falling for her, and I wanted to know everything about her, discover every part of her past she was willing to share. As Hadley turned the pages of the book, she explained every single one, opening us up to her world before we'd met in college. She'd recorded her life inside of the album—her memories, both good and bad, wrapped up in a bow.

When she got to the end of the book, Emilia frowned. "Why don't you have any pictures of your dad?"

"Oh, umm..." Hadley's face drained of color as she trailed off. "My dad wasn't around a lot when I was a kid. It was just my mom and me."

"That's sad." Emilia pouted. "Don't you miss him?"

"Nope. You can't miss someone you've never really met. Besides," she held Emilia a little tighter, "I have the best family in the world. I have you, your mom, Adam." Her eyes met mine. "And your dad."

Emilia stared at the picture for a little longer, then shrugged her little shoulders, satisfied with that answer. She turned toward me. "Can we have ice cream for dessert?"

"You got it, Em." I lifted her from Hadley's lap and pulled her into my arms. She squirmed, trying to get down as I planted kisses on her chubby cheek. I placed her back on the ground and nodded toward the playroom. "Why don't you grab your paint stuff? Hadley needs a few new decorations for her room."

With that, my daughter hurried off. Maybe I'd regret the request later, when she'd covered the kitchen with globs of paint, but Emilia's creations always made Hadley smile. And right now—with the way she still ran her fingers along the pages of the album—it seemed like she needed it.

"Hey," I said as I sat down next to her. My fingers wrapped around hers and guided them away from the photo album. "You okay, Hadley?"

She nodded, but a sheen coated her eyes. "It's hard to look at some of these. They might paint a pretty picture, but my childhood..." She let her voice trail off. "It wasn't the best."

I squeezed her hand. "You don't have to talk about it,

not if you don't want to. But if you do, I'm always here to listen."

She gave me an apprehensive smile. "It might change the way you see me."

My hand grasped her chin, forcing her eyes to meet mine. "I don't think you understand what I meant when I said you're mine, Hadley McKay. It means I want all of you, even the things you hide in the dark. Nothing, and I mean nothing, is going to change how I feel about you. No matter what happened when you were a kid, it made you the woman in front of me, and I think she's fucking incredible."

Hadley searched my expression, almost as if she wasn't sure she believed me. But whatever she saw written on my face must have been enough to convince her, because she leaned forward, lightly kissing me. It differed from any other kiss we'd shared. Don't get me wrong—those were amazing, full of fire and longing and everything we refused to say aloud just yet.

But this?

This kiss was quiet, comfortable. It tugged at that knot in my chest, binding me to Hadley just a little more.

"My mom wasn't the best parent. She tried—at least she did at first. But after years of thinking the world owed her, she got mean and started to drink. At first, it was a couple of extra sips at dinner, a bottle of wine when she was watching TV." She exhaled a shaky breath as she stared down at the picture. "It didn't take long for those to spiral into benders. Then one day, she just...disappeared. No call, no note. I thought she was dead. But I kept waiting, hoping there was another explanation." Hadley laughed bitterly. "And when she finally stumbled into our apartment, she didn't even acknowledge what happened. Never apologized. She just patted me on the head and told me to keep quiet so she could get some sleep."

My jaw tensed. "How old were you?"

"Eight."

A curse flew out of my mouth. That was only two years older than Emilia. I wanted to scream, wanted to rage, to track down her mother and unleash all kinds of hell on the woman. But I kept my mouth closed, letting Hadley continue.

"Eventually, I stopped keeping track, just trying to get through each day on my own. My upstairs neighbors helped. I'd spend a lot of nights at their place, and they always made sure I had enough to eat." Hadley brushed the page with her fingertips. "But then someone called CPS. After they found me alone and hungry because my mom had been missing for almost a week, they had no choice but to put me in emergency foster care."

"Shit, Hadley." I took her hand again. "I'm so sorry."

"Don't be," she said. "I got lucky. My foster parents were amazing, and not everyone gets that. They took good care of me, but it was hard to understand what was happening. I was so angry—at my mom, at the people who'd called, even at my foster parents. They took me to a therapist to talk about why I'd been removed, and after a good number of sessions, it helped. I let go of some of that rage, so thankful I had people who cared enough to stick with me during the hard times." She scoffed. "Until my mom got out of court-mandated rehab. Almost a year of stability, and the judge ripped it all away and dropped me back into her house."

Hadley turned to me and softly smiled. "I wish I could say I hate her, but it's so much more complicated than that. No matter what she's done, she's the only parent I have. No matter how tempting it might be, I can't cut her out of my life. I don't like to let most people in about my past. It warps their perception of me, like somehow, my mother's shitty behavior is a mark on my record."

"Hadley," I said as I shifted closer to her. "Nothing's changed for me. If anything, I'm even more amazed by you."

She rolled her eyes. "You don't have to say that, Cam."

"I mean it, Hadley. You've overcome so much, and you didn't let it harden you. Instead, you use it to bring love to everyone you care about. People are better when they have you in their lives." I brushed her hair away from her face. "I am."

Hadley let out a damp chuckle. "Damn it, sarge. You're making a girl swoon."

"About damn time, woman," I laughed as I pulled her into a hug. As she nestled into my lap, a packet hanging out of one box caught my eye. It was bound in a spiral coil, a sleek blue cover surrounding the document. Without jostling Hadley in my lap too much, I reached out and plucked it from the box. "The Sunshine Academy?"

Hadley instantly stiffened in my arms, staring at the document in my hands. She tried to swipe it from me, but my arms were longer. I shifted, holding it just out of her reach while she stretched to grab it.

"Is this a business plan?" I asked, scrolling through the pages in awe. I might have almost failed my only business class in school, but from what I could tell, the plan seemed on point. It was thick and very thorough. There were neighborhood reports, pricing models, even a five-year expansion plan. Graphs and projected numbers lined all the pages. Someone had clearly put a lot of time and effort into making this plan a reality.

With one last huff, Hadley grabbed the portfolio and

chucked it back into the box. "It's nothing." Her tone was dismissive, but there was something else lurking within it. Disappointment? Resignation? I didn't know, but I hated the sound of it. She snuggled back into my lap. "Are we done with the show and tell part of this night? Because whatever you're cooking smells amazing, and I could use some sustenance after the workout you gave me earlier."

"Come on, menace," I laughed as I pulled her up with me. "Don't want you telling anyone I starved you."

But as soon as Hadley turned around, I grabbed the document and shoved it into my workout bag, desperate to learn more about the woman quickly stealing my heart.

Hadley

After my talk with Cam, I felt better, lighter. When Cam first asked about my past, I wasn't sure how he'd react. With so much judgment lurking in my history, I never expected him to take it as well as he did. Cam surpassed my expectations, and his words healed a part of me. His unwavering support washed over me, reminding me my past wasn't a weakness. For the first time, I didn't have the weight of it pushing me down.

He was right—while I'd wished to change my circumstances so many times, if I had, where would I be now? My childhood might have been more idyllic, but I wouldn't be sitting at this table, laughing with two of my favorite people in the world. The only time I paused was when he pulled out my business plan. The thing was practically a relic, part of my senior thesis, discussing why I wanted to pursue education. With the help of a few business majors, I was proud of the final product, especially when my professor said it would easily secure funding for the future. Once it was finished, I'd planned on showing it to Victoria, but it was right around the time she left for her brother's wedding

—where she was re-introduced to Adam, and her life changed. So, in the box it sat, covered in dust like the dream itself.

It was hard not to be a little resentful. It was always meant to be our dream. But the more time went on, it seemed like it would never come, and no matter how hard I tried, I couldn't convince myself to pursue it alone. So there it sat, at the base of my closet—until the roof caved in. It was tempting to throw it away, but that seemed like too far of a leap, so I stuck it into a box, closing the lid on it and any other dreams I had of becoming an entrepreneur.

When Emilia yawned, Cam hauled her into his lap and kissed the top of her head. She had gotten so big, so fast, but he lifted her like it was nothing, holding her tight to his chest. It was the sweetest sight in the world, and I grabbed my phone, snapping a photo of them to hold on to it for a little longer.

Cam must have sensed me staring, because he lifted his head and winked at me. My entire gut twisted, and heat filled my cheeks. This man was crawling underneath my skin, and there was no way to pry him out—not that I wanted to. It was almost as if we'd been fighting this connection all along, relying on our animosity to bury any lingering feelings.

"C'mon, sleepy bug." Cam stood, Emilia still nestled in his arms. She snuggled against his chest and rested her head on his shoulder. "Let's get you ready for bed."

She nodded, then turned toward me. "Are you going to be here tomorrow?"

"Yup." I reached to rub her back. "Laila and I are here until your mom gets back, and then we'll see what's going on with the carriage house."

"Yay." Emilia yawned. "I like when you're here with us."

"Me too." Cam's eyes twinkled as he glanced down at me. Emilia waved goodnight, and it warmed my heart. It hadn't taken long, but we had a little routine I loved. While I used to pretend I wanted my space, it was nice being here with Cam and Emilia. Normally, on nights when Cam was home, I made myself scarce, retreating to the carriage house alone. While Laila was there, it wasn't the same as having the two Sedas around. They made me smile, made me laugh even on my worst days. After a lifetime of not having a family, things had shifted, and I was becoming more entrenched in their world.

Emilia let out a loud laugh upstairs, and the sound broke me out of my thoughts. My work was piling up—I had an entire stack of math tests to grade—but I remained in my chair, too overwhelmed to even move. The past twenty-four hours had been a lot—the days before too, if I was being honest.

Things were shifting between Cam and me. While we'd said a lot of things out in the carriage house earlier, I chalked them up to our heightened emotions during sex. That, I could handle. Words whispered against flushed skin, promises made while desire pulsed through your veins—those were easy to write off.

But what did it mean that I still wanted those things, hours later, when we were fully clothed? I might have craved his touch more than my next breath, but I wanted more than that. I wanted everything. The quiet nights together, talking about our days around the kitchen table. Cheering him on at his home games and talking through his away ones too. I wanted to carve open my chest and tuck him inside all my most painful, brittle memories, knowing Cam would always keep me safe.

Those familiar alarm bells started ringing in my mind, the kind that loved to remind me that the good can't last forever, especially with Cam. Sure, we'd agreed this meant something, but what was it? Were we just filling the time until Victoria got back, and then we'd retreat to our separate corners?

That idea soured my stomach; I couldn't to imagine life like it used to be. I knew too much about Cam now, had seen his softer side. If he wanted to walk away, I had no choice but to let him, though I wasn't sure I'd survive it.

"Get it together," I hissed to myself. There were plenty of other times I'd had to start over, times when my life upended itself and left me spiraling. I'd survived all of those —I could survive losing Cam too.

At least, that's what I tried to tell myself when he walked back into the kitchen and scooped me into his arms. As we ascended the stairs, I waited for him to turn left to my borrowed bed. Instead, he turned in the opposite direction and took me into his room.

"Cam," I said. "What are you doing?"

"Did you think I'd let you sleep away from me?" He pressed a kiss to my neck. "Not happening, menace. We're not sleeping in the same house but in different beds."

"But what about Emilia?"

Cam frowned for a moment, like he hadn't quite figured that out. He shrugged. "Emilia's a pretty good sleeper most of the time. Unless there's a storm, she probably won't come in here."

"And if she does?" I insisted. "How are you going to explain it to her?"

"Tell her you're a big scaredy cat and had a nightmare."

He laughed against my skin before pressing another featherlight kiss to my pulse point. "That you needed me to keep all the big, evil monsters away from you."

"Cam," I snapped.

He shook his head. When we crossed the threshold into his room, he placed me down on my feet. As soon as the door closed behind us, he approached me, unfurled desire radiating off his skin. "I don't know what I'll say, Hadley. Probably the truth. That I like you, and I want you close to me. I've already been inside you, and yet I haven't had you in my bed."

"I'd leave off the last part."

"No shit, menace." Cam shifted a little closer, his hand drifting over my hip. "If you're not comfortable, I get it. I'd never force you to do anything if you're not ready."

I chewed on my lower lip as I looked over at his bed. The idea was tempting, too damn tempting. I'd never shared a bed with anyone, choosing to end my dates once we finished fooling around. Sleeping with someone seemed too intimate, but not with Cam. Instead, the idea of spending the entire night wrapped in his powerful arms soothed me.

But as I glanced back out into the hallway, it reminded me we were both guests in this house. I was pretty sure Victoria didn't intend on us christening her guest room when she asked us to stay.

"Don't you think it's a little disrespectful?" I said. "This is Victoria's house."

"And you don't want to cross that line in her home." I waited for him to argue, but he just nodded. "I get that, and I can respect it, Hadley. It's already a complicated situation, so we need to establish boundaries."

"Yes," I answered, relieved he understood me. We'd

already crossed a million lines, but I was determined to keep this one. I couldn't deny the connection between Cam and me anymore—I gave up fighting it—but with this bond so new and complicated. We needed to draw a line in the sand, especially when Victoria didn't know about us. We still had almost two more weeks until she came home, and I wasn't ready to think about what would happen when the time came.

"Done," Cam said. "Nothing's gonna happen here. But if it's any consolation, I just wanted to spend the night next to you. No ulterior motives. I'm fucking beat after earlier."

I moved closer to him, running my hands along his abs. "Can't keep up with me?"

"You know I can." He smirked. "But you fucking wrecked me, baby, body and soul."

I stared up at Cam, trying to read through his words. But I didn't have to think about it. I trusted Cam. He'd proven time and time again that he'd respect my boundaries —he knew when to push me out of my comfort zone and when to leave things alone.

"Okay," I said. "I'll sleep in here."

With the way Cam smiled at me, you would have thought he just took home the championship trophy. He leaned forward and kissed me. "And I'll keep my hands to myself. But I want to run something by you."

"Okay..."

"Go on a date with me."

"What?" I spluttered.

"A date." He arched one of his brows. "It's this thing people do when they like each other. Go out to eat, maybe watch a movie, and if you're lucky—fuck each other all night long."

"What did we just say about that?"

"You said I couldn't fuck you here," Cam said. "But after this next travel stretch, we have two days off. I was thinking we'd find a place in the city, go out for some drinks, then spend the night. So if you're willing to wait until after the series ends…" His voice trailed off, letting me fill in the blanks. God, that sounded amazing. An entire night to explore this thing between Cam and me? With no one else around to judge or disapprove? That sounded like perfection.

I smirked at Cam, not willing to concede that easily. "I'll consider it…" Stepping into his space, I leaned forward and brushed my chest against him. "If your team wins this next series."

His jaw tensed. "We're going up against LA."

"So?" I ran my fingers over his skin.

"They have the best record in the league right now."

"Sounds like an excuse to me, Seda. I thought you were this major league hotshot. Are you going to let one team stop you from spending an entire night, alone, with me?" I cocked a brow.

"You don't play fair, menace."

I kissed his cheek and then scurried out of his reach. "Never claimed to, sarge."

Hadley

The next morning, I woke up before my alarm went off. While my eyes slowly opened and adjusted to the early morning light sneaking in through the curtains, I smiled like a content kitten. Most nights, I tossed and turned for hours before drifting off to sleep, unable to shut off my brain long enough to let myself rest. But laying nestled in Cam's arms all night, I slept better than I had in years, enjoying the secure comfort of his hold.

As I stretched my arms out, I glanced over and checked the time. Barely even five. I still had another thirty minutes before I had to get up and start my day, and I wasn't going to waste a single one. Shifting around to face the other side of the bed, I grabbed for Cam, but his side of the bed was empty.

I burst up, fearing the worst. Was this a mistake? Did having me in here trigger some kind of internal alarm, and now he needed to get some space? Past anxieties made my heart stutter an uneven beat, hating how sitting in his bed alone sliced open past wounds. Luckily, it only lasted for a couple more seconds. The bathroom door opened, and steam billowed out into the rest of the room. Cam stepped out, running a towel through his damp hair, already dressed in his travel uniform of a suit and a collared shirt. The dark gray material clung to Cam's muscles, and it made my thighs ache, cursing the boundaries we'd put into place last night.

"Not fair," I grumbled, tucking myself back under the covers. "You shouldn't get to look like that first thing in the morning."

"Can't help being this handsome, menace." Despite already being dressed, Cam slid back into bed next to me. As his arms wrapped around my waist and pulled me against him, he groaned. "Fuck, Hads. Having you in here is the best kind of torture."

"Why is that?" I pulled the blankets to my chin.

"You pressed up against me all night? Knowing I couldn't make you feel good?" His nose trailed along the column of my neck. "Took everything in me to hold back."

"Thank you." I shifted to face him. I reached up and brushed some of his hair away from his brow. "For listening to me. But if it's too hard—"

"Don't finish that sentence." Cam leaned down and kissed me softly. "Told you last night, I want you in here with me." I was about to lean into the kiss, tempted to throw my rules out the window, when his phone rang on the end table. "Shit." He dropped his head onto my shoulder. "That's Damien. He offered to pick me up and drive me to the airport."

"Leaving already?" His schedule was hectic, even more than I ever thought it would be when I first saw the game line-up. There was little downtime, only a day or two between series, and most of the time, he was traveling to the next city with the team. He worked so hard. I wanted nothing more than for Cam to achieve his dreams, to become one of the best players in the league. However, constantly watching him leave was also getting harder, especially when he'd be gone for a long stretch like this one. I plastered a smile on my face, forcing away any lingering doubts.

"Yeah," he said. "Gotta be in LA for the game tonight. But I'll be back on Friday afternoon."

I nodded, trying to ignore the ache in my chest. Despite the newness of our relationship, it was like he took a piece of me with him when he walked out the door, but I refused to let that show on my face. "Be safe, sarge."

"I will, menace." He leaned down and kissed me one more time. His hand darted up to my hair, holding me close for a few more seconds. "Fuck, Hadley," he whispered against my skin. "This is harder than I thought."

"I know what you mean," I said. "Normally, I'd revel in you leaving for four days, but now, it's like torture."

He nodded, pressing another kiss to my forehead. "I'm going to call you guys tonight. Do me a favor—sleep in here? It helps knowing you're waiting in my bed."

My throat dried at his request. The idea of going back to Victoria's room never crossed my mind. Even though Cam wasn't here, I wanted to be in his space, to hold on to his presence despite us being states apart. I swallowed, trying to force away the knot forming in the back of my throat. "I can do that."

He leaned down and pressed his lips to mine, long and luxurious, like we had all the time in the world. And maybe we would—when the season was done. But for now, his team depended on him.

"Go," I insisted, pushing on his chest. "The sooner you leave, the sooner you come home to us."

He grinned back at me. "I like the sound of that—coming home to you."

———

"GO. GO. GO!" I screamed at the television, not caring how loud I'd gotten. It was the second game of the series, and LA had clinched the first win. Now, the Hawks were battling hard for the second game. Cam had played most of the first seven innings and was doing incredibly well in the outfield, despite his initial concerns.

Over the past few hours, the living room had transformed into a miniature version of the stadium. Snacks and hard seltzers filled the coffee table, and we'd all worn our favorite Hawks jerseys. The game was blaring on the television in the center of the room, and we'd jumped to our feet during the last inning, unable to sit with all the anticipation coursing through our veins. Even Brianna, who only came for moral support, was getting into the game, screaming almost as loud as me when LA's outfielder dropped the ball.

We waited with bated breath as the ball flew through the air, trying to beat Damien's speed, but it was no match. After meeting Damien twice, I never would have guessed what a beast he was on the field. The man raced toward the base, his legs moving faster than should have been humanly possible, and dove just as the second baseman's mitt stretched out to catch the ball. As he turned to tag Damien, he slid right into the base, looking up at the umpire for the final call.

"Safe!"

The entire room erupted, almost eclipsing the announcer, when Damien stood and dusted off his pants at second base, leaving only first open for the next batter. The score was close, but the Hawks built a ton of momentum in this inning. If they did well, it would be LA's game to lose.

"Okay, boys. Just a couple more runs, and you've got this on lock." I took a sip of my drink. "Get some runs before we get to the end of the batting order."

"Hadley, I'm like a proud momma duck right now." Ollie smirked as she settled back on the couch. "Considering you didn't know a ref from an ump a month ago, you sound like a seasoned pro."

"That's because my daddy's teaching her." Emilia smiled next to her. She looked adorable in her bedazzled Hawks' jersey, the Seda on the back now sparkling with small rhinestones. We'd just finished it an hour before the game, and she insisted on wearing it every single time her daddy played.

"Love that!" Ollie squealed as she jumped out from the couch. She looked over at Brianna. "You want another drink?"

Brianna looked down at the almost-empty can in her hands. "Oh, I'm not sure. Todd might get upset if I have more than one."

"Because he doesn't like you driving after drinking?" I asked. "There's a lot of game left. You're more than welcome to crash here if you're not sober enough to head home."

Brianna shook her head. "Nothing like that. I'd never risk drinking and driving. He just doesn't like it when I go out, especially if alcohol's involved."

"Todd sounds like a barrel of laughs," I muttered to myself, but as soon as the batter started walking up to the plate, I shushed everyone. "Oh my God, Cam's up! Emilia—Daddy's up!"

A phone chimed from the other side of the room, but I

ignored it, too focused on the screen in front of me. "Hadley, that's your phone," Briana said as she shifted to pass it to me. "It's your mom."

"I'll call her back later." I wasn't letting another one of her guilt trips ruin tonight for me. It had been a while since we spoke, mostly because I knew she'd find some reason to make my happiness about her. Instead, I turned around and motioned for Emilia to join me.

She danced up next to me, and we clutched hands as Cam grabbed his bat and walked up to the plate. The heavy bass of his walk-up song blared through the stadium, all eyes on him. I could only imagine the pressure on his shoulders right now. With the bases almost loaded, it was up to him to get the guys home, especially because they only had one more out. If he fucked this up, LA might win the game and take the series.

"Come on, baby," I whispered the words and clutched Emilia's hand like a prayer. "You've got this. You can do it."

The pitcher eyed Cam down, looking too serious for his own good. But Cam didn't seem phased, keeping his eye trained straight ahead. Nothing seemed to bother him when he was in the game, too focused for anything to get in his way. He belonged on that field. Even with my limited baseball knowledge, I could see that. And with all his hard work this season, everyone else saw it too. He had the speed, the agility. Now, he just needed to get this hit to bring his team home.

The first ball flew before I even saw the pitcher move. Cam didn't bat; he just let it fly into the catcher's hand.

"Ball one!" the umpire shouted, and the announcers echoed it to the crowd.

Shit, my heart was about to give out under this pressure. How on Earth did Cam survive 162 games of this every year? If I was freaking out while watching thousands of miles away. How did Cam cope?

If the pressure weighed on him, he didn't show it. He just shook his head, keeping an easy grin on his face. The pitcher wound up and threw the ball so fast, it was barely a blur on the screen.

But Cam saw it.

With a crack of his bat, he swung as hard as his body allowed, throwing all his power into the hit. The ball soared past the infield, heading toward the upper left half of the stadium.

"Keep going! Keep going!" Ollie shouted behind me.

And it did.

The ball flew right over the outfield and up into the stands, where dozens of people volleyed to get it. I smiled when the camera panned to a little boy, not much older than Emilia, holding it triumphantly in the air.

But the grin on Cam's face eclipsed that joy. His first major league home run. He leisurely ran around the bases, slapping the hands of the coaches and teammates as he passed them by. The crowd went wild, but Cam didn't gloat. His smile was gracious, not at all cocky, but the elation in his eyes was clear.

He'd done it.

The dugout rallied around him once he got back inside, full of claps on the back and other congratulations. Before he sat down, one of the relief pitchers dumped a bottle of sports drink over his head. Cam grinned, shaking his head so it flew over the rest of the players. It tugged at my heart, knowing he was so far away during this pivotal moment. Emilia hugged my legs and beamed up at me. Her pride in her dad shone through her eyes—I probably had the same expression.

The batter after Cam struck out, ending the inning. While the team changed positions, a reporter came on the screen, Cam standing at her side.

"Cam, that was your first home run since you've joined the Hawks. How did it feel?"

He broke into a wide grin. "Pretty damn amazing, to be honest. I didn't want to let my team down."

"I'm sure you didn't." The reporter smiled up at him and placed her hand on his forearm. My hands clenched, not appreciating her touching my man. *Woah.* Where the hell did that come from? I wasn't a jealous person, at least, not normally. But Cam meant something to me, maybe more than I even realized, and it was causing my inner possessive side to rear her ugly head. The reporter continued, "Is there anything you'd like to say to your friends and family back home?"

"Yeah," he said. "Emilia, I hope you're watching, because that was for you, little one. And to the rest of my family back home, I miss you more than you know." He winked, and I knew the message was for me. "When I get back, we're celebrating."

I couldn't agree more.

THIRTY-FIVE

By the time I reached my hotel room, I was exhausted from celebrating with the team. We'd won the second game, tying us with LA as we entered the last game of the series. Despite the amazing turn tonight had taken, I was ready to be home. The weekend had already been a lot, and I wasn't looking forward to another game tomorrow. At the same time, I was still riding high from my home run, my first in the majors.

Holy shit.

The moment my bat collided with the ball, I knew it was going the distance, but I held my breath, hoping it didn't end up in one of the outfielder's gloves. But it soared right into the stands, and when the crowd cheered, aware-ness prickled in my chest. It was one of those pivotal career moments; at least, that's what the reporters kept saying when Benny shoved me into the media room to debrief after the game.

But as good as it felt, something was missing—or should I say, someone was missing. I glanced at my phone, trying to figure out the time back home. It was late here, which meant it was in the middle of the night back home. Hadley had sent me a couple of texts during the game, but I hadn't had time to read them until hours later.

MENACE

OMG SARGE!! THAT HIT!

You were amazing, baby. I'm so proud of you.

I read the messages again, knowing damn well I was smiling like a fool. God, I was fucking gone for this girl. Even when we lost last night, she was right there, cheering me on, despite being across the country. Tonight had been the same. When I called Emilia for our pre-game ritual, Hadley showed me their little set up to watch us play. During the game, she sent me updates of her girls' night at the house, along with pictures of her and all her friends wearing Hawks jerseys with pride. In the middle was my little girl, her grin bigger than I'd ever seen.

As if she knew I was thinking about her, my phone chimed with another text. As I clicked open the attached photo, my jaw tensed, and all my blood rushed to my dick. Hadley sent a picture from my bed, where she was curled up in the blankets. She wore one of my shirts, and the hem rose enough that I could see the pale pink of her boy shorts peeking out underneath.

MENACE

Missing you, sarge. Can't wait for you to come back to me.

Not waiting another second, I clicked on her contact, pulling up a FaceTime call. My dick hardened as I thought about the picture, wishing I was there to push the fabric up a little further, to explore her smooth, lush thighs with my fingers and tongue. As the phone rang, I closed my eyes, picturing her perky nipples pebbling in anticipation of my touch. I loved how responsive her body was, how it ached and screamed for me. By the time Hadley answered the phone, my erection was ready to bust through my sweats.

"Cam?"

Sleep tinged her voice, making it softer, more melodic. Hadley rubbed her eyes and squinted at the screen. With the way she smiled at me, like talking to me was the highlight of her day, I forgot about my straining cock.

"Sorry if I woke you, baby." I placed the phone on the nightstand as I undressed, pulling off my shoes and tugging my shirt over my head. "Wanted to say goodnight to you properly."

"It's okay. I can't sleep," she mumbled. "Keep thinking about you and how empty this bed is without you. It's too cold."

"Only using me for my body heat?" I quipped as I grinned back at her. "Should've known."

"You caught me," Hadley answered. "Well, that and your baseball tickets. I'm getting major brownie points from my students because I get to go to Hawks games." She shifted and settled on her stomach. "Speaking of games—I keep watching clips of your hit. It was so fucking incredible, Cam. I'm so proud of you."

"Thanks, Hads. Wish you were here to celebrate with me."

"Maybe the next one, I'll be there."

"If I had my way, you'd be there every time. I play better when you're watching me." I studied her tired expression. Her blonde waves fanned out over my pillows, her hands curled up under her head. She looked angelic.

Gratitude settled deep in my chest. How'd I get so

lucky? I could have missed this—missed out on Hadley. Thank fuck I pulled my head out of my ass and kissed her that first night. If I hadn't—I shook my head, refusing to even entertain the thought. As I pulled off my jeans and laid on the scratchy bed cover, I turned back toward the phone. "Tell me about your day, baby."

"While you're sitting there in your boxers?" Hadley rolled her eyes. "My day is the last thing on my mind."

"Keep your mind out of the gutter, Hadley."

"Impossible when you look like that, sarge."

"Hadley," I snapped, using that no-nonsense tone I knew she loved. "Talk to me, baby. I miss you, miss your voice. Tell me what you've been up to all day."

Hadley sighed but relented, telling me in great detail about her school day. With only a couple of weeks left in the year, she was almost done for the summer, but she didn't sound excited. In fact, when she spoke about leaving her class, her voice cracked a little.

My jaw tensed, debating whether to push her. She might not have told me outright, but after reviewing her business plan, I knew it was something she really wanted. When we were in school, I heard her talk about opening an early childhood center, but I wrote it off as another one of her whims. But there was nothing impulsive in her business, another clear sign I'd been so wrong about her.

It was easy to buy that she was just another party girl, not looking for anything serious in her life. After all, she almost always wore a smile and never seemed to let life get in her way. But now, I saw the woman underneath, the one who kept fighting even though life had failed her so many times. It took so much strength to keep going after dealing with her circumstances, and it only made me respect her more. And what was even more impressive—

she wanted to use her past to help others, to make sure other children got the support they needed to achieve their own goals, for parents to have a support system in place to help guide them through the challenging parts of early parenthood.

I knew that struggle all too well. While I wouldn't trade Emilia for the world, becoming a dad was the scariest moment of my life. I was only nineteen and had barely done anything with my life—made countless mistakes because I thought I knew best. The moment Victoria showed up at my door and showed me those two pink lines, my life's course changed irreparably. Many dreams got shelved, pushed aside for a stable life for my daughter. Even playing ball had been put on the back burner. Before Emilia, I'd planned on signing up for the draft, wanting to go pro as soon as possible. With an infant at home, though, it wasn't an option. Luckily, things worked out better than I'd imagined, but what if they hadn't? Would the resentment and regret have eaten away at me until I'd transformed into a shell of myself?

I glanced back at the phone and stared at Hadley once again, amazed by what she'd already accomplished on her own and hoping I'd be there for whatever she decided to do next. Her dark blue eyes searched the screen, and I smirked back at her, a devious plan forming in my mind. I'd do anything to erase those worried lines from her face, even if I couldn't physically be with her right now. I shifted onto my side. "Did you do anything else tonight, Hadley?"

She furrowed her brow. "What do you mean?"

"You sent me that photo knowing damn well what it would do to me. Did you touch yourself in my bed, baby? Did you play with your clit, knowing that perfect pussy was aching for me?"

Hadley's mouth fell open before she shook her head. "I didn't—I didn't think you'd be okay with that."

"About you getting yourself off?" I grinned as I flipped onto my back. Hitting a button on the screen, I flipped the camera to show the effect the idea had on me. "Baby, picturing you in my bed, touching yourself until you come, is making me hard as fuck. Are you going to be mad if I jerk myself off to thoughts of you? If I grip my dick wishing it was your tight little cunt?"

"No," Hadley breathed. "Fuck, Cam. You're killing me here."

"Are you wet, Hadley?" She nodded. "Good. That's so fucking good, baby. Now, stick one of your fingers inside yourself and show me. Show me how much you want me, even from far away."

Hadley chewed on her lower lip as she propped the phone up on her pillow. She dragged her finger down, lifting my shirt up to expose the bare expanse of her stomach. She continued down until she reached the edge of her boy shirts, smirking as she glanced back at me. "Keep fucking going," I growled.

"So bossy." She grinned, lowering her hand until it disappeared under the pale pink fabric. When she brought it back out, the tips of her fingers glistened with her desire, and my mouth watered at the sight.

"Suck on them," I said, tugging my sweats down my legs. "Taste yourself, baby. See how fucking incredible you are. Sunshine and goddamn honey."

Hadley didn't hesitate, sticking out her tongue and dropping her finger on top of it. God, my dick was practically stone. When she sucked it into her mouth and moaned, it took everything in me not to come. My fist tugged on my shaft as I watched her, wishing more than anything to kiss away the flavor, using my tongue to lap up every spare drop. "Fuck, baby," I groaned, quickening my movements. "Touch yourself. Please. I need it. I need to hear you come, baby."

"Cam," she breathed. Her cheeks brightened, turning a darker shade of red as she toyed with her entrance.

"Move the phone down, Hadley. Now."

She did as I asked, using her free hand to shift her phone so her pussy was on full display. Her fingers worked in and out of her core as her thumb circled her clit. She was so wet, probably aching for release.

"God," I groaned as my fist tightened around my cock. "Look at you, baby. So fucking needy, dying to come already. Are you picturing me there with you?"

"Yes," Hadley whispered, her fingers quickening with my words. "I wish it was your mouth on me. You make me feel so good, Cam."

"Same," I bit out. "I wish I had your tight pussy clenched around me right now. I need it. Nothing I want more than to sink deep into you and make you scream my name."

"Cam," Hadley called out, and her body pulsed with a mind of its own.

"Fucking come for me, Hadley. Let me watch your beautiful face when you do."

Hadley's hand shook as she adjusted the phone, highlighting her panting face. I wanted to lick every drop of sweat from her skin, to lap up her release like the sweetest candy. As her back arched off the bed and she chanted my name, my balls tightened, that familiar tingle of ecstasy cascading along my spine. Hot, thick cum coated my stomach and hands as Hadley crashed over the edge with me.

As our breathing slowed, we stared at each other, both wearing matching smirks. Hadley's blue eyes sparkled in the darkness, and I couldn't look away. She'd become my personal addiction, so fucking beautiful, it made my chest clench in appreciation.

We both turned away from the camera to clean ourselves up, but neither of us moved to disconnect the call. When I returned to the hotel bed, Hadley's face was the first thing I saw, and I couldn't hold back my grin. She was quickly becoming everything to me, and even though there would definitely be an uncomfortable conversation with Victoria in the future, I didn't regret what was happening between us.

Not for one moment.

No matter what happened next, I would fight to hold on to Hadley. I'd learned the hard way that baseball and relationships didn't mix well, but for her, I had to try. There wasn't an alternative. Her eyes drifted closed with a satiated smile on her lips. I reached out, and like a sap, I traced her cheek with my finger, counting down the minutes until I could hold her for real.

Hadley might only be mine during stolen moments and hidden nights right now, but as I drifted off to sleep, all I could dream about was how I wanted so much more.

THIRTY-SIX

Hadley

My leg shook under my desk as I stared at the clock on the wall. Even for a Friday, the time ticked down way too slowly. Only fifteen more minutes, and we'd start packing up, which meant the weekend was finally here.

Cam would be home tonight.

"Ms. McKay!" one of my students called out. Emmanuel smirked as he held up his creation. "Look what I made!"

"That's amazing, bud!" I beamed back at him. "You're becoming quite the engineer."

He responded with a toothy smile before he went right back to building. Friday afternoons were my favorite part of the week, and not even for the reason most people would expect. When Brianna and I talked about the schedule, I asked if I could take the last thirty minutes of the week and let the kids do some STEAM activities. One teacher I'd worked with back in Texas did it with her class, and it was incredible to see what the kids could create with only their imagination. It was a free-choice, less structured activity, but even in my brief tenure here, I saw how much they loved getting to explore different materials and concepts.

As I turned to talk to another group about their project, my phone vibrated on my desk. I walked over to look at who was calling. I never liked to keep my phone on while I was teaching, but with Cam out of town, I needed to make sure Emilia's school could get a hold of me if there was an emergency. But that wasn't who was calling. Instead, my mother's number scrolled across the screen. I instantly hit the side button, sending her to voicemail. She'd probably rant and rave in my voicemail, but there was no way I was dealing with her in the middle of the workday.

After checking on another group of students, Brianna came over to my desk, clutching her coffee cup. I tucked my phone into my purse and joined her on the other side. As I looked her over, I arched my bow, noting the dark circles under her eyes. "Late night?"

"Nights." She emphasized the "s" with a worn weariness. She glanced down at the group of students working next to my desk and lowered her voice. "Todd and I have been...disagreeing about certain things. It's been a little tense at home, so I haven't been sleeping well."

"Anything I can do to help?"

"No, but thank you. I keep trying to tell myself it's just a rough patch, that things are going to go back to normal soon enough, but..." Her voice trailed off as she shook her head. "There's another part of me that wonders if this is our new normal, if our relationship has changed so much, we'll never get back what we once had."

I reached out and took her hand. "I'm sorry to hear that, Bri. If you need anything at all, even if you just want to get drunk and scream about the idiocy of men, I am only a phone call away."

"Thanks, Hadley." She softly smiled back at me, but it didn't reach her eyes. "Then again, you might be the worst person to commiserate with right now. You have that new love glow all over you."

My mouth dropped open, and I stared at my friend like she had just betrayed me in the worst way. "I'm not!"

"Liar, liar." Bri tucked her smile into her coffee cup. "There's no point in trying to hide it. We all saw you when Cam got that home run. You almost jumped through the TV into his arms."

Her words ripped through the thin veneer I tried to tuck my emotions behind. Cam and I weren't supposed to be anything to each other, but I failed at holding back with him. It was slow, like raising the temperature in a pot. It became even more evident now after he left. I hated being alone in the house, counting down the minutes until the game ended and he'd call to talk about his day. Even though we'd had plenty of steamy moments through texts or Face-Times, those were almost becoming secondary to our conversations. Even with the pressure of playing profes-sional ball, Cam always devoted equal time to hear about my days. He'd follow along with my stories—even started to recognize my students through our conversations. It felt like a partnership, at least what I thought one should be. I'd been alone for so long, I wasn't used to having someone in my corner.

It was the most comforting and terrifying experience. As much as I wanted to fully dive into my relationship with Cam, it was almost a little too good to be true. I kept waiting for that moment, the one when he decided we weren't worth all the effort. I debated lying to Brianna, keeping my cards close to my vest. It was easier to hide what was happening between Cam and me, just in case it all fell apart, like most relationships in my life tended to do. But the idea of denying it—denying us—twisted in my stomach.

I chewed on my lower lip. "It's new..."

"I knew it." Brianna beamed at me like she'd been waiting for this confirmation all week. Apparently, I didn't hide my feelings for Cam as I'd hoped. "But what does this mean? Are you two together, or is this only a temporary thing?"

My mouth fell open, but no sounds came out. In truth, I did not know. I knew I cared about Cam, and we'd grown closer, but that didn't erase the thick, bold line between us. Right now, we were in a bubble—the past unable to touch us. But soon enough, Victoria would be back, and we'd have to face what we'd done. We only had one more week together, and then, everything might change.

For the first time, I no longer counted down the days until my best friend came back home. Embarrassment colored my cheeks, knowing I was being incredibly selfish. Emilia missed her mom terribly. We'd even put Post Its all over the fridge, and every day, she pulled off one more. When she realized she was down to single digits, she smiled so brightly, it lifted away the storm clouds in my mind.

Some best friend. Here Emilia was, ticking off days like waiting for Christmas morning, and I had mixed emotions about Victoria's return. Maybe she'd come home, and we'd never have to talk about Cam. But that meant I'd need to end things with him for good, and that no longer seemed like an option. Despite wanting to take the coward's way out, that wasn't an option.

I needed to talk to Victoria, needed to let her know what had transpired between Cam and me, no matter the consequences. Not just because of her history with Cam, but because she was my person. She shared in all my highs and lows, my biggest supporter and cheerleader. Not that I didn't adore Bri and Ollie, but Victoria and I forged our bond over years of shared history, there for each other during the most challenging times. No matter what had already transpired with Cam, it would never be truly real until I told her about it.

Brianna's brow furrowed. "But things are good, right? He's treating you well?"

"Yes," I said. "God, yes. The man is so good to me, so kind. He's the best dad in the world, which only makes me like him more. But..." I looked up at the clock, noting the time. After I called out for our students to start cleaning up, I ushered Brianna into the corner of the room, where we could supervise but the kids wouldn't overhear over our conversation. "It's almost too good."

"What does that mean?"

"Cam and I spent the better part of a decade hating each other. Or at least, strongly disliking each other. Now, it's like poof!" I snapped my fingers. "All the tension has changed from *I can't stand you* to *I can't stand being away from you*. It's all too much, especially knowing Victoria is coming back soon."

"And you don't trust it." I nodded. "I mean this in the best way, Hadley, but I think that's a good thing."

"What do you mean?"

Brianna continued, "It means you're invested. I think you're scared. That means you have something to lose. In the past, have you ever felt like this?"

I scanned through my memories, searching each of my relationships to see if I reacted to them like I did with Cam. But no one came close, not even Josh, who I once called the love of my life. Looking back, what we shared wasn't love—more like excitement, a sense of experimenting with new emotions we were too young to handle. Our break-up might have been devastating, but it didn't take long to realize the betrayal hurt more than the end of the relationship. For the longest time, I'd never risked my heart because I hadn't given enough of it away.

Everything was different with Cam. If he asked for a piece of my heart, I'd hand him the whole damn thing without hesitation. Cam was the first person I allowed close enough to break me, but holding back wasn't an option. He'd become as integral to me as the other people I loved: Victoria, Emilia, Adam, and now, Ollie and Brianna. But my need for him ran so much deeper, like a soothing balm to my tattered soul.

Fuck. I was falling in love with him. That explained why I couldn't ignore the pull between us. When I used to picture falling in love, I thought about the exhilaration of sledding for the first time. One girl from school invited me over, and considering that my mom was sleeping off another bender, I joined her. When I first saw the hill, I was terrified, but once I got onto the sled, the gentle glide made my heart soar. It was the closest I'd come to flying, and when the sled finally slowed, all I wanted was to do it again.

But that wasn't the case with Cam.

There was no slow, gentle glide when falling for him.

No, this was more like cliff-jumping, where all you could do was hold your breath and hope you landed safely. No turning back, no undoing what had already been done. From the moment Cam's lips touched mine for the first time, I'd taken the leap, and now, I just had to have faith he'd be there to catch me.

As my heart pounded a steady, heavy beat against my ribs, my phone chimed in my hand.

Cam:

At the stadium. Left your ticket at will call. Can't wait to see you.

And after the game, you're all mine, baby.

Brianna laughed at my side as she walked past me to help a student with their mail. "Told you," she called. "You're head over heels, Ms. McKay. Might as well accept it."

THIRTY-SEVEN

Cameron

Fuck, it felt good to be home. Not just back in New York, but in our own stadium, ready to face another long series. We'd barely gotten off the plane from California when we got called in to practice. After hours in the batting simulator and doing drills on the field, my body thrummed with anticipation, waiting for the crowd to fill the stadium.

Who the hell was I kidding? There was only one face I wanted to see.

I'd texted her a few times today, after we'd gotten off the plane and headed toward the stadium. She didn't respond right away—pretty common for her. The girl could never find her phone. Last time she lost it, she'd left it in the freezer after she'd pulled out an ice pop for Emilia. As much as I tried to let it go, her lack of a response grated on me. After so many days apart, I needed to see her, needed to know we were still in a good place. Sure, we'd talked on the phone every night, but it wasn't the same. I needed to hold her, needed to let her warmth consume me.

I needed to get a fucking grip.

Practice continued around me, and I had to rub my

hand over my face to get my head in the game. Baseball was supposed to be the priority, but Hadley had taken over much more of my attention. I tried to focus on the field, but it was becoming more challenging to think about the game when she was on my mind. A barked command from my side made my spine straighten, and I immediately regretted losing focus. Benny was watching me, as if he knew my mind had drifted to other places.

"Shit," Parker groaned at my side, rubbing his eyes under his glasses. "Benny's on a fucking warpath. You'd think we were last in our division with the way he's riding us today."

I nodded across the field, pushing thoughts of Hadley aside so I could focus on our opponents. They lined the other half of the field, stretching and warming up before the game.

This series was a big deal—we were finally facing one of the other New York teams, the Rebels. They were one of the top legacy teams in the league and had the wins to show for it. Everyone dreaded when they came to town, and now, it was our turn.

Tonight was one of the biggest games of the season. Tickets sold out months ago. The league billed it as an upstate/downstate competition, and our fans were dying to show the city guys how capable our team had become.

As I watched Benny's scowl turn toward them, I shifted closer to Parker, trying to remember our GM's history. "Think it has something to do with the other team? He's riled up about us beating them."

"Benny used to work for the Rebels." Parker and I both turned as Damien's voice broke through our conversation. When I last checked, he'd been over by the dugout, having a tense conversation with Jace. Our second baseman looked like hell. Dark circles lined Jace's eyes, and his beard looked unkempt, like he'd given up trimming it. His pants hung a little too loose on his waist, as if he'd dropped weight. My gut twisted as I looked at him, trying to ignore all the red flags waving around him. When he walked out onto the field earlier this afternoon, Damien gave him the same once over, scowling like he didn't like what he saw either.

Damien shook his head. "Before the Hawks hired Benny, he worked for the Rebels. The new manager used to be his assistant." He jutted his chin toward the other side of the field, where a short, stocky man stared out at his players. He crossed his arms over his chest, nothing easygoing about his presence. Benny might be tough on us, but he was also fair. Nothing about this guy seemed like he enjoyed baseball, much less wanted to motivate his team. "Carter went behind Benny's back and told upper management he was the reason for their losing streak. That Benny was failing as manager, and if they wanted a winning season, they needed to let him go."

"And that worked?" I asked, palming the ball in my glove.

"Nah." Damien shook his head and glanced back over his shoulder. "But it was enough for them to question all of Benny's choices, which pissed him off. He called it quits mid-season. Which worked out well for us, because the Hawks scooped him up quick."

We all watched as a group of suits joined Benny on the field, barely bothering to look at the other team. As they swarmed him, Benny shook his head, but that didn't seem to stop the conversation. Eventually, the rest of the men left the field, barely bothering to watch the practice. As soon as they disappeared back into the building, Benny gave a resigned sigh, scanning through the group of our players until his eyes stopped on me.

"Seda! Get your ass over here."

"Shit," I muttered under my breath. What the hell did Benny want with me? Unease swirled through my gut. The last time I got pulled off the field mid-practice, it'd been because Benny didn't like how I handled the ball and chewed me out to get my head on straight before the game.

"Don't stress it." Damien tossed a ball over to Parker. "Probably wants to talk to you about the All-Star game."

"You serious?"

He nodded. "Hell yeah, kid. You've been on a hot streak. He's gonna put you up for it."

"But I'm a rookie—"

"Don't play that game, boy scout." Jace stepped next to me. "You're fucking killing the game right now. You earned a spot."

For a moment, I just stared at the guy, unsure if he'd ever lobbed a compliment my way before. I cleared my throat. "Thanks, man."

"Ah, shit." Jace smirked back at me. "Don't let it go to your head. Now, get your ass in Benny's office and figure out what he wants. We need you in the game tonight."

———

AS SOON AS the door closed behind Benny, my blood pressure skyrocketed. He wasn't the only one in the small office space. The room was pretty minimal—Benny was a zero distractions kind of guy. Besides his desk and a couple of white boards mounted on the wall, a worn leather sofa took over the left side of the room.

On it sat the team's General Manager, Russ Burton. My

blood cooled in my veins. It was never a good thing to see the GM behind the scenes. While Benny ran our day-to-day, Russ shaped the team, responsible for all the trades and player acquisitions. The man owned players during their contracts, able to shape your future with a single phone call. You never wanted to get called into a private meeting during the season.

"Cam," he said as he stood, holding out a hand to greet me. I took it while stealing a glance at Benny, who had settled behind his desk. His scowl was set in place, as if he liked Russ being in his space less than I did.

"Mr. Burton," I greeted him as I stood against the wall, my arms crossed over my chest. Next to him sat another member of the upstairs office, a notepad in his lap. He didn't make any move to greet me, so I acted the same, keeping that wall up until I knew what was about to go down.

"I'm going to give it to you straight, Cam," Burton started. "We've had a lot of teams reach out about a trade for you."

Ice burned through my sternum. Out of all the conversations I imagined walking into, this was the last one I expected. One of the unwritten rules of baseball? Never get too comfortable, especially early in your career, when you could get traded without notice. Burton's dry, no-nonsense tone burned, and it took everything in me not to rub my chest. Fuck. This was not how I thought this conversation would go. I cleared my throat, glancing over at Benny. "Am I leaving?"

"No," Benny insisted, his voice firm until he exchanged a look with Burton. "At least, not right now. There's been some good offers, but I told Russ we can't lose you. You're keeping our outfield strong, and you've earned your place on this team."

"But—" Russ interrupted. "The trade deadline is not for a couple of weeks. If another team comes back with a competitive offer, I can't say for sure you're going to be a Hawk for the rest of the season. We love having you, Cam, but you know this game. Things always change."

I nodded, trying to resist the urge to vomit. This was bullshit. Sure, the game always changed, but that didn't mean I wanted it to. I had high hopes for sticking around for a few years, especially with Emilia now in school. She couldn't drop everything to come visit me during the season, and I barely got a break, much less time to travel around the country to visit my daughter. I'd just gotten used to seeing her every day, getting to know her world in a way I'd missed out on for the past year. And fuck, it was everything. The idea of leaving now, just when I'd gotten a taste of it, was the worst kind of torture.

And then, there was Hadley.

My heart stuttered in my chest as I thought about her. We were good, so fucking good together, it almost knocked me on my ass. Even though she'd talked about wanting to travel and see the world, it had always been on her terms, not tied to a guy she'd barely see for months at a time. She wanted an adventure, and all I was offering her were lonely nights and baseball-filled days. A lot of wives and girlfriends said they'd be there for their partner at the beginning of their careers, only to leave when the reality came to light. It was a lonely life, one I didn't want to pressure Hadley into. It'd be cruel to tie her down in that way, especially right now, when her life was just getting started, akin to trying to catch the wind.

Benny stood. "I want to make this clear, Cam. This isn't something I want. You earned a fucking place on this team, and you've made me proud with what you've accomplished in a short time. But this game is a bastard, and we don't always get a say about who walks out onto the field every night." He shot a glare over to Burton, who almost cowered for a moment. "If my opinion matters, you're not going anywhere. But I'm only one cog in this machine, and you deserve a heads up."

"Appreciate it, Benny." I dropped my head, unsure how the fuck I'd go out onto the field tonight, knowing my future was up in the air. If they wanted to trade me, I needed to prove I was worth keeping, that I'd bring it all to every game.

Without another word, I walked out into the clubhouse and stared at my name on the wall. I hadn't even noticed it earlier. The crew must have put it up while we played in LA. That sign was supposed to be the first goal, the first in a long line I wanted to achieve with the Hawks. Now, it felt mocking, like a future I almost had in my grasp but lost at the last second.

Hadley

"Answer the phone," I growled as my mother's voicemail clicked on again. The same familiar message filled my ears, reiterating that her voicemail box hadn't been set up despite my dozens of reminders. With an annoyed huff, I chucked my phone back in my bag, too frustrated to keep playing her games. No doubt, she was punishing me for ignoring her calls over the past week, or she was deep into self-destruction mode. Either way, I'd done my part, tried to call despite her hostile voicemails. I couldn't worry about her right now, not when I was running so late.

I'd gotten stuck at work a little longer than I'd planned, pulled into an impromptu parent meeting about grades in the pickup line. By the time I checked my phone, I saw more messages waiting from Cam, but he would already be on the field, so I didn't bother to reply.

My legs burned as I rushed through the stadium, hating that my rideshare had dropped me off at the furthest corner. I must have accidentally crossed under a ladder, or Laila must have traipsed in front of my path, because the universe was determined to keep me from the game.

My heartbeat slowed as I got to our section, rushing down the concrete steps to find Ollie waiting for me. As soon as I slouched down in my seat, she handed me a hard seltzer. "You look like you could use this."

"You are an angel." I took a long sip, letting the cold bubbles soothe my anxieties. Running late was nothing new for me, but I hated I'd missed so much of the pre-game, especially talking to Cam. Just as I settled in my seat, the music amped up, and the announcer called out the starting lineup.

I reached into my bag and grabbed my Seda jersey, throwing it over my tank top, ready to cheer on Cam and his team. I waited for him to show up with his signature smile, but when he walked out onto the field, it was missing. In fact, his mouth formed a tight line and his hands clenched at his sides. It was so different from his usual persona, it took me a minute to realize it was Cam.

The team stood in the dug-out, waiting for the game to begin. It was hard to see Cam from over here, but once he went out onto the field, I had the best view in the stadium. Thank goodness, Ollie and I changed our seats to the edge of the right field, where we could watch Parker and Cam in action. The box might be a nice luxury, but it seemed a little out of touch, too distant from the rest of the crowd. I preferred being out here, in the middle of a crowd of Hawks fans as they excitedly chanted their favorite players' names.

A lot more Seda jerseys filled the crowd now, almost equal to the other big name players. It filled my chest with pride, knowing how long Cam had wanted this and that he was playing so well. I never thought dedication to a sport would be such a turn-on, but here we were.

While the team prepared to start the game, Ollie and I whooped and cheered for our boys. Yes, our boys. It was useless to deny it. Ollie might still firmly be in the just friends' camp, but I was too far gone for that. After my conversation with Brianna, the words "you're falling for Cam" repeated in my mind like an oath.

The announcer called out Cam's name and number, and I jumped up from my seat, screaming as loud as my lungs would let me. He turned over to our section and gave me a wave, but it lacked his usual excitement. Dread pooled in my core—had something changed for Cam too?

He must have seen the distress on my face, because he turned back toward me, mouthing the words "I missed you." They soothed my churning insides a little, but not enough to ignore all the warning bells going off in my mind.

After the announcer finished, he darted to the outfield, warming up before the visiting team started batting. Normally, Cam looked confident on the field—not in a cocky way, more like confidence in his skills. But tonight, his movements felt different, as if he'd lost that trust in himself. As he threw the ball with the other outfielders, his throws seemed a little off, as if he was too in his head.

"Hey, Sarge!" I called out, not caring who heard me.

Ollie tugged at the edge of my jersey. "Hads, he's not supposed to talk to us. If he does, he'll get fined."

"It's okay," I said as his face perked up and he met my eye. He gave me a tentative smile, but it was there—the first one he'd cracked since he walked out on the field. "Remember our bet!"

He shook his head, unable to hide his wide grin. "Thought that was just for LA?"

"Yup," I shouted back. "But I'm always down to raise the stakes."

"You've got a deal, menace." Cam winked up at me, and warmth spread through my chest. "See you after the game."

"Give 'em hell, baby!"

The other outfielders turned to watch our conversation, probably confused about what was happening. One guy must have said something, because Cam shot him a warning look. His eyes narrowed and his forehead creased, but it wasn't enough to break the smile on his lips when he turned back to me. His umber eyes searched mine, and for a moment, my heart beat a little faster. It was the expression usually reserved for rom-coms and epic, sweeping romances, when the guy realized he never wanted to live without his love interest again.

Or it was wishful thinking on my part.

As the first batter stepped up to the plate, Cam's attention turned back to the game, that fierce determination back in its place.

I settled back in my seat, and Ollie handed me a beer. Her eyes burned into the side of my face as she smirked at me. "What?"

"Nothing." She smirked. "Just wondering when you finally figured it out."

"Figured what out?"

"That you're in love with Cam."

This was the second time today someone had told me as much.

But unlike earlier with Brianna, I didn't deny it.

UNFORTUNATELY, the brief joy in Cam's eyes was gone by the second inning. The Rebels were crushing the Hawks, and they seemed to know every play in their handbook. I'd chewed my nails down to the beds while watching, especially when I looked over at Cam waiting in the dugout.

Frustration lined every inch of his body, from the clench of his fists to the tightness in his brow. It took everything in me to stay in my seat, wanting nothing more than to run to him and take some of his pain away.

"It's fine," Ollie muttered in her seat, more to herself than to me as Parker stepped up to bat. Her hands wrung together, and her eyes never left him. "You can do this, Park. You've got this."

As his walk-up song blared through the stadium speakers, Ollie hummed along absentmindedly. Not surprising, considering Ollie almost always picked Parker's walk-up songs. According to her, he had the worst taste in music, and it was her duty as his best friend to remedy that. She'd been making him playlists and helping him since high school, and it seemed like it wouldn't end soon.

Her words turned hushed as Parker turned slightly, staring directly at our section. Just as Cam always found me in the crowd, he always looked for Ollie. Parker shot her a sly smile before turning to face the pitcher with a determined stare.

The pitcher wound his arm back, throwing the ball through the air with almost inhuman speed. Parker didn't bite on the first swing, instead standing still as the umpire called "strike". Ollie muttered a sharp curse under her breath as the pitcher repeated the motions, but this time, Parker tried to hit the ball.

And missed.

Before my mind caught up, the umpire called out a second strike. Parker shook his head, muttering a sharp curse under his breath. Ollie reached out and took my hand, clenching it as hard as possible when the third pitch came. But it was no use. The sound when the ball collided with the catcher's glove echoed in the crowd, everyone almost silent as Parker walked off the field. When he reached the dug-out, he chucked his helmet down, screaming out a frustrated groan. Cam gave him a commiserating pat on the back before turning to watch the next couple of batters step up to the base. A single. Another single. Enough to get on base, but not nearly enough to tie up the score.

By the time Cam stepped up to bat, the Hawks were still five runs behind the Rebels, and the tension was so palpable, it clouded the whole stadium. Ringing filled my ears, blocking out the hum of the music and the cheers of the crowd. All I could do was close my eyes and pray Cam would pull off another flawless hit.

But as we watched pitch after pitch, that didn't happen. Ball after ball landed in the catcher's mitt, Cam's timing off by a second or two. My heart jumped into my throat. This wasn't like Cam. This wasn't the team I'd grown to love. When the third strike called out, Cam looked like he was ready to murder someone. His hands tensed on the bat, as if he was tempted to break it into pieces but didn't want to rack up any fines. By the time he walked back into the dugout, he slouched down on the bench, far out of sight from the crowd.

"Holy shit," I said to Ollie. "I can't believe that just happened."

Ollie reached out and squeezed my hand. "They're having an off night—it happens. There's still a lot of game left."

But even with her reassuring words, her eyes never left Parker's, as if she was struggling with being on the sidelines as much as I was.

"Do you think it's my fault?" I asked, unable to look away from the dugout. Where was he? Was he okay? Cam put a ridiculous amount of pressure on himself, constantly trying to prove his place on the team. If I'd somehow messed with his head—

"No," Ollie insisted. "It's a bad night. They all have them once in a while. Don't put that on yourself. If anything, you helped Cam. We all saw it. He was in a mood before he ever stepped out onto the field."

"How do you help Parker on nights like this?"

"I get him drunk and then take him to an all-night laser tag place. Something about taking out overly-competitive teenagers makes him a little less mopey." Ollie took her hand and linked our fingers. "Honestly, it depends on what's going on in his mind. Sometimes, he needs a distraction, and there are other nights he needs to talk through the game. All you can do is be there for them. This is a long season, and they're going to have a couple of rough nights. As long as they get back up again tomorrow, ready to do it again, that's all that matters."

Without another thought, I let go of Ollie's hand and pulled her into a tight hug. "Thank you."

"For what?"

"For all your advice and support so far. I don't know what I'd do if you weren't here with me."

"Awww, Hads," Ollie said as she pretended to flick a tear away. "Same to you, babe. Even though you're no longer a member of the platonic best friend's club, you'll always have a place next to me."

THIRTY-NINE

Cameron

Guilt churned through my gut as I stared up at the scoreboard. The fans had already fled the stadium, leaving with their heads hung in defeat. The field lights turned off one by one with an audible thud, but the score remained, lighting up our failure for the world to see.

It wasn't even a close game. We couldn't pretend that a couple of wrong moves caused the loss. There were so many errors, it was hard to keep track. And a lot of them happened in the outfield, the blame landing squarely on my shoulders.

My whole body sagged as I dropped my head between my knees. The rest of the team filed out when the umpires called the game, ready to hit the showers and wash away our defeat. But I remained, looking out at the field, wondering if I just hammered the final nail into my coffin. A small, pathetic part of me wished other teams would give up after my poor performance. However, a much larger part of me wanted to earn my place on the Hawks, to prove that I was an asset on the field.

Our social media manager, Melanie, walked out onto

the field, her heels clicking in a strange rhythm on the grass. She let out a quick breath when she spotted me. "Oh good, Cam. Weber wants you on camera. Media room in five minutes?"

"Do I have to?" I ran my hand over my face. "I can't promise I'll play nice tonight."

"Try." Melanie gave me a tight-lipped smile. With her wavy black hair tucked into a tight bun, and her signature dark red lipstick, she might have looked like a corporate angel, but there was no messing with Melanie's work. She was the first one to get players in line and made sure we were cordial with the press.

Without another word, I rushed into the locker room, taking a quick shower before making my way into the media room. The Hawks logo behind the table felt like a mockery, our mascot hung his head in shame.

As the media pestered me with questions, I tried to keep on a placid expression, one that showed my disappointment, but made the fans believe I'd be back in it next game. But would I have the chance to redeem myself? Or would there be another closed door meeting in my future, where I was told to pack my stuff and head off to some other city?

After the last reporter finished questioning me, Melanie unceremoniously dropped me back at the locker room, muttering something about wrangling interns as she stomped past.

When I walked inside, my teammates sat silently in front of their lockers. Normally, we'd chat and talk after the game, whether we won or lost. Each win was celebrated, and the losses were a chance to grow and improve. Not tonight. Instead, the air in the clubhouse clawed at my throat, heavy as fuck and thick with the sting of this loss. And sure, there were two more games left in the series, but the first one set the tone. The Rebels kicked our asses, and we couldn't even blame it on their superior skills.

I gathered my stuff and muttered a quick goodbye before rushing out to the crowd, hoping that there wouldn't be too many fans waiting for me. All I wanted was my girl. Like that ray of sunshine at the end of a rainstorm, Hadley's face was the first one I saw. She said nothing as I walked up and pulled her into a tight hug. No, she just let me hold her, not caring who watched us. Her nails ran through the back of my hair when my head dropped onto her shoulder, and her spring scent washed all my worries away. She didn't say a single word as I held her, didn't even squirm, even though I held her too tight.

This was something. *We* were something. No matter what happened next, this thing between us had to be enough to overcome it. Because seeing her here, giving me exactly what I needed, was the best thing that had happened in a long time.

Even if the worst happened, and the Hawks traded me, this brief period would be worth it because I got to be with her.

Hadley pulled back and brushed her fingers along my jaw. "Ready to get out of here?"

I nodded and took her hand. We walked side by side down the hall toward the player parking area. Once we cleared security, I tugged her back to me and kissed her lips. *Quick, soft.* Nothing like what I'd planned to do to her tonight. But right now, my head was too messed up to even think about anything more.

"About tonight..." I shook my head. "I'm in a shitty fucking mood, Hads. If you want some space—"

She placed her hand over my mouth. "I don't care, Cam. If you need space, I'll give it to you. If you want to beat the crap out of a pillow and gorge yourself in chips and dip, I'll do that too." Hadley pulled her hand away, but ran her fingers over my jaw. "Just let me be there for you."

I took her hand in mine and kissed her fingertips. How had I been so wrong about this girl? I wanted to go back and kick my past self for my assumptions about this girl. Hadley was the opposite of flighty and weak. She was a well of strength, and instead of hoarding it for herself, she used it to help others.

"You're the best thing that's happened to me in a long time, Hadley McKay." The words came out quietly, almost like a solemn oath between us. Her deep ocean eyes flicked up to meet mine, and her mouth fell open. Maybe it was too much too soon, but I no longer cared. Everything else in my life was up in the air. My housing, my career, shit, even the next day, wasn't guaranteed. The only thing I knew for sure? I wanted Hadley in my life.

For the longest time, I'd convinced myself that all I needed was Emilia and baseball. As long as I had those two things, nothing else would matter. I buried any doubts and loneliness down so deep, even I'd believed the lies. At least, until Hadley showed back up in my life. And the moment that we'd connected, all the answers became clear. It wasn't about having a person by my side, a nameless person to slide into the role—I needed Hadley.

I reached down and tugged her into my arms. Once Hadley wrapped her arms around my neck, I lifted her up in the air, carrying her over to my truck. She smacked me on the arm. "Cam! Let me down! You're going to hurt yourself."

"Baby, you're out of your mind if you think that's the case." I placed her in the passenger side of my truck and used my body to cage her in. She beamed up at me, her lower lip tucked between her teeth. I used my thumb to loosen it, then traced the indents left behind. "You sure you want to stay with me? If you'd rather go home, I understand."

"How many times do I have to tell you, Cam? You're not getting rid of me." She rolled her eyes, but a smile played on the corners of her lips. "Better get to used to having me around, you stubborn ass."

"Yup," I smirked as I leaned down to kiss her. "And you have no idea how much I like the sound of that."

THANKFULLY, I'd already checked into the hotel before the game, so we avoided the crowds in the hotel lobby. Word had spread among some fans that some of the team crashed at this hotel on game nights, and the bar was likely already full of people hoping for autographs or more. Most nights, I didn't mind. Hell, it was an honor to sign their balls or other mementos from the game. But tonight, I had zero interest in reliving the evening, recounting all my fuck-ups for the world to tear apart. I just wanted to be alone with Hadley.

As the elevator doors closed, she let out a quiet sigh, and I reached out and took her hand. Even with just the two of us, she didn't breathe easily until the doors opened and she scurried off into the hall.

I took an extra second to watch her walk away. After a few steps, Hadley paused, realizing I wasn't with her. She turned back to me with an uneasy grin. "You okay, Cam?"

No. Not even a little. The trade conversation had fucked up my head, and there was nothing else I could do. It hung over my head like an axe. Every time my phone jostled with a message, I bristled, wondering if this was the moment everything changed.

But as I stared at Hadley with her welcoming smile, and for the first time, I wondered if it was all worth it. If I'd be willing to give it all up for her and Emilia. What would life be like if I weren't a baseball player? I'd never imagined doing anything else, but it might be time to reconsider. If playing the game meant another five years of moving around the country, never sure when I'd see my family again, then I wasn't sure I could do it.

Hadley's brow furrowed, staring at me like she knew where my thoughts had wandered. I swallowed, the weight of my words settling heavily on my tongue. All I wanted was to tell her the truth, to lay everything on the line. But everything was so new, and I didn't know where Hadley stood. She'd already proven to be a flight risk, and I didn't want to push her until she was all in like me.

So instead of laying all my secrets at her feet, I stepped off the elevator and took her hand, expecting her to lead me down to the room. But even as I moved, she stayed planted in the same spot, tugging me until I had no choice but to pause as well.

"I'm fine, Hadley."

"No, you're not." Her voice hushed but soothing. She reached out with her spare hand and ran her fingers along my jaw. "Is it about the game?"

I forced myself to nod, even though she'd broken me out of that haze when I found her waiting for me outside of the locker room. But how did I explain I was already mapping out our future break-up when she still hadn't committed to me? Sure, she'd reluctantly admit to being mine, but we'd never discussed anything beyond the next moment. No talks of the future, no confessions that made me think she wanted more.

"I'm trying to shake it off," I said. "Haven't played that crappy in a long time, and it's taking me longer than I'd like. I'm sorry I ruined our date night."

"You didn't ruin anything, Cam." Hadley's hand tugged mine until I met her eyes. They softened as she smiled up at me. "I don't need anything fancy. I just want you, sarge. Everything else is just extra."

"I'm dragging you down with me, Hads. You should call Ollie, see if she wants to hang out tonight. She's gonna be better company than me."

"Cameron Seda." Hadley released my hand and placed her own on her hips. She glared up at me, her nose crinkled in annoyance. "Do you want me to leave?"

"No." The word flew out of my mouth, even though it was selfish of me. I wanted her here with me, wanted to soak in her honey and sunshine scent for as long as she'd let me.

"Then stop telling me to go." Hadley poked her finger into my chest. "I want to be here for you, Cam. So goddamnit, let me! Or did you think I only stuck around for the great sex?"

I started to answer, but she put her fingers up to my mouth to silence me. "Cam, I care about you. And that means I'm sticking around through all of it. The wins, and yeah, the shitty losses." She pulled her fingers away, but dragged them along my jaw. "So let me be there for you, Cam. Trust me to be a safe place for you to land."

There were no words that could summarize the fluttering in my chest. Maybe it wasn't everything, but it was enough. With the way Hadley stared at me, there was no way she wasn't falling just as hard as me. It might have taken us years to find our way, but now that we had, no force on earth could get me to leave this girl's side.

I dropped my bag at my feet and cupped my hands on Hadley's hips, lifting her up into the air. She giggled as she wrapped her arms and legs around me. My mouth claimed hers, leaving no question about how I felt. Because this girl was mine, and I'd do anything in my power to keep us together, to return the favor, and always be her safe place to land.

I pulled back, searching her expression with a sly smile. "Great sex?"

"Of course that's what you'd hold onto." Hadley rolled her eyes. "Yes, sarge. Great sex. Amazing even. Is that what you want to hear?"

"It's a start." I reached down and grabbed my bag, but kept Hadley in my arms. "Rather hear you screaming my name right now, menace."

Her eyes widened as my steps quickened. "I thought you said you weren't in the mood?"

"Changed my mind." I shrugged. "Besides, if anything in this world can make me feel better, it's you, naked in front of me, begging for my cock."

Hadley

The moment the hotel room door closed behind us, Cam and I collided. Our clothes ended up in a pile on the floor, our bags tossed aside without a care for their contents. The only thing on my mind was touching and tasting every inch of the man in front of me.

There was more on his mind than the loss tonight. After growing up with my mother, I'd inherited an extra sense, able to tell when people were on edge or if they were trying to hide their pain. With my mother, it always told me when to steer clear or if it was the right time to question her. By the time I was a teenager, I no longer cared about what was bothering her, knowing it was some slight she'd blown out of proportion.

It was different with Cam. I wanted to bear the weight of his secrets, wanted to be a pillar for him to pull strength from. I wanted to shower him with love so he never had to question his worth in my eyes.

Cam reached around my back, unclasping the lace material of my bra. It slid along my arms and joined the rest of my clothes on the floor. Cam pulled back, running the back of his fingers over every inch of my exposed skin. "You're fucking stunning, Hadley. If I went blind right now, I'd be a lucky man with you as my last sight."

I shook my head, my cheeks heating with his words. "You probably say that to all the girls." A dumb joke, but a tiny kernel of truth lurked in it.

Cam's hand reached up, pinching my chin between his thumb and forefinger. "There is no one else, Hadley. No other girls. From the time I wake up to the moment I close my eyes, you are the only fucking girl I see." It was hard not to squirm under the weight of his stare, but he held me tight. "Tell me you understand, Hadley."

I swallowed, searching his eyes. The intensity lurking in them made my knees buckle. No one ever looked at me like Cam, as if I was the only person in the world who mattered. It was the same way he looked at Emilia, like his world would fall off its axis without us at his side.

As much as I loved it, it also brought a flurry of nerves to the surface, worried I was undeserving of such a gift. But Cam didn't give me a chance to question him, not when he backed me up against the bed until my knees folded. As my ass hit the comforter, he brushed his thumb over my lower lip.

"I've been dreaming about fucking this devilish little mouth for so long, menace." Another stroke of his finger. "Will you let me?"

I nodded, not trusting my voice. Despite everything we'd already done, Cam had never let me taste him—too busy getting me off to let me return the favor. He palmed his hardening cock through the thin material of his boxers, and my mouth watered at the sight, already craving the exquisite ache. I reached up as I slid off the bed, dragging the fabric down his muscular thighs. I kissed the bare skin, savoring the way his skin pulsed under my touch.

"Fuck, Hadley. You're driving me insane, baby, and you've barely touched me."

The first few swipes of my tongue were tentative, testing to find where he was most sensitive. But soon, my lust took over, and I couldn't help but suck him into my mouth, my tongue tracing the thick veins on his shaft. His hands remained clenched at his sides, trying desperately to hold back. That wouldn't do. I hollowed my cheeks, sucking him deeply into the back of my throat.

His knees wobbled, and he leaned forward, a string of curses flying from his mouth. "Jesus, baby. You're fucking gorgeous with my cock filling your mouth." His thumb traced my cheek as I continued to work him. "You like that? Knowing you're ruining me every time we're together?"

I moaned, loving how this man came apart at the seams for me. He might have the world's attention on the field, but I held his all the time. It was the most intoxicating sort of power, the kind that made you want to fly out of your skin and never come back down.

"Can't hold back anymore," Cam muttered through gritted teeth. "Gonna get a little rougher with you, baby. But you can handle it, can't you?" Another groan left my throat, vibrating around him. Spit filled my mouth, and my jaw already pulsed from trying to take him, but nothing on Earth would have made me stop.

Cam's hand tangled in my hair, adjusting me to take him deeper. His first thrusts were gentle, testing my limits, but when my nails dug into his muscles, he quickened and hit the back of my throat. It constricted around him, and he tried to pull back, but I refused to let him, wanting more of that power.

His eyes widened as he stared down at me in awe. "Damn it, Hadley. You feel too damn good. I'm never gonna last like this." His head fell back, and the tendons in his neck pulsed. "Touch yourself, baby. I need you to make yourself come until I can take care of your aching pussy."

As he directed my mouth, one of my hands snaked in between my legs, circling my already swollen clit. The first couple of slips already made my head spin. I was so fucking turned on by the look in Cam's eyes, it wouldn't take long for me to fall apart. Just as I found my rhythm, Cam suddenly stopped, pulling out of my mouth.

My eyes widened as I stared up at him. "Why the hell did you stop?"

"Because if I didn't, I was going to come down your throat, and we can't have that."

"Why not?"

Cam smirked as he reached down and brushed away the spit from the side of my mouth. "Because I've been craving you for days, baby. I'm not wasting another minute without filling you. Been dreaming about your pussy ever since that phone call, and I need it strangling my cock when I come."

My cheeks flushed, and I climbed up on the bed before Cam crawled over me, lining up with my entrance. His lips dusted my chest and my neck he took my hands, licking my desire from my fingers. After they were clean, he kissed each pad of my fingertips. He held me close as he entered me, his eyes never leaving mine. Each thrust was reverent, as if he was paying penance instead of fucking me. His hands travelled along my sides, keeping me close despite his movements.

As my release climbed up my spine, my eyes flashed open, searching Cam's expression as I tensed around him.

"You feel that, Hadley?" he asked quietly, such a stark contrast to his usually filthy words. "This is us, together. It's not great, it's not amazing. It's fucking life changing. You're made for me, baby, every single inch of you, and I'm never letting you go."

Between his hushed promise and sacred movements, my heart cracked open. The last lines of my defense imploded, unable to stand up against his words. As my release crashed over me and Cam growled his own, I held him close, hoping he could sense the fundamental shift.

There was nothing left of my formerly jaded heart. He'd repaired it day by day, and if he listened close enough, he'd realize it only beat for him.

FORTY-ONE

The next morning, my phone alarm blared from... somewhere. My hands fumbled through the sheets, trying to find where it ended up last night. Finally, I reached down to the floor, dragging my jeans closer and grabbing it from the pocket. After hitting snooze, I tossed it right back into the pile of clothes, unable to exert any more energy, too exhausted from a full night with Hadley.

We'd barely slept, too busy making up for lost time. Every time I closed my eyes, it was only a matter of time before she rubbed up against me, making me hard as a fucking rock, or she climbed on top of me, riding me until we both saw stars.

All the clouds from last night cleared from my mind in the early morning sun, destroyed by Hadley's touch. Without even trying, she pulled me out of the haze. I reluctantly opened one eye, finding her sitting up in bed next to me, typing away on her laptop, papers surrounding her side of the bed.

My knuckles dragged up her bare spine. Hadley

jumped, then turned and grinned at me. "You're supposed to be sleeping in, sarge."

"Hard to do when you're next to me, menace," I grumbled. "Sleep's not what's on my mind right now."

"You better try." Hadley leaned down and pressed a kiss to my temple. "You've got to kick the Rebels' asses tonight."

My entire body tensed at her words, remembering we'd have to face our opponents for two more nights. Refusing to dwell on it until I needed to leave for the stadium, I sat up and placed my chin on Hadley's shoulder, reading what was on her screen.

"Field Day proposal?"

"Yeah..." Hadley said, her voice suddenly meek. "I guess the school always had one, but they weren't able to secure funding this year, so they cancelled it." She shook her head. "The kids have worked so hard, and I want to give them a good send-off, so I'm trying to reach out to different places that might work with us."

"Why are you planning this?" Hadley's eyes narrowed into a glare. I shook my head. "No, not like that. I'm just wondering why this responsibility isn't falling on the principal, or the PTO, or someone else like that."

Hadley tucked her lower lip between her teeth. "They've tried, especially the principal. The PTO is out of funds because they already donated a lot to the after-school programs and the fifth grade moving up ceremony. With a lot of our federal grants getting defunded, there's not a lot the principal can do." She let out a long sigh and looked back out the window. "No one asked me to do it, but I hate the idea of our kids missing out because of bureaucratic red tape. I can't solve all our problems, but I can at least create something memorable for them."

"That's a great idea." I rubbed my hand along her back,

immensely proud of my girl. Hadley was determined. There was no doubt in my mind that if she wanted to do something spectacular for her students, she would make it a reality. I just hated that she was in this alone.

I grabbed a pamphlet from her side, thumbing through the information. "You're reaching out to the football team?"

Hadley's mouth parted as she glanced over at me. "Oh, yeah! They do a lot of community outreach, and I thought if we could get a couple of players to show up..."

"You know another team does a lot of community support as well." Hadley's eyebrow arched. "My team, baby. I'm talking about us."

She shook her head. "I can't ask you to do that."

"Why not?"

Hadley huffed, staring at me like the answer was the most obvious thing in the world. "Because it wouldn't be fair. Some schools work for years to make these partnerships happen, and I'd be jumping the line just because you've seen me naked."

I closed the lid of her laptop; Hadley turned to snap at me, but I didn't give her the chance, instead pulling her into my lap. She brushed against my length, and we both sucked in a sharp breath, all too aware of how little fabric separated us. But that wasn't what I wanted right now. My fingers pinched Hadley's chin, guiding her eyes down to meet mine.

"First, as much as I love seeing you naked, that's only one reason I like having you around. Another is because of your fierce heart, menace. I've never met anyone who fights so hard for the people in their life." Hadley opened her mouth to protest, but I silenced her with a hard stare. "Second, you know more than most people—life isn't fair. Sometimes, you have to use the advantages handed to you. If our team was to help, it wouldn't be just because I care about you."

"It wouldn't?"

"No," I laughed, brushing my lips along Hadley's cheek. "It's because I've seen how hard you work, baby, how much you pour into your career. You're determined to make your students' lives a little more exciting, and it shows when you talk about them."

She wrinkled her nose. "You make me sound powerful."

"The most powerful woman I've ever met." My lips dusted across her collarbone. "The most beautiful." Another touch to her pulse point. "The most aggravating."

Hadley snorted. "And you love it."

I pulled back, snaking my hand around the back of her neck. "You're damn right I do."

I TRIED to convince Hadley to spend another night in the hotel with me, but she wanted to head back to the house. It was tempting to see if I could convince her otherwise, but I also wanted to see Emilia before my game. If anything could shake away my nerves, it was a couple of hours with my daughter.

Ever since she went to the game earlier in the season, Emilia had developed a love for the game. She'd been going to them since she was in diapers, but this was the first year she started asking questions, wanting to learn everything I could offer.

"Em's been asking to play catch," Hadley said from the passenger's seat of my truck. She turned and smirked at me. "You get this goofy smile when you're thinking about Em.

Hate to break it to you, Cam, but you're not as hard to read as you think."

I rolled my eyes. "Was thinking about getting her a glove, but I need her to come with me. Want to make sure it fits."

"She'd love that." Hadley let out a sigh when I hit the blinker, turning the truck into the driveway. "Only a few more days until Tori comes home."

"Yeah…" My jaw tensed. "A lot of things are going to change around here."

Hadley nodded, dropping her head onto my shoulder. "I don't want some things to change." I said nothing, but I gripped the steering wheel a little tighter. "When she gets home, are you going to look for an apartment?"

My spine stiffened as I tried to answer her innocent question. I hadn't gathered the courage to tell Hadley about my possible trade, and after last night, I was in no rush to ruin our morning. "Yeah." I ground my teeth. "As much as I love these guys, a little space will be good for all of us. Plus, I'd like to be a little closer to the stadium. I don't mind the drive, but it's hard on late nights. I've already talked to a real estate agent. She's going to send over some listings later this week."

I pulled into my parking spot and turned off the engine. After dropping the keys into my pocket, I reached down and linked my hand with Hadley's. "When they come through, will you take a look? Come with me and see if we find any we like?"

Her eyes widened as she stared up at me. "You want my opinion?"

"Of course," I said, tugging her a little closer. I reached up with my free hand and brushed some of her hair behind her shoulder. "If I have my way, you'll be spending a lot of nights there with me. I want to make sure you'll be comfortable."

Hadley's mouth hung open, and for a moment, I thought I'd gone too far. Maybe she wasn't as ready to take our relationship into the real world as me. Instead, she surged forward and captured my lips, making elation gather in my chest. "I'll take that as a yes?"

"I'd love to," Hadley answered. "So this is it? We're really doing this?"

Just as I was about to tell her yes, that she was one of the most important people in my life, a knock sounded on the driver's side window. Hadley's face paled as she looked over my shoulder. I followed her gaze, and the world stopped spinning as I met Victoria's smirk.

"When I said I wanted you two to get along, this was not what I had in mind."

FORTY-TWO

Hadley

"Fuck." The word came out more like a squeak, my voice unable to produce much more. Out of all the ways I expected Victoria to find out, this never even crossed my mind. So much for the gradual conversation about what happened between us. I'd pictured this moment a million times in my mind, trying to figure out exactly how to tell my best friend I'd fallen for her ex. I expected tears, and hopefully, some understanding, but that was only if I framed it right. And this? Her walking up and finding us making out in his truck? That was the wrong way to break the news.

My heart thundered in my chest as I stared at her, trying and failing to find the right words to say. Cam just shook his head as I spluttered out. "Wh-what are you doing here?"

"I live here," Victoria said, her dark eyes glinting with amusement. "I think the better question is, what have you two been doing here?"

If the Earth could've swallowed me whole right then, I would have welcomed it. Where I was the picture of anxiety and unease, Cam just chuckled, climbing out of the car and sweeping Victoria into his arms. "When the hell did you get back, Vic?"

"Last night." She looked at me. "Are you going to get out of the car, Hads?"

"Depends." I leaned back in my seat. "Ar-are you mad?"

Victoria's brow furrowed. "Why would I be mad? About you and Cam?" She rolled her eyes. "Do I wish you had given me some kind of heads up? Definitely. That was not what I expected to see when I opened the door. But if this means I can finally host a dinner party without the two of you screaming at each other, I'm all for it."

"Dinner party?" I asked as I got out of the truck. "Did we secretly slip into the sixties?"

"Shut up," Victoria teased as she rushed to my side. I tensed when she came closer, still not fully trusting she was okay with what she'd just witnessed. But when her arms wrapped around my shoulders, it felt like coming home. It didn't take long for my arms to settle around her waist, holding my best friend close. God, I'd missed her. It was a phantom ache, the type you didn't realize you needed until it came back into your life. It was like going home after a long stretch and remembering how much you loved the quiet comfort of the town. "But after all your teasing about Adam, you better believe I'm giving you hell about this."

She pulled back, and a wide, genuine smile filled her face. The girl was glowing, pure happiness radiating from her pores. Still, my guard remained raised, waiting for her warm disposition to change. Cam walked up to my side and wrapped his arm around my shoulders. I tried to step back, but he refused to let me, holding me close.

"Okay, Vic, I know you've got questions. Let's hear them."

She rolled her eyes at his flippant tone. "First, let's go

inside. Cole's going to drop Emilia off in an hour, and I want to hear everything before she gets back." She stepped toward the porch. "You guys want some coffee?"

"Only if it's spiked with something," I muttered under my breath. As Cam guided me toward the house, I stopped, tugging his arm so he stayed back with me. "Why are you not freaking out right now?"

"About Vic finding out?"

"No, about Christmas coming early." I smacked his bicep. "Of course about Tori finding out! I'm about to throw up in the bushes, and you're acting like this is a regular Saturday morning."

Cam stepped closer and enveloped me in a tight hug. His head rested on top of mine as he rubbed soothing circles on my back. "Why are you upset?" He leaned back and searched my expression. "Did you want to keep us a secret?"

"What? Of course not." I didn't miss the flicker of relief in Cam's eyes. "It's just... I thought we'd have time to figure out what we were going to say, have some sort of plan in place. I don't want her to hate me for this."

"Hey," Cam said, tipping my chin up to meet his expression. "She won't hate you. I don't think she's even capable. I agree this wasn't the best way for her to find out, but it might be even better. We've ripped the Band-Aid off, and now we can talk about it together."

I shook my head. "But we haven't even talked about what we are, what all of this means, the two of us."

"I know I want to be with you." Cam reached down and took my hands. "Maybe we haven't defined what we are yet, but I know in my heart you're the person I want to be with. I like being around you, like the way you make me feel. And no matter what insults you hurl in my direction, you want to be with me too."

"You're so cocky."

"Not cocky if it's true, menace." He shifted closer and kissed my temple. "Tell me I'm wrong. Tell me we don't belong together. The world makes more sense as long as we're facing it side by side."

I stared up at him, searching the soulful brown eyes I loved so much. The words couldn't come. They never would, not when I'd already surrendered my heart to Cam. He leaned forward, brushing a soft kiss on the side of my mouth. "That's what I thought."

"I DON'T KNOW what's more shocking—that the two of you are together, or that you got Hadley to sit through an entire baseball game."

Victoria sat on one side of her dining room table, Cam and I on the other, like errant teenagers facing down their parents. Nerves still tittered along my spine, but Cam clutched my hand, giving me something concrete to hold on to.

My best friend's eyes tracked our every movement, as if cataloging each one for later. Despite her calm demeanor and accepting words, I had a hard time trusting the sight in front of me. Even though my last relationship had ended a long time ago, I probably wouldn't handle the same situation in stride. Cam's phone chirped on the table, and his face paled as he looked down at the message. He grabbed the device and kissed the top of my head. "I'll be right back."

Questions sat on the tip of my tongue; I wanted to find

out what had caused his face to fall, but the weight of Victoria's stare kept me in my seat. I turned back toward her, searching her expression for any signs of anger. "Okay, Tori. What's really going through your mind right now?"

"What do you mean?"

I groaned and dropped my head on the back of the chair. "You cannot possibly be okay with this. It's Cam. Scream at me, curse me out, flip the damn table if you have to. Just get it all out, because I don't want this to ruin our friendship."

She leaned closer. "Would that change anything?"

I pondered her words. As much as I wanted to say yes, I couldn't bring myself to do it. No matter what happened between us, I refused to regret Cam. After years of searching for a place in this world, it was like it had always been waiting for me in his arms. He and Emilia were my world, and as much as I loved Victoria, I loved them just as much. "No," I quietly admitted. "It wouldn't."

"Good." She smiled at me, reaching out to take my hands. "I'm not upset, Hads. Was I shocked? Of course. But that was more because I know the history between the two of you. I honestly would have been less surprised if I came home to caution tape."

"There were moments when I wondered the same thing," I chuckled. I cleared my throat then, and my voice took a more serious tone. "I'd never do anything to intentionally hurt you, Tori. You're the light of my freaking world. But Cam..." I tried to swallow the lump in my throat. "He's everything to me."

She smiled boldly back at me. "That is all I've ever wanted for you, Hads. For someone to love you just as fiercely as you love everyone else. I never imagined it'd be Cam, but now that it happened, it makes perfect sense. You two complement each other—when you're not trying to kill each other."

"So you don't think I've lost my mind?"

"No," she smirked back at me. "This might be the best decision you've made in a long time."

"And you're sure you're not mad that I'm dating your ex?"

"Hads, I love Cam, but we haven't been together in a long time. I barely remember what we were like together, especially now that I'm with Adam. All I've ever wanted is for Cam to find happiness. And you, Hadley, you make him so happy. I haven't seen him like this in years, and I've only been back for a couple of hours." She paused, chewing on her lip.

"What?"

Victoria tilted her head. "Are you all in with him?"

Her question caught me off guard. As much as I wanted to explore things between Cam and me, I was still holding back, refusing to give my feelings a voice. He'd alluded to caring about me, but without knowing his mindset, I refused to dive completely into this new relationship. It was my last line of defense, only the rubble remaining of my once-fortified walls. While Cam had already knocked down most of them, I couldn't completely give in, not just yet.

"I want to be," I said. "I-I'm trying."

Victoria squeezed my hands. "That's all I ask. Because Cam—he'll move the world for you if you ask him. But if you're not all in with him, it'll break his heart, and I don't want to see that for either of you."

I nodded, soaking up her words, when my phone rang, breaking the tension. I released Victoria's hands, pulling my device from my purse. When I saw my old neighbor's name and number, my heart froze in my chest, terrified about what she had to say. Mrs. Majors never called me, not unless there was an emergency. Victoria's brow furrowed across the table. "Everything okay?"

No. It wasn't. But as I stared down at my phone, I couldn't bring myself to answer, terrified of what waited on the other side of the line. After a moment, the call clicked off, and I breathed a sigh of relief—at least until the voice-mail notification sprung up on the screen. I lifted myself up from the chair, my legs already shaking with adrenaline. "I should check this. Be right back."

As soon as the porch door closed behind me, I lifted the phone to my ear, hearing the scrambled message. Words like hospital, ambulance, and intensive care rose above the rest, making me almost cry out with guilt. My hand shook as I tucked them back into my pockets.

My mother had a heart attack.

While I was having the time of my life, my mother had been alone, fighting to survive. Now, she was sitting in a hospital room, unsure if she'd see another day or two. I rushed inside, telling Victoria I had to go, telling her I'd call her later to explain what happened. My feet barely touched the stairs as I rushed into Cam's room, grabbing my bag and shoving a couple of outfits inside. As I rooted around my stuff, trying to find my car keys, the door opened.

My throat constricted as I turned around and locked eyes with Cam. "Hadley, what's going on?"

FORTY-THREE

Cameron

"Nothing yet."

The words from my agent should have given me some relief, but it only added to the anxiety brewing in my chest. I'd asked him to look into the trade conversation after my meeting in Benny's office yesterday. There wasn't anything Theo could do to stop it, but I couldn't live with this hanging over my head for another month. With the trade deadline not until the end of July, it would be weeks until I'd be able to fully exhale, knowing my future was secure until the end of the season.

I ran my hand over my brow. "And you haven't heard which teams are asking about me?"

"No," Theo answered. "I've tried asking informally, but teams are protective about agents poking around mid-season." He paused, and from experience, I knew this next statement was going to hurt. Theo was one of the best sports agents out there, having moved from representing actors to athletes in the past couple of years. I was below his usual radar, but Gray reached out to him on my behalf. Theo was a shark and would go to battle for his clients. He'd been instrumental in getting me to the Hawks' farm team, all because he knew this was where I wanted to be.

"I'm going to be honest with you, Cam. If there is a trade option on the table, the Hawks might take it, and there's not much we can do about it."

"I'm aware of that," I ground out.

"All you can do is keep your head down and play the best game possible. Make yourself invaluable as a player. They won't trade you if they think you'll take them all the way."

I exhaled slowly, staring out at the vast valley below me, highlighting the lake anchoring the town. Was I that player anymore? The last few games, my mind hadn't been in the game, to say the least. Between Emilia and Hadley, baseball was becoming less of a dream and more of a barrier to the life I wanted. If I could have it all, I wanted to grab the opportunity with both hands, but if I had to choose, my direction was clear.

"If the trade happens, would you be able to get me out of my contract?"

Theo sucked in a sharp breath. "Are you serious right now?" My silence answered him. "Fuck, Cam. Maybe, but it's going to come with some serious fines. We can ask them to release you, but you've got a lot of years left on paper."

"I know."

Theo muttered something under his breath. "I'll read through your contract again and see what options we have. But if you make this choice, there's no going back. You're too new to change your mind in a year or two. So, if you want to go down this path, make sure you're fucking sure. Don't throw your future away because you're pissed."

That was the thing—I wasn't throwing my future away. Sure, my life would look different when it no longer revolved around baseball, but every day I spent with Emilia and Hadley, the more I was sure they were my future. I wanted to spend my days with them, not video chatting from the other side of the country. It was one thing if I got to come home to them during the season and spend my nights in Hadley's arms. But leaving them behind for long stretches, unsure when our paths would cross again, wasn't an option anymore.

Theo interrupted my thoughts. "No decisions have to be made today, Cam. Play tonight and push this out of your mind. Pretend that the trade conversation never happened. If these are going to be your last games, you want to enjoy them."

I STEPPED BACK into the house and found Victoria waiting for me in the foyer. Nerves prickled my spine when I didn't see Hadley at her side. My throat dried up. What happened when I stepped outside? As much as I wanted Victoria to accept my relationship with Hadley, my loyalties had shifted over the past few weeks. I still cared about Victoria as the mother of my child, but Hadley was my future, the woman I wanted to build my world around.

"Where is she?" I bit out, unable to keep my tone light.

"She's upstairs," Victoria said. Before I asked what happened, she held up her hand. "Nothing to do with us. Hadley and I are good. She got a call, and when she came back in, she was white as a ghost and rushed upstairs."

"Fuck." My legs moved before my brain caught up, taking the stairs two at a time. As soon as I got to my room, my heart stuttered in my chest, watching as Hadley rushed between the closet and the open bag on our bed.

Her shoulders caved in around her, as if standing took too much energy. Red rimmed her sharp blue eyes, fresh tears spilling down her cheeks. I took a step closer, and her eyes darted up to meet mine. My chest cracked in half. "Hadley, what's going on?"

She squeezed her eyes together, and I rushed toward her, pulling her into my chest. The moment my arms wrapped around her, she collapsed against me, needing my strength to keep from falling to the floor. I ran my hand over her hair. "What happened?"

"My...mom..." she said through shaky breaths. "She's in the hospital."

"Shit, Hadley. I'm so sorry." I kissed the top of her head as I held her a little tighter. Her breaths shuddered against my skin and my shirt dampened from her tears, but I didn't care. I'd hold her forever if that was what she needed. Her fingers clung to my shirt, clutching me closer. "Tell me what you need, baby. I'm here."

She shook her head against my chest. "You have a game tonight."

"Fuck that," I bit out. I shifted us so she faced me. "You are more important than any game, Hadley. Tell me what you need, and I'll make it happen."

She swallowed and slowly nodded. "Can you get me a car? I need to get to Boston, and I can't drive like this. Shit, I can't take Laila with me. She's going to need someone to watch her."

"Don't worry about Laila, I'm sure Emilia and Vic will be happy to keep an eye on her. As for the car, I'll drive you out there."

"No." Hadley stepped out of my hold and resumed packing. When I tried to hold her again, she moved out of my reach. Her eyes narrowed at me. "Cam, you need to go to tonight's game. Your team needs you."

What the fuck? The caving in my chest suddenly intensified, hating the cold way Hadley stared at me now. I shook my head. "I'll talk to Benny. He'll understand—"

"I said no." Hadley's voice rose, shaking with anger. "I don't want you to come with me, Cam. This is about me. About my mother. The one I've been ignoring because I've been living in this fantasy with you. And now, she's lying in a hospital room, alone, and it's my fault." She let out a saccharine laugh. "Please, Cam. Just go. I can't think about you, about anything but getting to my mom right now."

I stared at the woman I loved, wishing I had told her the truth earlier. Because, right now, when her world was falling apart, she had no idea how much I wanted to be there with her. She was more important than any game, more important than my career. I'd worked for twenty-five years to play at the professional level, yet I'd walked away without a single glance back if it meant spending the rest of my life with her.

Reaching out, I brushed a piece of hair behind her ear. Hadley inhaled sharply, and I hoped it meant she was regretting her words. I knew her, and when the devastation faded from her mind, she'd wish to take them back. "I'm going to go, Hadley. Not because I want to, but because I'm going to respect your wishes. If you need anything, I'm only a phone call away."

It took a herculean effort to let her go. The moment the door shut behind me, it felt like I had left my heart in Hadley's hands.

FORTY-FOUR

Hadley

Two days. For two days, I sat in this sterile hospital room, trying to ignore the scent of antiseptic spray and the steady beats from the machines attached to my mother. She'd been in and out of consciousness for days, waking up only long enough to voice her disappointment that it took a medical emergency for me to come visit her.

The white walls mocked me, begging for a splash of color or something else to break up the barren space. It made my heart ache, missing having a place of my own. Even though Victoria's home was comfortable, it wasn't the same. After a lifetime of delaying putting down roots, the urge overwhelmed me, clinging to the idea of something permanent.

As she slept, I watched my mother, searching for any hint of myself in her. We had the same eyes, same pout to our lips, but that was where the similarities ended. She'd aged since I last saw her, as if her lifestyle choices took their toll on her physical appearance as well. Small lines marred her forehead and cheeks, but none of them seemed from laughter or happiness—more like her ever-present scowl had been marked on her face for the world to see.

When I was a kid, I looked up to my mother, seeing her as a free-spirit, something to emulate rather than fear. But seeing her now? It was clear she wasn't that person. Instead, she was selfish and bitter, using her anger at the world for an excuse to hurt others. She wasn't a role model—she was a cautionary tale.

My phone chimed on the end table, and I reached out to grab it. Another message from Cam. My heart ached to reach out to him, to explain I didn't mean a single word I said to him when we parted. My fear and guilt about my mother's health had shifted into something vile and ugly, taking what we had and twisting it into something darker.

But despite that knowledge, I couldn't bring myself to call him, couldn't even return a simple text—not when I knew the moment I heard his voice, I'd want to rush out of here and back into his arms.

It wasn't just Cam I missed.

I missed my hurried morning routine with Emilia, blaring Ivy Abrams on the stereo as we drove to school.

I missed sitting at the stadium with Ollie, trying to keep up with the game and laughing about the team's antics.

I missed Brianna, with her stoic patience and always-waiting smile, and how each day was a little brighter when I walked into my classroom.

While the ache of missing Victoria was a familiar friend, it was even harder knowing she was home and I was the one who'd left. I was dying to talk with her without the awkwardness of our last conversation, needing to share about how Cam had stolen my heart.

I missed everything.

Standing, I walked over to the window, staring out at

the city below. Boston wasn't a place we came to often when I was a kid, so it didn't feel like home. My childhood home was about thirty minutes outside the city, but this was the closest hospital with a cardiac specialty wing. The gray clouds over the bay mirrored my mood. It had soured more each day I spent here, waiting for the results of my mother's testing.

A groan came from the hospital bed, and I whipped around, finding my mother trying to sit up. "Mom, take it easy," I said as I stepped to her side. "You're not supposed to move too much."

"I'm fine," she ground out. "Can you pass me a cup of water?"

I did as she asked, pouring some fresh water from the pale blue plastic pitcher. Her hands shook as she reached out. The doctor warned it would be a while until she regained her strength, and she shouldn't try to push it.

While she sipped on the cup, I sat down on the edge of the bed, weariness overtaking me. Three nights sleeping upright in a vinyl chair was catching up to me, and I had no idea when I'd get to go home.

"Are you ready to talk about what happened?"

My mother's dark blue eyes jumped up to meet mine. "You already know."

"No," I sighed. "I know you had a heart attack. What I didn't know was that your doctor warned you this might happen. How long have you been on blood thinners and high blood pressure medication?"

She scoffed at my question. "Don't act like you care, Hadley. You've had years to come around and check on me, and you've never bothered. I'm shocked you even showed up now."

"Mom, I—"

A knock sounded on the door, and my mother turned, smiling as her doctor walked inside. Dr. Leeds was a young and handsome doctor who'd been overseeing my mother's care since she got admitted. With dark hair and tall, confident swagger, I could see why my mother always brightened up around him. Hell, if we'd matched on an app in the past, I definitely would have swiped on his profile. But now, I barely noticed. No one compared to Cam in my mind. He was the only one I wanted, and my chest ached with the need to get back to him.

Dr. Leeds smiled as he walked over to my mother's bedside. "You're looking much better, Ms. McKay."

"Oh, please." My mother smiled up at him with all the warmth of a bright summer's day. Give me a fucking break. Even half-dead, the woman was trying to charm her way through life. "I already told you. Call me Colleen. After all, you're my savior."

"Mom, he's a doctor. It's his job to help you heal and get better."

"Ignore my daughter." My mother sat up straighter in bed as Dr. Leeds pulled out his stethoscope and examined her pulse. "So, Doctor, when do you think I'll be able to go home?"

"After a major cardiovascular event like that, we'd like to keep you a little longer to make sure there are no other complications. We have a couple more tests to run, but if those come back clear, we should be able to get you home in a few days."

"And you still aren't sure what caused the heart attack?" I asked, moving closer to the bed. "Our neighbor said—"

"Hadley..." my mother cooed, but I saw the warning in her eyes. Back off. She smiled back up at the doctor. "Thank you for taking such great care of me. I haven't felt this great in years."

I suppressed the urge to roll my eyes, waiting until the doctor left the room to ask my questions. "Did you ask about why your medication wasn't working?"

My mother shook her head. "Hadley, don't start. The doctors have all the information they need. Stop trying to stir up drama."

"It's not dramatic to wonder why your blood pressure medication stopped working. We need answers before you're discharged so this doesn't happen again."

My mother shook her head again. "It'll be fine. You can come with me to the follow-up appointments and we can ask them. Stop bothering these nice doctors."

My steps faltered as I took in her words. I crossed my arms around my chest and shifted closer to her bed. "Wait— do you think I'm coming back home with you?"

Her eyes widened, and her mouth contorted into an annoyed scowl. "You aren't? You're going to leave your mother in her time of need?"

"Mom, I have a life, a job, I'm seeing someone—"

"Ah." She inhaled, then leaned against the pillows. "There's the truth. You've met some guy, and now you're turning your back on your family."

I squeezed the bridge of my nose. This was my penance for opening up to my mother. I just shook my head and moved closer to the window. Despite not responding to her comment, my mother continued, "I was like you once."

My eyes closed, trying to force out her words, even though I hung on every one. My mother had never opened up about her past, and as much as I wanted to shut her out, I'd always wondered about her life before I came along. I shifted, propping my hip on the windowsill.

She shook her head as she toyed with the edge of her blanket. "When I met your father, I had that same sparkle in my eyes. I thought it was the start of our lives. He came from money, someone who'd make life worth living." She darkly chuckled. "Instead, he took off, left me alone with no way to get in contact."

"And what does that have to do with me?"

She smirked. "You're the same as me, Hadley. You always had stars in your eyes. I saw it with that boy from high school, and look how that turned out. And what? Now you have some new man, and you think you're going to run off into the sunset like those books you used to read?" My mother laid back onto her pillow, her eyes slowly drifting off to sleep. "Don't make the same mistake as me, Hadley. Get out before you're trapped. Don't shape your life around a man. It'll only end in heartache."

FORTY-FIVE

I stared through the windshield of my truck, waiting as the clock ticked down. There were only a couple more minutes until Emilia got out of school, but the quiet was too much. A country song hummed on the radio, and parents chatted in the other pickup line, but none of it was enough to soothe the ache in my chest. I'd spent the last couple of years alone, but I'd never been this lonely, not since Hadley walked out the door without a promise to return.

Fuck, I missed her. For too long, I took her presence for granted, not realizing how much I needed her in my life. She was the warmth, the reason for most of my smiles, and the person who mattered most, alongside my daughter.

The sound of giggles broke through the noise of my truck, and my eyes darted up, finding a hoard of kids exiting the school. It took a couple minutes, but Emilia came running outside, beaming when she saw me waiting. I hopped out of the truck, moving to the passenger side. She ran over to me and jumped into my waiting arms.

She pulled back, pressing her small hands into my cheeks. "Daddy! You don't have a game today?"

"Not tonight. Mommy and Adam are at the house, but I wanted to grab ice cream with you before heading back. How does that sound?"

"Perfect." She smiled. "With extra sprinkles?"

"If that's what you want, Ems."

I lifted her into the back seat and buckled her into her booster. After I climbed into the driver's seat, I grabbed my phone, opening my music streaming app to pull up Emilia's favorite playlist. But as I pressed the button, a call came through the speakers. My heart pumped a little faster when I saw Hadley's name. It had been five days since we'd spoken, five days since she walked away from me. All I wanted was to run to her, but she'd made it clear she didn't want that. Right now, she needed to focus on her mother, and I'd be a distraction.

I cleared my throat as I pressed the answer button. "Hey, Hadley."

"Cam..." she said, her voice almost pained. It broke my heart to hear her whisper my name like that, giving me hope she missed me just as much as I missed her. "Ho-how are you?"

"Not that great," I admitted. "Missing a certain menace in my life."

"I miss you too. So much." She sighed, and the defeated sound broke me. "Are you with Emilia?"

"Yeah," I said, looking into the rearview mirror and motioning for Emilia to unbuckle and come closer. "Just picked her up from school."

"Hi, Auntie Hadley!" My daughter beamed up at the screen. "Daddy's taking me for ice cream."

"That sounds incredible, Emilia Bedelia. Are you going to get strawberry or cookies and cream?"

"Cookies and cream," my daughter answered. "With lots of sprinkles."

"Man, you're making me jealous, kid. All I've been eating is hospital food, and trust me, it's not the best." She huffed a humorless laugh through the phone, and I gripped the steering wheel, wishing I had her in front of me right now. "How's Laila?"

"She's good," I said. "Emilia's been taking great care of her. I've been sneaking pieces of meat into her bowl, so I'm taking your place as her favorite."

"I'll remember that," Hadley mused. As I started to tell her how much I missed her, another voice broke through the line, more urgent and hushed. Hadley groaned. "Cam, can I call you back later? The doctor has an update for us."

"Any time, Hads. I'm here whenever you need me."

Without another word, the line clicked off, the silence deafening. I dropped my head and ran my hand over my face. The distance never felt like a bigger hurdle, as if every day Hadley was gone, she slipped further away from me.

Emilia climbed into the front seat and sat on the center console. She placed her head on my shoulder, her soft sigh echoing my own. "I miss Hadley, Daddy."

"Me too, kiddo."

She looked up at me, her brown eyes wide, blinking back tears. "Do you think she'll come home soon?"

I pulled a breath through my teeth, warring with the choice to lie to my daughter or tell her a heartbreaking truth. I didn't know if Hadley was coming back. If her lack of communication was any sign, then she wouldn't be returning soon. She'd left everything behind, including us, and it stung more than I ever thought it would. How dare she make me fall in love with her, only to disappear from my life?

From our limited conversations about her mother, I'd figured out they had a complicated dynamic. The woman seemed like a narcissist, using her daughter as more of a bargaining chip than her pride and joy. I reached my arm around Emilia, holding her close to me. My heart broke for that younger version of Hadley, the one who dreamed of having a family, only to have the door shut on her every time. Despite all the harm her mother caused, she still opened up to us—let us into her world and her heart.

"She's coming back," I said to Emilia. The words might not have been the full truth, but it was the one I held on to. I wasn't giving her the option. Hadley McKay stole my heart, collecting the different pieces until she held the whole thing in her hand. "She's going to come back to us."

"Because you love her?" Emilia smirked up at me, too much awareness in her expression for a six-year-old.

"Yeah, baby. I love Hadley." I ran my fingers through her thick brown curls. "Almost as much as I love you."

"Mommy says if you love someone, you should always tell them." She narrowed her gaze at me. "Have you told Hadley you love her?"

I chuckled as I shook my head. "Not yet, Em."

She shook her head. "Oh, Daddy. First, we're getting ice cream. Then, we need to make a plan."

I furrowed my brow as she climbed back into her booster seat and buckled herself in. Looking back in the rearview mirror, I stared at my daughter, whose brow creased again in deep concentration. "A plan for what?"

She shook her head, as if I was trying the last bit of her patience. "For you to tell Auntie Hadley you love her."

LATER THAT NIGHT, after I tucked an exhausted Emilia into bed, I headed down the stairs. Sleep had eluded me over the past week, my bed feeling cold now that Hadley wasn't lying next to me. As I opened the fridge and grabbed a bottle of water, someone stepped up and tapped my shoulder. I almost jumped out of my skin as I turned to find Victoria behind me. "Shit, Vic. You scared the hell out of me."

"Sorry, I called out to you, but you seemed too distracted to hear me." Her brow furrowed as she took in my tired expression. "Heading outside?"

"Yeah." I ran my hand over my eyes. "Can't get to sleep just yet."

"C'mon." She nodded over her shoulder. "I'll keep you company."

As we stepped out onto the back porch, I let out a long exhale, taking in the world's beauty. With summer officially started, the sky was taking its time turning to night, leaving behind lines of dark reds and pinks across the valley. Victoria settled onto one of the Adirondack chairs while I took the other, letting the tranquility wash over me.

Victoria turned and stared at me. "Do you want to talk about it, or are you going to keep brooding?"

I closed my eyes and dropped my head back. "I'm not brooding. I'm...contemplating."

"Ah, is that what we're calling it now?" Victoria let out a little huff. "Have you talked to Hadley?"

"For about ten seconds. She called earlier, but she needed to talk to her mom's doctor. Tried to call back, but it went right into voicemail."

Victoria hummed at my side. Her fingers tapped along the side of her mug, a rhythm to accompany her thoughts. We sat easily in the silence, the kind forged by years of friendship, love, and everything in between. Once, I was sure Victoria was the love of my life, but now that I'd been with Hadley, I knew the difference. Victoria was a cozy comfort, the kind you sought on a cold winter's night. Hadley was a raging wildfire, consuming every part of me until all I saw was her.

Victoria and I slipped easily back into the role of friends, like that was always what we were meant to be. With Hadley, there was no way I'd ever be able to be her friend, unable to stand at her side without holding her close.

"I don't know what to do, Vic."

My shaky voice broke the silence between us. She turned and smiled at me, the soft kind, filled with empathy. "Has Hadley told you about her mom?" I nodded. "I don't want to speak out of turn, but the woman did a real number on Hadley. She made her think she ruined her life, that Hadley caused all her pain. She doesn't trust that someone can love her—at least, not the authentic version of herself. Hadley hides a lot behind smiles and sunshine because she doesn't believe she's worth the effort."

"She's worth more than that." My voice took a hardened turn, grateful I hadn't gone to the hospital with Hadley. There was no way I could look at that woman, after everything she'd done to the woman I loved, with a smile on my face.

"You and I both know that, but it takes time with Hadley." Victoria leaned forward, resting her elbows on her knees. "Do you love her?"

"Yes." I answered without hesitation, without an ounce of fear. "Pretty sure she's it for me, Vic."

"Then you need to prove it, and not just with grand gestures, though, trust me, Hadley would love those too. She needs someone who is going to see her, who will support her even when she doesn't ask." She smirked over at me. "And remember—if you hurt her, I will have to kill you."

I grinned. "You're supposed to defend me, Vic."

"Eh." She shrugged. "You might be Emilia's father, but Hadley's my soul sister. She's the other half of me, and if you were to mess this up, I'd have to seriously consider murdering you."

I thought about her words, running through all the stuff Hadley had confided in me without asking for help. But there was already a list in my head of ways I wanted to help, wanted to make sure all her dreams came true. An idea from last week wiggled into the front of my brain, and I turned toward Victoria. "Hey, what can you tell me about Sunshine Academy?"

FORTY-SIX

Hadley

After five days of sitting in the hospital room, I was going out of my mind. Every time I thought my mother might get discharged, something else came up, whether it be her blood pressure, her temperature, or another ailment. I hated that she still wasn't back to her full health, but another part of me hated watching her fawn all over the doctors, only to act like I was an ungrateful brat the moment the door closed.

My only moments of reprieve were during her tests, when I would get an hour to myself. Most of the time, I'd close my eyes, but my dreams almost always consisted of Cam and Emilia and how much I missed being with them. I missed them more than words, but I couldn't bring myself to call, not when I was unsure about my future.

My mother needed help and would need it for the foreseeable future. Even though she was recovering, someone needed to monitor her and make sure she followed the doctor's orders. She'd assumed that person would be me, telling all the doctors and staff I would be moving back in with her without even asking if that was what I wanted.

Later that afternoon, after the nurses rolled her bed

away for another round of tests, I made my way into the visitor's lounge, checking the time on my phone. Cam had a game later today, and I refused to miss it. I tried to watch all his games over the past week, but my mother made it difficult. Between her comments and her questions, I couldn't focus, but from the brief glimpses I'd gotten, Cam played well, though his spark had dimmed. I was selfish enough to admit I hoped it was because he missed me.

If I left, would he fight for me? A voice in the back of my mind said no, reminding me he was a pro athlete. Hundreds of women vied for his attention every day. I'd seen his private messages on social media. Women and men alike flooded his inbox, asking for a bit of his time, but every one remained unanswered. As the players warmed up on the unfamiliar field, I tugged my phone out of my pocket, pulling up his account. It was almost an addiction, needing to see his face, even if I couldn't bring myself to call until I had answers.

Cam's page had only a couple photos of teammates and the field. He and Victoria agreed to keep Emilia off their social media; she deserved the privacy. My thumb hovered over his profile and clicked. As it loaded, my heart caught in my throat, finding it drastically different from the last time I'd checked.

Instead of the dozen pictures that lived there before, now, there were almost a hundred, and most of the photos? They were of me.

Pictures of Cam and me throughout the years, with Victoria nestled between us. Pictures of me holding Emilia with her face blurred out. And then there were the ones he must have taken during our time together, hidden moments when I didn't even realize he was watching, much less capturing us on his phone.

I clicked on the first post, the one filled with the most recent pictures. As I read the caption, tears pricked the corners of my eyes.

My everything.

So simple, yet it meant the world to me. Cam was notoriously private, hating the idea of talking to the press about anything other than baseball. I never expected him to talk publicly about our relationship, much less show these moments to the world. It meant more to me than I realized, being so publicly claimed, like Cam was proud to be seen with me as opposed to the shame I'd experienced in the past.

A familiar chuckle broke my attention, and my eyes darted up, finding my best friend standing in the doorway. A smile stretched across my face as I stood, rushing over to capture her in a tight hug. "What are you doing here?"

"Did you think we'd let you disappear on us?" Victoria asked.

"We?"

As the word left my mouth, I noticed the others following behind her, Ollie and Brianna each holding one of Emilia's little hands. When she spotted me, Emilia dropped their grip, dashing toward me with a loud shriek. "Auntie Hadley!"

"Wow," Ollie chuckled. "I'm a little insulted. No one's ever dumped me like that."

Emilia rushed into my waiting arms, and I held her closer than I ever had before. After a week of treading water, a warmth settled in my stomach. I was home. It wasn't a place, wasn't somewhere checked off on a map. Home meant being with the people I loved and who loved me back in return.

After letting Emilia go, I embraced Ollie and Brianna,

still pinching myself that they'd all showed up for me. "I can't believe you guys came all the way out here for me."

"We missed you," Brianna said. "Work hasn't been the same since you left."

"I'm sorry about leaving you like that." My cheeks heated in embarrassment. "I never wanted to abandon the kids—"

"Woah," Brianna said as she stepped closer. "You didn't abandon anyone, Hadley." She opened her bag and pulled up a stack of handmade cards. "They know why you had to go, and while they miss you, they get it. It doesn't hurt that you gave them the most epic field day ever, even without being there."

"Field day?" I asked, wracking my brain for what she meant. I'd spent weeks trying to get something together, but I'd abandoned it when I got the call about my mom. "What are you talking about?"

Brianna pulled out her phone, showing me pictures of our students playing various games and making crafts out in the back field of our school. My eyes widened. "Is that?"

"Yup." Brianna beamed back at me. "Almost all the Hawks volunteered to come play games with the kids. They ran a miniature baseball clinic and even brought shirts and balls to sign for everyone."

"B-but how?" I asked. "I never reached out to the team."

"Cam," Victoria said. "He knew you were upset about the kids not having a sendoff for the end of the year, so he pulled some guys together."

"Yeah, he called the principal and made it happen the very next day," Brianna added. "The guys were all out there setting up at six in the morning, ready for the kids as soon as they got off the bus."

I stared at the photos on her phone, swiping through

until I found one of Cam. His wide smile was so genuine, it made my chest ache. He'd done this for me. He didn't even call to tell me what he'd done; he just went above and beyond to make sure my kids got the end of the year celebration they deserved. Fresh tears filled my eyes as realization struck me.

"Oh, I know that look," Ollie teased. "Please tell me we're planning some big, romantic statement." As the other girls turned and stared at her, Ollie just shrugged. "What? You all know you want to see it. Wasn't that the whole point of coming out here, to bring Hadley home?"

Home. Suddenly, there was nowhere else in the world I'd rather be. After almost a week of being at my mother's beck and call, I was done catering to her needs. As much as it pained me to walk away when she needed someone, it had to be done. To my mother, I'd been nothing more than a burden, a convenient support when she felt down. Her love was conditional on what I could do for her, as opposed to the unconditional love of the people surrounding me now.

"Yeah," I said, handing Brianna back her phone. "I think it's time I tell Cam how I feel."

"Because you love my daddy?" Emilia asked.

I leaned down and took her hand in mine. "Yeah, Em. I love him. Is that okay with you?"

She beamed back at me. "Yup. And that's good, because he told me he loves you too."

Maybe earlier, her words would have shocked me, when I was too busy doubting my worth to see what was right in front of me. Now, though, there was no question that Cam loved me. He'd been showing me all along, but I'd been too jaded to see it. "Give me a couple of minutes, and then we can get out of here, okay, Em?"

She nodded as I turned down the hall, needing to tell

my mother I was leaving. But as I turned the corner into her room, I ran smack into Dr. Leeds. We bounced apart, and my hand flew to my chest, trying to soothe my panicking pulse. "I'm so sorry, doctor."

"No problem." He smiled. "I was looking for you. We're going to discharge your mother today. Between her new medicine regime and some healthier lifestyle choices, she should make a full recovery."

He handed me a list of her new prescriptions, and my brow furrowed as I read the names. "She's already on a lot of these meds. Are you increasing the dose?"

Dr. Leeds brow furrowed. "Your mother didn't disclose she was on any of these medications. Has she been taking them?" I started to answer, but no words came out. Almost all the bottles in my mother's bag were full. I never second guessed it, assuming she'd just gotten them refilled.

"I-I'm not sure." My eyes remained glued to the paper in front of me. "If someone prescribed these medications, but she refused to take them, what could happen?"

"I think you already know the answer to that."

Unbridled rage danced along my skin. Suddenly, everything snapped into focus—my mother's evasive answers about her medication, her quieting me every time the doctors stepped into the room. Ringing sounded in my ears, blocking out all other noises, a sharp awareness of everything my mother had put into motion. While she might not have guessed the outcome, she had to realize the risks when she stopped taking her prescribed medication. No wonder she believed I was going to move back home with her. It'd probably been her plan to begin with.

The realization snipped the last string tying me to my mother. After a lifetime of living in her shadow, I found the strength to step out of it, needing to get home to my real family. I handed the papers back to the doctor. "My mother is going to need to find someone else to drive her home. Here." I opened my wallet and handed a couple of twenties over. "That should be enough to get her back to the house."

"Wait," he called as I turned to walk away. "Where are you going?"

"I've spent enough time away from the people I love. I'm going home to them. And after today, you can tell my mother she's not one of them."

FORTY-SEVEN

Cameron

"Seda, I need to talk to you for a minute."

My hand gripped my phone, staring at the blank screen, hoping for a message or call to come through at the last second. Emilia had already called earlier, checking that off my pre-game list before Victoria and the rest of Hadley's friends hopped in the car to drive to Boston.

It was only a four-hour drive. They should have arrived at the hospital early this morning, but the only message I received was a quick check-in from Victoria, nothing else. I kept staring, hoping Hadley's name would glide across my screen, telling me she was coming home to me.

There was so much left to say, so many words I'd held back for fear of getting distracted. As much as I wanted to go for a ride to Boston and bring her home myself, I also needed Hadley to make that choice. I needed her to *want* to come back to me.

Benny's eyes found me across the clubhouse, motioning for me to hurry and join him, but my legs felt like lead. Despite my improved performance, my fate was still on the line. I tried to ignore the trade deadline, channeling all my frustrations into the game. However, it always lingered above me like a guillotine, waiting for the last thread to snap.

When I walked inside the office, I scanned the room, happy to see there was no one else waiting for me.

Benny settled into his chair behind the desk, kicking his feet up. "Gonna make this quick, Cam, because I know this has been bothering you for a while."

Dread pooled in my stomach, unsure what would come out of his mouth next. I'd already made my peace with leaving the league, willing to lose this part of my life if it meant holding on to everything else. But the reality of it sucked all the breath out of my lungs. "Where'd they trade me to, Benny?"

"Nowhere."

My eyes jumped up to meet his, a slow smirk forming on his face. Nowhere. I wasn't leaving. The word didn't quite compute, as if I'd already settled for the loss. My hand jumped up to my mouth, blocking the shocked laugh that barreled up from my chest. "Wait, so I'm sticking around?"

"Hell yeah, kid." Benny shook his head. "The suits upstairs might be out of touch, but they recognize talent when they see it. You've been steady since you got here, and with more time and consistency, you'll be a standout on our roster."

I shook my head, dropping my elbows down on my knees. "I, uh—thanks, Benny. Got to be honest, I didn't think this was how it was going to go. I was thinking about hanging up my jersey for good."

Benny leaned forward. "I've been there, kid. Maybe my life would look a lot different if I had." He dipped his finger, slamming it into his desk. "We leave everything on that field for one-hundred sixty-two games a year. Injuries, pain, heartbreaking losses. But we don't owe this game our lives, Cam. If you want to give it all up, I'm not going to stop you." He sat back in his chair, crossing his arms around his chest. "However, if you want to give this a shot, I think we can shape this team into something great, something worthy of the time and effort we pour into it."

MY SMILE WAS WIDE and bold as I stepped back into the clubhouse, ready to take on the world after my conversation with Benny. I was sticking around. Life wasn't always going to be easy, but at least I was going to be close to my family and would get to see Emilia as often as our schedules would allow. It might change in the future—God knows most baseball players don't spend their entire careers in one city—but at least it was a shot. A chance.

With another hour until we had to hit the field, I walked over to my locker and grabbed my phone before settling on the couch. When I unlocked the screen, my brow furrowed as I took in the notifications piling up. I opened my social media app, finding more notifications than I'd ever seen in my life. Unsure what was going on, I pulled up my account and saw someone had tagged me in several photos.

I clicked on the first one, a photo of me doing karaoke back in college. The team decided we'd all dress up on Halloween and hit up a bar in Austin. Victoria even tagged along, leaving Emilia with family for the night so we could all hang together. We'd dressed up as Sonny and Cher, me wearing the long, black sequined dress and her rocking a seventies style mustache. But in this picture, it wasn't the two of us. Instead, it was of the moment I fumbled on the stage, too nervous to get the words out despite the number of shots I'd had beforehand. In true Hadley fashion, she'd jumped up onto the stage with me, belting out the words without a hint of shame. My cheeks may have been dark red, but I watched her, smiling wider than I had in a long time.

As I shook my head, I read the caption. *Because you never back down from a challenge.*

Hadley. It finally clicked she'd tagged me in all the photos, linking our two accounts. When I'd posted the photos of her, a part of me worried I was going too far, but I couldn't hold back anymore. I wanted to claim her for the world to see, wanted everyone to know that somehow, this beautiful girl was mine, and I was completely and utterly hers. Even if it all blew up in my face, I'd always belong to Hadley.

I kept scrolling through the pictures Hadley tagged me in. I couldn't help the wide smile across my face. They were pictures of our lives together—when we were friends, when we hated each other, and when we'd finally fallen for each other's charms.

And they were all captioned with simple phrases: because you know how I take my coffee, because you're the best dad in the world, because you always make me smile.

By the time I reached the end of the photos, my heart was incredibly full. Hadley had laid out all the reasons she loved me, even without saying the words themselves. My head bolted up, my eyes instantly finding the clock on the wall. Only forty minutes until game time. Normally, I'd be deep in prep mode, trying to relax before I stepped out onto the field. But right now, I couldn't relax, couldn't think of anything else but getting to Hadley.

I jumped up. "What the fuck am I doing here?"

No one answered, but it didn't matter. I might not be

able to get to Boston right now, but if I left right after the game, I'd get there before the sun came up. At least then, I'd be able to tell Hadley in person how I felt. Until then, though, I needed to call her, needed to hear her voice.

I pushed open the doors of the clubhouse, clutching my phone in my hand as I stepped into the hall. Before I pressed her contact card, someone cleared their throat in front of me.

"Another reason I love you? You have impeccable timing."

As soon as my eyes connected with Hadley's, I dropped my phone, rushing forward to scoop her into my arms. I held her close, inhaling the sunshine and honey scent I'd come to depend on. Hadley held me just as close, and in that moment, I knew it was all worth it. The fights, the stress, the doubt—everything had led Hadley into my arms, and there was nothing I wanted more than to keep her forever.

I pulled back. "I love you, Hadley McKay. I love you so much."

She smiled brightly back at me. "So much, huh? I thought I was just a menace."

"You are." I leaned forward and captured her lips, sealing us together. Hadley's fingers knotted in my hair, and I groaned at the sensation. "You're my menace, Hadley. And I'm going to need you to keep tormenting me for a long, long time."

She grinned up at me. "Then I guess it's a good thing I love you too, Cam. Besides..." Her blue eyes twinkled with mayhem. "You still owe me a date."

FORTY-EIGHT

Hadley

THREE WEEKS LATER

"You let a guy blindfold you one time in the bedroom, and suddenly, he's dragging you all over the city with a mask over your eyes."

Cam chuckled behind me, his firm hands guiding me inside what I assumed was an apartment. At least, I hoped it was. Ever since I got back from Boston, we'd been inseparable, only spending nights apart when he went on the road. Luckily, Cole, Victoria's brother, was well-versed in construction, so he repaired the carriage house's roof one weekend. It ended up being perfect timing, because Adam returned from Australia two days after I moved back in, but this time, Cam joined me.

And as much as we loved being close to our family, Cam and I were ready to find a place of our own. The goal was to have two places: one apartment in the city and a house closer to Tori and Emilia.

With the break for the All-Star game coming up, we figured it was the perfect time to hunt for a new home. But everything we'd seen so far had been too small or too far from the rest of our friends. When Cam told me he had a surprise waiting for me today, I'd crossed my fingers, praying he'd found us somewhere to call our own. Even though Cam's season was only half-way over, I was off for another five weeks—enough time to get settled before the new school year started.

Despite my initial hesitation, I'd taken the maternity leave position at the school. Victoria and I had been talking more about our early childhood center, and it seemed like we were taking more steps toward making it a reality. With her wrapping up her MBA in the fall, the stars were finally aligning, and our dreams might just become a reality.

There were still a lot of steps to be taken, but at least we were taking steps forward. We'd eventually have to find a place, especially if we wanted to update our business plan to reflect the local population. For now, though, we were working more on the internal workings of how we'd want our center to run.

I reached up to itch my nose as we walked further into the space, and Cam wrapped his arms around my shoulders. "Are you trying to peek, menace?"

"If I was, what would you do about it?"

He inhaled sharply, his nose pressing against the length of my neck. "Don't tempt me right now, baby. The listing agent's going to be here soon, and I can't have her walking in on us." Cam kissed the side of my neck. "But if you're a good girl, I'll make it worth your while later."

"I like the sound of that." I turned to face him, looping my arms around his neck. "As much fun as this blindfold has been, can you take it off now?"

"Impatient, menace?"

"You know it, sarge." I let out a little sigh. "I'd love to have a place before your break ends. That way, we can come straight home after the games."

"You have no idea how much I like the sound of that, Hads."

With a quick tug, the black silk fell away from my eyes, and I had to hold my hand up to my mouth to stifle my gasp. It was criminal to call this place an apartment, especially after the lackluster ones we'd seen over the past couple of weeks. One wall was all windows, showcasing the skyline of Erie City, complete with the Hawks' stadium in the background.

It was only after I stared at the view for a couple more minutes that I dared to look at the rest of the place. The apartment was the perfect mix of rustic and modern, with warm, wood accents and exposed brick, painted black pipes running along the ceiling. The open floor plan let you over-look the living room from the kitchen. As I walked into the living room, my hand ran along the back of a dark green velvet couch. Whoever furnished this apartment needed to be my best friend. It was like they pulled all my dream elements out of my brain. Everything was mix-matched but flowed together, the perfect eclectic elegance I loved more than any other style.

"Wait..." I said as I walked further inside, checking out the primary bedroom off the hall. The walls were painted my favorite shade of teal, the bed the same one I'd shown Cam earlier that week. As I moved closer to the dresser, I realized all the photos in the frames were of us, many taken from our public declarations on social media. As I picked up our most recent one from the game earlier in the week, I turned around to face Cam. "Why is all of this here?"

He gave me a sheepish smile as he held up the keys. "I hope you like it, or I'm going to be kicking myself all night. When the listing agent showed it to me, I just knew. I see us here, Hads. Mornings together, celebrating with Emilia, and everything else in between." Speechless, I just stared at him, trying to figure out how he pulled this off behind my back. He must have misread my silence as annoyance, because he took my hand and led me down the hall to the other two bedrooms, one that had already been painted in glittery purple, with the dream bedroom set to match. "This is Emilia's room, and then I was thinking we could use the extra one as a guest room, or an office, if you wanted a space at home."

When he finished showing me around, Cam led me back to the kitchen, his smile replaced with something much less shiny. "Shit, Hads. If you hate it, I'll go right back down and try to get us out of this. I just wanted to take care of you, and when I saw this place—"

My hand covered his mouth. "I love it."

His eyes glistened. As I pulled it away, he grabbed my wrist, leaving a soft kiss on my pulse point. "Are you sure?"

"Cam, you found us a home." Tears formed in the crests of my eyes. "And it's absolutely perfect. But I am mad about one thing..." My fingers trailed along his chest. "I thought we couldn't fool around because the listing agent was coming up here."

"Okay, so that was technically a lie. But there is one more thing you need to see before we can break this place in."

My brow furrowed, about to argue, when Cam took my hand. He pulled our joined hands to his mouth, leaving a kiss on my knuckles. We walked out of the apartment, and I looked over my shoulder in complete disbelief that we had a place of our own. Once we were in the hall, Cam passed me a key topped with a light blue key holder. "Lock up for me, baby?"

I did as he asked, beaming up at him when I pulled the key from the lock. "I still can't believe you did this."

Cam pulled me into his arms, kissing the top of my head. "I'd do anything for you, baby. After all, you're the one who's made my life more than I ever imagined. I want a full life with you. This is just the first step."

WHEN WE LEFT THE APARTMENT, I expected Cam to take us to a local restaurant or a coffee shop that would be our new place. Instead, when we reached the ground level of the building, he turned away from the car, directing me to where a bunch of empty storefronts sat, waiting for businesses to claim them.

"This building is brand new," Cam said as he tugged me along. "Just finished construction last month, but the plan is to make it a staple of the community. Not only quality housing, but local businesses to help the neighborhood thrive."

We turned the corner, and I saw an addition next to the building, a one-story set-up with an attached yard. My heart clenched at the sight, wondering if one day, I'd have a place of my own just like this, a place where kids could learn and grow.

I expected Cam to turn around and continue the tour of the neighborhood, but then the sign in the front caught my eye.

The Sunshine Academy.

"Son of a bitch," I muttered under my breath. Cam stopped, arching his brow in question. I shook my head. "It's nothing. It's just...the daycare Victoria and I always dreamed about? That was going to be its name. It was an inside joke, that she was the brains and I was the sunshine, and together, we'd make the perfect pair."

Cam laughed, nodding. "Think that's still the case?"

I furrowed my brow, following his line of sight until it reached my best friend, who grinned as she opened the door and walked outside. For the second time today, I was stunned silent, too busy hoping the sight in front of me was real.

When Cam let go of my hand, I stepped up to Victoria. "What are you doing here?"

"Thought you'd want to check out our first location." She held up the keys. "Because a certain benefactor of ours just bought the building, and he wants to make sure both the owners approve before we sign on the dotted line."

I whipped around to face Cam. "How did you even know about this?"

"I might have stolen your business plan," he admitted with a shrug. When my mouth fell open, he just smirked. "Sorry, menace. It was too good to sit in a box gathering dust. I knew you just needed a push to make it happen." He stepped closer, but this time, his expression didn't seem so confident. "If I overstepped, I'm sorry. You're an amazing teacher, Hads, but you've dreamed about doing so much more. Maybe I should have talked to you first, but you'd never let me help if I asked."

I stared up at him, too stunned to articulate all the emotions rushing through me. Instead, all I could babble was a shaky, "Why?"

Cam cupped my cheek in his palm. "I will always support your dreams, Hadley. No matter what comes next, I'm in this with you. If you wanted to run the world, I'd be right by your side, doing everything in my power to make it a reality. I believe in you, baby."

I rolled my lips, trying and failing to keep my tears from falling. Cam smoothed them away with his thumb. "Please tell me these are happy tears."

I launched myself into his arms. "These are ridiculously over the top happy tears." I pulled back and kissed him, pouring every ounce of devotion and appreciation into my touch. "But please tell me this is the last of the surprises. My heart can't take any more."

"This is it," Cam chuckled. "But you have to go inside and make sure it matches your vision. Vic checked it out last week, but we wanted you to have the final say."

I nodded, and Cam put me back on the ground. As I looked up at the building he'd bought for us, I reached out and took Victoria's hand. "So we're really doing this?"

She winked at me. "We always were. Sometimes, the right thing just takes a little longer to come along."

I glanced over my shoulder at the man who'd stolen my heart.

Truer words had never been spoken.

EPILOGUE
ONE YEAR LATER

You would think after spending the last year with a professional baseball player, I'd be used to the energy of a packed stadium, but the air at the All-Star Game was different, filled with excited anticipation and awe. This game might not affect any team's standings, but fans packed into the Dallas stadium, ready to cheer on the best in the league.

Including my man.

I smiled as I surveyed the crowd, proudly displaying the Seda name stamped across my back. In fact, we had an entire cheering section for Cam and the other two Hawks playing tonight. Damien's sister and her wife sat on the other side of our group, all five of their girls ready to cheer for their uncle. Ollie and Brianna sat together, wearing matching jerseys for Parker. They'd become close friends over the past year, especially since Brianna filed for divorce. When she had to sell her house, Ollie offered her a room in her condo, and they seemed to enjoy living together.

In Cam's unofficial cheering section, I sat with Emilia, Victoria, and Adam, as well as Cam's parents. I'd met them in passing over the years, but when we first flew out to

Texas so they could meet me as Cam's girlfriend, I was terrified. Not only did they remember me as Victoria's best friend, but they had high standards for their son. After a lifetime of never being enough for my mother, I convinced myself they'd see right through me, wishing Cam had found someone better to spend his life with.

But just like their son, they exceeded all my expectations. His parents welcomed me right into the fold. Where I viewed our shared history as a negative, it thrilled them, already knowing how much I loved their granddaughter. After years of being alone in the world, I finally had a family, and it was all thanks to the man about to take the field.

I couldn't lie and say there weren't days I missed my mother. At least, I missed the idea of who she could have been—the relationship we missed out on. In the year since we last spoke, she'd only reached out a handful of times, each message more belligerent than the last. In my mother's twisted mind, she probably thought I'd cave, guilt and shame eating away at my resolve. If anything, it had done the opposite, especially now that Cam showed me love didn't have to be conditional. These people were my family, the ones I counted on during life's highs and lows. There was no more room in my heart for someone who only saw me as a pawn.

As I turned to Victoria, ready to talk to her more about our newest idea for the Sunshine Academy, a voice called out above me. "Excuse me, miss? Someone asked to see you before the game."

I furrowed my brow. "Everything okay?"

"Oh yes." The attendant smiled back at me. "But please, we'd appreciate it if you came quickly, and bring Miss Emilia."

"Do you know anything about this?" I turned to ask Victoria.

She just shrugged, but a smirk teased the corners of her lips. "Nope. Guess you're going to have to find out what's going on."

I narrowed my eyes at my best friend and business partner. Despite the rocky start to our dream, the Sunshine Academy was thriving. We had a waiting list three months out for our flagship location, and were scouting new ones to potentially open next year. And the best part? I got to spend every day with my best friend. There was no one else I would have wanted to take on this challenge with, and I was forever grateful Cam pushed me to chase this dream.

When I stood, I grabbed Emilia's hand, and we followed the attendant to the lower part of the field. I kept waiting for someone to tell me what was going on, but the attendant remained stoically quiet as we took the elevator down to the locker rooms. As soon as the doors opened, Cam's grin greeted us on the other side. Emilia took off, leaping into her father's arms. He happily caught her, pressing a soft kiss into her hair.

"Hey, Em. Having fun so far?"

"It's so cool!" she exclaimed. "I got to meet so many players!"

At seven, Emilia had become obsessed with baseball, even asking her first grade teacher to start an after-school softball program. Cam fully supported the idea, and during the off-season, he volunteered to show the girls some tricks. He'd done so well, the school asked him to continue the program, but that all depended on Emilia and if her tastes changed in the future. But right now, her dad was her hero, and Cam loved every second.

After he set her back on her feet, Cam's hand found my

hip and pulled me in close for a kiss. It was a simple touch, yet I inhaled slowly, savoring his mouth on mine. I'd never get enough of it. He pulled back, brushing his fingers along my jaw. "Need a favor, menace."

"Okay..."

"We had someone lined up to throw the first pitch, but they had to back out."

"Oh!" I exclaimed, pulling out my phone. "Do you need me to text Adam? I'm sure he'd love to do it."

Cam shook his head. "Another time. Tonight, it's all you."

They probably heard the laugh that barreled out of me on the space shuttle. "Me?" I squawked incredulously. "Have you lost your ever-loving mind? I can barely throw the ball to Emilia, and she moves in closer for me."

"It's true, Dad," Emilia added in from our side.

Cam shifted closer to me, his fingers finding my chin and tilting it up. "Are you telling me there's something my girl can't do?" He leaned down and pressed his lips to mine. "Because I don't believe that."

"Cam, as much as I love your undeserved confidence in me, this is a professional baseball game with millions of people watching." I fumbled for my phone again. "I'll text Adam. He can fill in, and we can forget about this ridiculous idea of me pitching in a professional stadium."

"If that's what you want." Cam shrugged, his tone too casual to be real. "I'm disappointed. My girl never backs down from a challenge." He took Emilia's hand and sauntered away, but not before calling out over his shoulder. "It's okay, I won't tell anyone you're scared of throwing a ball, menace."

"I'm not scared!" I bit back, even though I was terrified. It was one thing to make a fool of myself in our backyard; it was another thing to make an ass of myself in front of *millions*. Plus, I had to live with the baseball community for a long time, thank you very much. I did not want to be the girlfriend who fucked up the All-Star game for the next ten years.

Cam laughed as he looked down at Emilia. "She sounds pretty scared to me."

The man was baiting me. I knew he was. The rational part of me was already heading back to my seat, telling Adam to get his butt down here before the game began. But Cam knew me too well—he knew I'd never back down after he issued a challenge. I let out a frustrated groan before I stomped after him.

Cam paused when he got to the tunnel. "You're making the right choice, baby."

"Just remember..." I leaned in closer, but instead of kissing him, I flicked his nose. "If I embarrass myself, I am going to make the rest of your life miserable."

He laughed as he looped his arm not holding Emilia's hand around me. "As long as I get you forever, baby." Cam's face turned serious as he looked down at me. "I'd never set you up for failure, Hadley. You can do this. It's just one throw, and then you can head back to the stands."

Maybe it was the adrenaline, or Cam's unwavering faith in me, but I believed him. He was right—it was only one throw. How hard could it be?

ON SECOND THOUGHT, this was a terrible idea. The moment I stepped out under the stadium lights, I could feel every set of eyes turn toward me, probably asking themselves what I was doing out on the field. Yeah, join the club.

Damn Cameron and his sexy-as-hell grin. I was going to tease and torture him for hours when we got back to the hotel tonight. The assistant coach reviewed all the steps with me before I headed toward the pitcher's mound, careful not to disturb it too much.

I expected to see a catcher on the home plate, waiting for me to toss him the ball. Instead, Cam's sure smile greeted me. "What are you doing?" I asked.

"Did you think I'd let anyone else catch for you, baby?" His eyes twinkled as he looked up at me. "C'mon, Hads. Show off your skills for everyone to see."

I rolled my eyes, but a blush still filled my cheeks. I might tease him, but I loved Cam's confidence in me. It bolstered my own, making me feel like I could conquer the world with him at my side.

An announcement echoed through the stadium, but I couldn't hear it over the pounding in my ears. Instead, I toyed with the ball in my hand, focusing on the glove in front of me. *Throw the ball into the glove.* How hard could that be? Answer—really fucking hard.

I started to wind up my throw when a sudden flash of movement made me pause, and Emilia came bustling up to my side. "Wait," she said, taking the ball from my hand. "That's the wrong one. You need to use this one."

I stared down at the one she handed me, already noticing that the weight was off. I turned it over and frowned. Someone had torn the stitches, leaving a wide hole instead. "Hold on, this ball's busted—"

But as I looked up, I saw Cam kneeling in front of me, taking my free hand in his. My heart leaped out of my chest, trying to connect words to the sight in front of me. "Are you...?"

"Yeah," Cam laughed. He took the ball from my hand,

squeezing the sides until the opening was large enough to reach inside. He pulled out a beautiful diamond ring, a princess cut with a halo of smaller stones surrounding it. "I've spent the last couple of months trying to find the right place to ask you to marry me, Hadley, but nothing seemed right. Not until I came to practice one day and looked out over the stadium. I fell for you the first time you came to my game, cheering for me despite claiming to hate me."

"I wouldn't use the word hate." I smirked.

"You definitely did, but it doesn't matter. Once you were up in those stands, I realized I always wanted you at my side, wanted to cheer you on like you did for me." Cam slipped the ring out of the box. "Baseball might have been my first love, but you are my forever. So please, baby. Marry me?"

"Of course!" I squealed as I leaped into him, arms going around his neck, kissing him with every ounce of love in my body. Cam held me tight against him, like he never wanted to let me go. But as soon as my senses came back to me, I remembered where we were and jumped off him.

I held my hand out, and Cam slipped the ring onto my finger, beaming brightly down at me. "What do you think, menace? You ready to spend the rest of your life with me?"

"I've never been ready for anything more, sarge."

ACKNOWLEDGMENTS

It is such a privilege to get to sit here, writing the acknowledgments for my FIFTH book. I am honored that you picked up this story, and I hope you fell in love with Cam and Hadley, just like I did.

With every book, it takes a village to come together, and I am so blessed to have the very best in my corner.

My family— I would not be here without you. You guys support me, encourage me, and inspire me. I love getting to share this journey with you.

My friends—thank you for not laughing when I said I wanted to pull out my rusty baseball knowledge. Thank you for listening to me screaming about this couple, and the entire series in general, and being incredible cheerleaders along the way.

Maeghen— GIRL! You are the whole reason this book exists. I'd probably still be staring at a blank screen without your amazing support along the way. Thank you for loving this couple as much as I do, and making me so excited to bring their story to life.

Lauren at laurenturnsthepage—I love working with you! Not only do you help me have more confidence in my stories, but your insights and comments always help me build the best version of my work. Thank you for all of your help!!

To Alexa at Fiction Fix—thank you so much for polishing this story into the best version of itself. I have your voice in my head while I'm editing, reminding me to check for extra that's and of's. Thank you for always taking such good care of my stories.!

Lemmy & the Luna crew— Thank you guys for your ARC management. You guys take so much off of my plate, and let me focus on writing. I love knowing that my books (and readers) are in such great hands with you guys.

To my amazing beta readers-- Meghan, Nikki, Cas, Katie, and Brandi, thank you so much for all of your input and invaluable feedback. I love reading your reactions and watching as you experience this story for the first time. Thank you so much for taking the time to help me mold my stories into the final product.

And last- to my readers. Whether you've been with me since the beginning, or if you are just finding my books now, thank you. Thank you for investing your time in reading this story, and I hope you enjoyed it.

Love you all!

ALSO BY K.C. BROOKS

SAINT STEPHEN'S LAKE SERIES:

(Un)Expected

A Dislike to Lovers, Small Town Romance

(Cole & Alex's Story)

(Un)Planned

A Grumpy x Sunshine, Workplace Romance

(Calla & Theo's Story)

(Un)Spoken

A Brother's Best Friend, Single Parent Romance

(Adam & Victoria's Story)

(Un)Rivaled

A Second Chance, Accidental Marriage Romance

(Devyn & Gray's Story)

ERIE CITY HAWKS SERIES:

Single Glance

A Single Dad, Baseball Romance

(Cam and Hadley's Story)

Double Down

A Friends with Benefits, Baseball Romance

Coming Fall 2025

ABOUT THE AUTHOR

K.C. Brooks is an avid romance reader who has always dreamed about turning her ideas into a book of her own. She lives for sunny days, iced cold coffees, and stories that make your heart ache for more. When not living in the fantasy worlds of her books, she resides in upstate New York with her husband, two children, and two fur babies.